Dangerous Crossing

Other books by R. Douglas Clark

Welcome to Maravilla
American Odyssey

Dangerous Crossing

R. Douglas Clark

SPEAKING VOLUMES, LLC
NAPLES, FLORIDA
2020

Dangerous Crossing

ISBN 978-1-64540-174-2

Prologue

October 2009

The snow came up to the bottom of the cowboys' stirrups, and their boot heels skimmed the surface, leaving narrow grooves in their wake. The flakes were falling slower now. The horses strained to break through the heavy accumulation. It was deep and wet, sliding in ponderous clumps from the pine branches above.

The two ranch hands had been searching the foothills all day and had not seen any of the missing cattle. Sometimes it would take a week or so to gather all the cows in the fall, but that was when there was no snow on the ground and food was still easy to forage. After the first snowfall, they usually came down willingly, gathered in a clearing and waited patiently to be picked up, like passengers expecting a bus. Without much coaxing they would shove their way into the cattle trailer, ready for a dry barn and green hay. Seventeen of them were already there, but three others were missing.

At dusk they called off the hunt, loaded up the horses and drove home. That night it snowed another four inches, making the search even harder. "In all my years here we never lost a cow," said the older ranch hand. "Much less three."

The next day they found one—a yearling that had fallen off a ledge camouflaged by the snow. It was still alive, but it had a broken leg. They were surprised that coyotes or a cougar hadn't gotten to it yet. Getting it back to the trailer through the heavy snow was not sensible, so they shot it in the head. "That's okay," said the older cowboy. "We need meat for the winter anyway." They gutted it, wrapped the meat in a blanket, and tied it across the haunches of his horse. They left the head and hooves and guts behind for the scavengers, and rode away from the red mess they'd made in the papal snow.

In the morning it was sunny, and much of the snow melted, leaving a terrain of thick mud to wallow through. They wanted to give it another day to dry out, but more snow was forecast the next afternoon so they went out early.

They crossed a bog of cattails and willows, clotted with mud. On the other side of the marsh, an old Douglas fir had caught most of the snow on its broad branches, leaving a bare spot under the tree encircling the trunk. And lying in that bare spot was a dead man.

"Holy shit!" said the younger ranch hand. "Is that what I think it is?"

"Looks like a dead body to me," said the elder.

It was a white man with a thick, dark mustache, thinning hair and a short, sturdy body. He was cold to the touch and stiff as a poker, although he didn't smell yet. He was dressed in jeans and a heavy flannel shirt with a bandana around his neck. There wasn't any blood on the snow nearby. He looked like he was asleep.

"Christ. We better call the police," said the younger man.

The elder ranch hand took out his cell phone. "No signal," he said. "Why don't we just tie him onto my horse and take him back?"

The younger cowboy looked up with surprise. "We can't disturb a crime scene," he said.

"Who says it's a crime? Besides, we can't just leave him here. What if a coyote finds him?"

"Okay, I'll go find a signal and call 9-1-1. You wait here and watch the guy until the police get here."

"No way! How are the cops even going to find me out here in the middle of nowhere? We'll go home and let the cops deal with it. We can show them where it is this afternoon."

"All right," the younger hand relented. "All right. Let's go."

The man hiding in the brush nearby waited a full five minutes, staying still as the corpse, before coming out into the open. He hoisted the dead man onto one shoulder and trudged to his car, parked on a Forest Service road half a mile away. He'd find another place to bury the body.

When the two cowboys got back to the ranch they told the owner of the ranch what they'd found.

"And you just left him there?"

"We thought if we moved him, we might be messin' up a crime scene."

"Oh, for Chrissake," said the rancher. "Could you find him again?"

"Yeah, I think so," said the elder cowboy. "Unless a snowfall covers up our tracks."

The owner called the New Mexico State Police and the County Sheriff. Within half an hour there were five cop cars at the ranch house. Everyone went inside, and the snow melted off their boots onto the parlor floor while the cowhands explained what had happened. The cops asked them to describe the man, and they did, and said that he didn't have a pulse, and that he was definitely dead.

"That's for the coroner to say," said one of the cops. "We need to conduct a search."

"Now?" asked the elder cowboy. "It's getting dark out and starting to snow again."

"But what if he's alive?" said a deputy. "We don't know for sure he's dead."

"He's dead. Believe me."

"He looked pretty dead to me," the younger man confirmed. "Besides, you're gonna have to wait 'til the snow melts to look for clues."

In the end, they decided to go out again in the soft snowfall and fading light to look for the body of the dead man. They held high-intensity flashlights to illuminate their trail. The only thing was, when they located the fir tree where they had found the corpse, the body wasn't there. The dead man was gone.

There was one set of tracks in the soft ground under the tree, boot prints leading to a trail in the snow where someone had come in and gone back out again.

"I guess he wasn't as dead as you thought," said one of the deputies.

They followed the trail through the snow until they came to a gravel road. No one was sure where they were. Some sloppy tire prints were pressed into the gravel where the car had pulled off the road onto the shoulder. It was like the dead man had gotten into a car and driven off. The cops took pictures of the tire tracks and said they'd come back in the morning for a more thorough search. Someone called a patrol unit and asked to be picked up. The state cops carried tracking devices for emergencies such as this. By the time a patrol car showed up, the snow had stopped.

The two ranch hands lived in a bunkhouse behind the main house. Each of them had a room with a sink, but they shared a toilet and a shower. They kept busy all year: caring for the cattle, mending fences, pruning the orchards, irrigating the fields, cutting hay. And now, add to the list, finding dead men in the snow.

One of the cowboys built a fire in the woodstove, and they spent some time passing a pint of bourbon back and forth, speculating on the missing man and the reason for it and whether or not he was, in fact, dead.

"Betcha he was a mule, carrying cocaine someplace."

"Then he musta got lost. We ain't that near to Mexico."

"I wonder how he died. I didn't see no blood."

"Heart attack? Stroke?"

"Overdose?"

"Poison!" The younger hand put another log on the fire.

"Maybe he was killed somewhere else and then dumped up here."

"And then someone came and got him? That don't make no sense."

"We shoulda taken him back with us in the first place," the older hand said. "Then at least we'd have a body."

"Well, hell."

"Maybe he *was* still alive, and another guy came to rescue him."

"Nope. I seen plenty of dead men in Iraq, and this guy was dead."

"Maybe he got lost and froze to death."

This stopped the conversation in its tracks. Neither man wanted to think about freezing to death. They went off to bed.

The police came out the next morning to see if anyone had remembered anything else they might have forgotten the night before, but no one had. The cops wanted to look at the site during the daytime, so they all piled into the sheriff's car. They drove in on the gravel road, and then followed the trail to where they had found the dead man. The police looked as well as they could over ground that had been trampled by men and horses, but they didn't find anything, and eventually they called it quits.

The police filed a missing person's report, identity unknown. The cowhands' description of the dead man was disseminated over a broad region, but no one fitting that description had been reported missing yet. Police throughout the Southwest and northern Mexico were all notified about the unidentified man. Twenty-four hours later, no one had responded.

Part One

Chapter One

After one more long, lazy cast, Eddie Maez slowly reeled in his line and laid down his fishing rod. He sat on the end of the pier, legs dangling, as the sun disappeared, washing the water, the waves and all the world in deep pink. But the fish weren't biting, and he was getting tired of pink.

Eddie was 62 now. On March 1 he had taken early retirement from the news staff at the Houston daily paper. He had done 35 years on the crime beat and the political beat. He'd grown weary of the nasty no-holds-barred, bare-fisted brawls that rule those realms. He had had enough hardball—being threatened by goons with big fists and foul breath, or bribed by slicked-down dudes in suits. He'd had his tires slit and his windows broken. Once someone had even fed poisoned meat to his dog.

Eddie had certainly seen the avaricious, venal side of human nature. In devoting himself to exposing the stink of evil deeds, he had sacrificed the satisfaction of leading a normal life. He had no family and few friends. He didn't travel or attend the theater. On a free night he would work out at the gym and take a sauna—alone.

The newspaper offered him a softer job—writing features for the Arts and Leisure section—but he had turned it down. He was done. Finished, fed up, gone.

Or so he thought.

Eddie had locked up his small brick bungalow in Houston and rented a cottage on the Gulf Coast. In late March, on Padre Island, it was a comfortable 69 degrees with a balmy breeze blowing in the afternoon. Eddie was enjoying himself, filling his days with fishing, reading mystery novels, watching old movies and drinking good booze. Before bed he would walk along the beach in the moonlight and let the warm water wash over his bare feet. He planned on staying there for two months, but that was before he got the call from his friend Brad Collins.

His cell phone rang as the pink turned to lavender and the first stars became visible. Eddie wasn't sure why he had brought his cell phone to the beach, and considered tossing it in the water to silence the ringtone forever. But years of habit plus a mild curiosity compelled him to answer it.

"Talk to me," he said.

"Eddie? Brad Collins here."

"Good to hear from you, man. What's the word on the street?"

"Since you ask, I do have a story for a discreet reporter such as yourself."

"I guess you didn't get the memo, Brad. I retired."

"Retired? You can't do that."

"Oh, no? At this very moment I'm watching the sunset over the Gulf. Gorgeous sky. Just one beer shy of perfect. Hold on." Eddie reached into the small cooler where he kept his bait and beer and withdrew a cold longneck. "There," he said, popping the top off. "Perfecto."

"Are you shitting me, Eddie?"

"No, sir. They offered to let me interview artists and write about style trends."

"Sounds dreadful."

"Right. That's why I turned them down."

"Well, congratulations, I guess. But Eddie. How about one more juicy investigation, just as a favor to me? I'll pay your fee. Make a little extra cash, expose a little corruption, maybe add a little gloss to your already legendary status."

"Why not hire a private eye? I'll give you some names."

"No, no, no. You're the one for this job, Eddie. And didn't you start out as a private eye?" It was true. Before he was a journalist, Eddie was a private investigator, a shamus, a gumshoe. He was still licensed to carry a concealed weapon.

Eddie took a long swallow of his beer. "What's the scoop?" he asked.

"I don't want to discuss it on the phone."

"Off the record, on the Q.T., very hush-hush?"

"It's delicate."

"It's not a divorce or a missing person, is it?" he asked, brushing sand off his bare feet.

"Nothing so mundane as that."

"I don't know, man. I'm kind of liking this laid-back lifestyle."

"Oh, come on. You're probably bored to death."

"Yeah, if I have to see one more beautiful sunset, I think I'll scream."

"Look, the sunsets will still be there when you're through with this job. Just do it for me. For old times' sake."

Eddie thought of a few witty retorts, but the truth was, he *was* getting a bit bored. Besides, spring break was coming soon and the coast would be transformed from a peaceful paradise to a purgatory of drunken college kids riding dune buggies.

"All right," he said. "One last splash. It better be a good one."

Eddie's childhood was as normal as losing your baby teeth. His father was an insurance man, who bought a brand new Chevrolet Impala every other year. He belonged to the Rotary Club and liked to mow his own lawn. Eddie's mother worked three days a week at Goodwin's Five and Dime, sang in the church choir and played bridge with other women every Thursday night.

The Maez family—Eddie had two sisters—lived in a mixed-race part of San Antonio, whites and Hispanics, no blacks, but Eddie always put character above skin color or social status—not intentionally: that's just the way he was. He and his parents were native Texans, although his mestizo heritage was evident in his blocky stature, broad face and reddish-brown skin. His hair was black and wiry.

Eddie Maez graduated from high school in 1966 with an eye to becoming a journalist, although he was voted "Most Likely To Be Ten Minutes Late." He got a part-time job selling auto parts and enrolled in English and Journalism courses at the University of Texas, but, not being a full-time student, he was soon drafted into the Army. The nature of Eddie's college courses kept him in a non-combatant position, writing for the Army's newspaper, *Stars and Stripes*. That was the good news. The bad news was that he got stuck behind a desk in Kansas City, writing watered-down press releases that hid more than they revealed. With visions of Hemingway clouding his thoughts, Eddie volunteered to report on the war from the front lines.

During the Tet Offensive in 1968, Eddie was attached to a squad of gutsy guys who had an unhealthy disrespect for danger and a swaggering confidence in themselves—soldiers who either didn't expect to die or didn't care. Their mission was to seek out and search the tunnels of Cu Chi, a vast network of underground passageways used by the Viet Cong for moving troops and transporting ammunition, food and medical supplies under the very boots of their American enemies. Eddie wrote hair-raising accounts of these "tunnel rats," who discovered booby traps, poisonous snakes and Viet Cong fighters in the subterranean battleground. In the interest of accurate reporting, Eddie explored a few tunnels himself, *after* they had been declared safe. It freaked him out to be confined. He felt trapped. He preferred to be on the ground, not under it, even when the open air was laced with the greasy smell of napalm.

Discharged in California, Eddie looked for work as a reporter in Los Angeles but struck out because he was haunted by his experience in Vietnam. Later in life he learned he had suffered from PTSD, but at that time post-traumatic stress disorder had not yet been parsed or even named by the psychologists. He went to job interviews drunk or hung over, afraid of what he might say or do if he were sober. Suspicious of anyone who looked at him twice, he carried a knife for protection. A hornet's nest of anger buzzed in his head, which would occasionally explode into violence, such as the time he received a routine sales call from the phone company. Eddie screamed at the caller and then took a hammer to the phone, smashing it until it was nothing but a pile of plastic shards. Finally he managed to land a job as a security guard for MGM. It was easy work but boring. After the tension and adrenaline highs of combat, Eddie had trouble sitting in a booth all day, checking credentials of movie people coming and going. Within a year, he quit his job and moved back to Texas where he went solo as a private investigator. He took on small jobs—mostly surveillance, missing persons, some background research. Gradually he adjusted to civilian life, but peace of mind remained elusive.

Eddie's career break came when he was hired to investigate a politician who, as it turned out, was skimming money from campaign contributions to pay off old gambling debts. When he brought that story to light, the daily newspaper in Houston hired Eddie as a stringer in Austin and San Antonio. He proved to be a stellar newshound, turning out a steady stream of stories about toxic chemicals, drug trafficking and corporate malfeasance. Before long he moved to Houston as a full-time investigative reporter where he embarked on a long and storied career. Now, it appeared, he had one last story to tell.

Eddie Maez was not the perfect journalist. He had the essential qualities of a good journalist—curious mind, agile writing skill, good listener, fearless questioner—but he had something else too: an opinion. As everyone knows, opinions belong on the editorial pages, not the news pages. For the most part Eddie was able to keep his opinion out of his reporting because if he did his job right—finding out who, what, when, where and why—the truth would come out and the public could draw their own conclusions. But when the evidence was inconclusive or the facts were incomplete, Eddie would fill in the blank with his own opinion, or at least employ a careful choice of words to imply a certain conclusion. Thankfully for his readers, Eddie had a pretty solid sense of right and wrong. Often, the only unanswered question was: Why?

Chapter Two

"I swear, that thing gets bigger every year," Brad Collins said, coming in from the garage. He had just finished pruning the viburnum in the front yard. Spring had snuck up on him.

"*Dad*-dee!" said his eight-year-old girl, exasperated by her slow-witted father. "Of *course* it's going to get bigger. It's a *tree*."

"Well, then maybe we'll have to move the house back a few feet to make room for it."

"No, Daddy. We can't do that."

"We can't? Why not?"

"It's too heavy, silly," she replied. "Besides, I'm doing my homework. That's more important, isn't it, Mom."

"Yes, dear," said Brad's wife, Olivia. "You'll have to move the house later."

Collins was the founder and CEO of a non-profit organization called Neighbors for Health, based in San Antonio. Its mission was to deliver medicine and medical assistance to poor farmers in Guatemala, El Salvador and Honduras. It shipped medical supplies from the border town of Laredo, Texas, 160 miles south of San Antonio. Collins's job was to solicit money from supporters, and goods from pharmaceutical companies, and to manage the Laredo facility. Neighbors for Health owned a small fleet of aging refrigerated cargo trucks to deliver the supplies to remote areas of Central America, providing the trucks didn't break down *en route*. Doctors and nurses volunteered for six-week residencies in the primitive clinics of the countryside, traveling from one makeshift clinic to another, administering vaccinations, setting broken bones, handing out antibiotics, stitching up cuts. To help defray the cost of this enterprise—and to help the farmers market their product—the trucks returned to the U.S. with heavy burlap bags filled with organic green coffee beans that Collins sold to a specialty coffee chain. The beans were then roasted and sold under a distinctive promotional label.

Brad Collins was a man of medium build who kept a pair of dark glasses nestled in the curly hair on top of his head. His usual attire was a rumpled corduroy sport coat over a dress shirt with jeans and sneakers. He had a four o'clock shadow by noon, and his dark unruly hair was always two weeks overdue for a cut. His ready smile revealed large white teeth that overlapped like shingles on a roof. His handshake was firm and strong.

Despite his disheveled appearance, Brad Collins was an engaging man, and everyone wanted a piece of him. He was honored for his successful humanitarian work and he was invited to speak at conferences. He sat on important boards and committees. His earnest face frequently popped up on television and in the newspapers, often alongside his striking Hispanic wife and their two handsome children, ages 8 and 11. Brad Collins was the very essence of goodwill and philanthropic leadership. His evident sincerity and passion for his cause brought out checkbooks and elicited pledges wherever he went.

His credentials were impeccable. Born and raised in Texas, he earned a master's degree in non-profit management from SMU. His father had been a Methodist minister who had died of a heart attack when Brad was twelve. His mother, Rosa, grew up in a Spanish-speaking working-class family in the barrios of El Paso, but she had worked hard in school and had become a registered nurse. After her husband died, she worked nights and weekends in order to raise her three kids and send them to college.

Spanish was Rosa's first language, but she encouraged Brad to speak English as a way to advance himself in a white society. He picked up Spanish slang and swear words on the street but was never properly fluent. He was quick with a quip, and only the stuffiest people could resist his bright laugh.

It was the weekend, so Brad pruned the viburnum, played with the kids, watched a critical Spurs game on TV, and went out to dinner with Olivia. He had also received an unexpected phone call from the World Health Congress. The caller apologized for bothering him at home on the weekend but explained that it was a matter of some urgency. Their annual conference was coming up in less than two weeks, and one of their presenters had cancelled. Would Brad be willing to take his place? The topic was "new developments in tropical illnesses," a subject Brad was intimately familiar with. Brad said he would check his calendar on Monday and get back to them.

"Good morning, Jasmine," said Brad to his receptionist on Monday morning. "I hope you had a good weekend."

"I did indeed. Very relaxing."

Jasmine sat behind a round counter, a central command post, equipped with all the techno-devices of a modern business. Hallways led off both sides, opening onto offices or conference rooms, with a uni-sex bathroom at the back. Jasmine was a twenty-something American who had grown up in a Jamaican household. She could speak in an island patois warm enough to melt an iceberg.

She also could speak the most immaculate English on the planet. It made you want to enunciate clearly and say intelligent things. Jasmine was smart and canny with an unerring sense of a person's character. Lastly, which should perhaps be firstly, Jasmine was a knockout. She was tall with skin darker than black walnuts. She braided her thick hair into scores of strands. Over a lacey camisole she wore a sheer white sleeveless blouse, edged with colorful Jamaican prints.

"Jasmine, there is a conference of the World Health Congress in San Francisco coming up soon. One of their speakers cancelled, and I've been asked to fill in. How's my calendar look for these dates?" Brad handed her a piece of paper; Jasmine checked the dates.

"Nothing that can't wait," she said.

"Good. Please call the WHC in New York and tell them I'll do it. Then get me a plane reservation. The WHC said they'd take care of the hotel and reimburse me for the flight."

"Yah, will do, mon. Olivia not goin'?"

"No, there's a big school event that weekend, which I'll have to miss, unfortunately. Olivia and the kids will be going to that."

"You be all alone in San Francisco? Oh, my!"

"I expect I'll be pretty busy."

"I'm sure you will be," said Jasmine with a smile. "I am sure you will."

The phone rang and Jasmine answered it. Brad patted the counter in good-bye and walked off to his office.

Brad's office was filled with light and provided an unbeatable view of downtown San Antonio, just above the treetops. He put his briefcase in a chair, sat down at his desk and swiveled to see the palm trees that grew below. It gave him great pleasure to sit looking out over the city. He was proud of what he had accomplished and grateful for his good fortune. He loved his family. He was aware of the gulf between his life-style and the lives of those he served, but had come to accept it. Life was not just; everyone's life was not equal. He would do whatever he could to even things out, but he knew that progress would be slow.

He could see the Alamo from his office, and he looked at it now, thinking of the vast changes that had taken place since that famous battle, 175 years ago. On the other hand, Texans were still trying to keep out the Mexicans, and the Mexicans were just as determined to get in. Some things hadn't changed.

Chapter Three

Neighbors for Health's facility in Laredo backed onto the Rio Grande River, bordered by a 12-foot chain-link fence topped with razor wire. Brad Collins had convinced his board to purchase the property from a former pipe supply company that had gone out of business when its owner retired. The yard was large enough for the fleet of trucks, and the enclosure included a loading dock and a storage facility into which Collins installed walk-in coolers to store the medicine waiting to be shipped out.

What Brad didn't know about the facility was that in one corner of the building, next to the loading dock, there was a small hidden door, flush to the ground, invisible to the casual eye. Beneath the door was a ladder leading to a tunnel that went under the Rio Grande and came out in a copse of scrawny trees in Mexico, half a mile from the nearest road. The tunnel was made of metal pipe, four feet in diameter, and the pipe lay in a slurry of gravel and mud just below the riverbed. A few inches of water sat on the bottom of the pipe, giving off the fetid smell of raw sewage.

The pipe had been installed in the 1970s when border security was lax and the construction activity attracted little attention. The owner of the pipe supply company, an opportunist named Oswald, installed the pipe as a means to smuggle stolen goods into the U.S. Couriers crawled through the tunnel carrying a steady supply of gemstones, jewelry, Mayan artifacts and other contraband. Occasionally there would be a stolen painting by a famous artist, such as Diego Rivera or Jesús Helguera, rolled up inside a metal tube. Oswald took the booty to a fence in Houston who sold it on the black market. This lucrative practice continued for several years. Then a Mexican *coyote* found out about the tunnel and convinced Oswald to open the tunnel to human traffic, specifically immigrants who wanted to enter the United States illegally to find work. All along the Gulf coast there was a strong market for cheap labor. These two smuggling enterprises, stolen goods and illegal migrants, coexisted peacefully for a time until a drug cartel moved into the area. The *jefe* demanded exclusive use of the tunnel to smuggle drugs into the United States. With a gun to his head, Oswald had little choice but to capitulate to the drug boss. The smuggling of contraband and of immigrants stopped, and the exchange of drugs for money began. Within a year, the drug lord and his associates got into a turf war with a rival gang called the Matamoros Cartel. The upstart gang, led by a ruthless madman called El Flaco, was so eager to seize power that it killed off all the competing gangsters before finding out the location of the tunnel. Oswald decided to get out while he still could. He shut down his business and, a few months later, sold the property to Neighbors for Health. He didn't mention the tunnel.

Once the old gangsters had been wiped out and Oswald had moved away, the only person who knew about the tunnel was a man named Delmore Briggs, who had been the yard foreman at the pipe supply company. Briggs was an unlikely man to have such a job. He knew nothing about pipes and had no experience as a foreman. He didn't even want the job, really. He just needed to make some money and keep a low profile while he figured out his next move. His last scam had ended badly. Briggs was smart and had a pathologically cheerful disposition, so he was able to talk his way into the job and then figured out the details as he went along. It wasn't brain surgery.

On one occasion, when working late, he had witnessed a man with a backpack emerging from the tunnel. In the gloaming, Briggs hid himself behind a truck. He saw another man, outside the fenced yard, with a similar backpack. The man outside the fence threw his backpack over the top, then drew a gun and held it on his counterpart while he sat on the loading dock with a flashlight and counted several bundles of currency. With that done to his satisfaction, the man inside threw his own backpack over. It was filled with bricks of heroin, quickly counted. Without exchanging a word, the two men parted: the first man disappeared down the tunnel, while the second man walked off into the darkness.

The next day, Briggs told his boss what he had seen. At first Oswald pretended surprise and outrage, but when Briggs threatened to go to the cops with his story, Oswald had been forced to take Briggs into his confidence. He outlined the history of the tunnel and divulged the drugs-for-money exchange. He said he received a "small fee" for allowing the use of the tunnel—but emphasized that the drug runners had threatened to kill him if he did not go along with the scheme. He raised Briggs's salary to keep him quiet. At that moment Briggs saw his future unfolding. He understood the nature of power and felt its lure. He thanked Oswald for the raise but said it would take more, much more, to keep him from spilling his story to the press as well as the cops. Oswald refused at first, but by the time he walked out of Oswald's office, Briggs had gotten what he wanted: a bundle of cash. This was his first taste of raw power, and he liked it.

El Flaco, the new drug lord, had heard rumors of the tunnel but failed to find anyone who had firsthand knowledge of its location. It was then that Oswald seized the opportunity to sell the property to Neighbors for Health. After they moved in, Briggs kept an eye on the tunnel. He saw no activity coming or going, and he concluded, correctly, that no one else knew about the tunnel, including the new owners.

A plan began to form in Briggs's mind.

Chapter Four

The bellboy had worked in room service at the well-regarded San Francisco hotel for almost two years. He worked part-time for minimum wage, not nearly enough to feed his family of five and pay for their small apartment in Richmond. Like many undocumented Mexican workers, he had learned ways to earn extra cash on the side. In the bellboy's case it meant working for Jimmy Flores, a room service captain who ran a ring of call girls. The bellboy had a small but important job: seeing to it that the right doors would be unlocked at the right times. He was just one of many cogs in a well-greased machine.

Jimmy told the bellboy when and where to hide a key card. If he did his job right, the bellboy would just be turning the corner in one direction when the john and his escort were approaching the room from the other direction. He got $20 for each key drop. When there was a big conference at the hotel, the bellboy could make $100 a night. And when the job was more complex—such as when it involved installing equipment like cameras or tape recorders—he could make even more because he would usually get a tip from the camera crew as well. At the conference of the World Health Congress, he made $300 for 15 minutes of work.

It was easy for Delmore Briggs to find out who ran Neighbors for Health. It was almost as easy to find a suitable event for his plan. Going online, Briggs searched for gatherings related to health in the Third World. Within an hour he discovered that an organization called the World Health Congress was having its annual conference in two weeks at a hotel in San Francisco. Briggs didn't know if Brad Collins was planning to attend the conference, but that didn't matter. The WHC had posted the schedule for its conference online. Brad Collins was not listed as a speaker or a panel member. *Perfect*, thought Briggs. *I can fix that.*

Really, the only tricky thing for Briggs was finding out who ran the show at the hotel. For that he had to fly to San Francisco and book a room. A few discreet bribes later he was face to face with Jimmy Flores.

"I have a job for you," said Briggs. "A delicate one."

"Our specialty," replied Flores.

Briggs outlined his plan. "She has to know her stuff, like a real doctor."

"No problemo," said Flores. "We got one young lady who is putting herself through med school working for us."

"How much?" asked Briggs. Flores gave him a number. Briggs took out a roll of bills and peeled off several of a large denomination. He started to hand them to Flores but pulled back his hand at the last second. "If this operation goes awry," he said, "I expect a full refund."

"Don't worry, boss. Ain't nothing gonna go wrong." Briggs handed him the money.

The next day Briggs placed a call to the main office of the World Health Congress in New York.

"This is Dr. Wilbur Cook in Miami," he said. "I'm scheduled to give a talk at the upcoming conference in San Francisco?"

"Yes, Dr. Cook. How can I help you?"

"I'm sorry to say something has come up, a family emergency to be frank, and I won't be able to make the conference. I'm going to have to cancel, I'm afraid."

"That's a shame, Dr. Cook, but we know how it is. These things happen."

"If it's any help," said Briggs, "I can recommend a replacement."

"Well, yes, that would be helpful, with the conference starting next week. Who did you have in mind?"

"A colleague of mine in San Antonio, name of Brad Collins. He runs a non-profit called Neighbors for Health."

"Oh yes, I've met him. Charming man."

"Indeed. And he knows as much about dengue fever as I do, probably more. He's on the front lines, you know. I'm just a lab rat."

"Don't sell yourself short, Dr. Cook. Both ends are important."

"Yes, I suppose that's true. Anyway, I think Brad would do an excellent job. Would you like me to contact him for you?"

"No, that won't be necessary. I'll give him a call. I'm so sorry you can't come yourself. I hope you can resolve your family matter."

"Thank you. I'm sure we will. And again, my apologies."

Initially, Briggs thought he had to figure out a way to keep Dr. Cook from attending the conference. He considered several ways to accomplish this from kidnapping to a bribe to an unfortunate accident. But none of these seemed to be the right solution. Just like a proof in mathematics, Briggs believed, a crime should be simple and elegant. His initial ideas were complicated, expensive and risky. The solution came to him like a voice whispering in his ear: he didn't have to do anything. Let Dr. Cook come. What difference would it make? There would be some confusion at the session with both Brad Collins and Dr. Cook showing up to speak, but so what? The important part of Briggs's plan would already have been completed. Mission accomplished, simply and elegantly. Then Briggs could take the next step.

Chapter Five

At the San Francisco airport, Brad stood outside the baggage claim area looking for a taxi. He spotted a taxi queue and walked toward it. He arrived at the end of the line simultaneously with a young cocoa-colored Latina.

"Oh, excuse me," she said to Brad.

"Not at all. After you."

Brad studied her from behind. Her jet black hair, velvet in the sun, reflected shine and shade. When she turned her head, Brad admired the shape of her cheekbones. Her clothes were charmingly rumpled after a day of travel and hoisting bags into the overhead bin.

When she reached the front of the line, the taxi wrangler asked where she was going. She named a prominent downtown hotel.

"Excuse me." said Brad. "Are you going to the WHC conference?"

"Yes," she said. "You too?"

"Yeah, would you like to share a cab?"

"Perfect!"

She was not a ravishing beauty. She was tall and thin with small breasts, a big smile and a hearty laugh. Her smile was the key. Nothing else mattered after she flashed that smile. It cleaned the slate.

Her raven hair was long and messy, held together with clips and bobby pins, yet fetching the way it sprouted out here and there, barely contained, threatening to come loose at any moment. She would often push it back with her hands, combing it back with her fingers, and blowing it up, away from her face, only to have it float down again. Brad found it sexy.

They introduced themselves. Brad Collins, Gen Phipps.

"It's actually Genovesa, but everyone calls me Gen."

"Have you been to this conference before?" Brad asked.

"Yes. This is my seventh year. How about you?"

"Oh, I'm just a rookie. I've never attended before." He paused a beat. "I'm presenting," he said.

"Oh, you are? What's your topic?"

"'Fighting Dengue Fever in Central America.'" Brad laughed. "Does that sound boring or what?"

"No, not at all. When is it?"

"Tomorrow at 10:00."

"Good time. What room?"

"I'm not sure," he said. "Aspen? Maple?"

"I'll check the schedule. Maybe I can come."

They leaned back into the bulgy cab seats. Gen interlaced her fingers and looked out the window. "Do you know San Francisco?" she asked.

"Oh, a little. Just from conventions and so on."

"There's a sweet little Japanese fusion restaurant not far from the hotel, if you're hungry. I mean…. I'm sorry, that was very forward of me. You probably have other plans."

"Not that I know of." Brad said. "I'd love to join you, although you'll have to order for me. I know nothing about Japanese fusion, whatever that means."

"Oh, you'll love it. It's like a Spanish tapas place. We can order a lot of small plates of different dishes, all of them delicious."

They made small talk the rest of the way. When the cab pulled up to the hotel entrance, Gen said, "How 'bout I meet you in the lobby in an hour."

"Great. See you then."

Brad Collins loved women. He was completely loyal to his wife, Olivia, but he enjoyed flirting with pretty women. He was gracious and good-looking himself, so women were frequently flattered by his attentions. Some women found his casual, rumpled look to be attractive or cute. But going out to dinner with a woman he had just met—that was stretching the boundary.

An hour later—tidied up a bit—Brad waited for Gen in the lobby. She arrived a moment later, her long hair now tangle-free and brushed to a luster. She wore dark slacks and an ivory-colored satin blouse. Gen had made reservations and, after walking the three blocks to the restaurant, they were right on time. The kimonoed waitress sat them in a private alcove with a curtain drawn across the entrance. They were seated on a floor strewn with thick rugs. A set of candles infused the room with a low, flickering light.

The food was excellent. They started with a wakame salad with radishes, scallions and a ginger dressing. Brad had trouble mastering the chop sticks, so Gen placed them in his fingers and demonstrated the technique. Her fingers felt smooth and strong to Brad. The awareness of her touch filled the front of his consciousness. If anything, her touch made his hands more awkward. Gen picked up a pickled radish with her chopsticks and fed it to Brad.

"See? Easy!" she said.

Next, they had shimeji mushrooms braised in sake with butter, lemon and spinach. Between exclamations praising the food, they talked about their work, their families, their ambitions. A main dish arrived: thin slices of wagyu beef, medium rare, succulent and tender. This was accented by an assortment of roasted vegetables with a balsamic glaze. The Brussel sprouts, which Brad had always hated, melted in his mouth like candy.

Gen said she was an orthopedic surgeon with a specialization in shoulder and elbow surgery. She found a card in her purse and handed it to Brad. It said, "Genovesa Phipps, M.D. Orthopedic specialist." It gave a phone number and address in Phoenix.

The only thing Brad knew about elbow injuries was Tommy John surgery, named after the pitcher whose surgery had pioneered the procedure. Gen knew a lot about Tommy John surgery—reconstruction of the ulnar collateral ligament, she explained—but nothing about Tommy John, so Brad talked about the great pitcher's years with the Dodgers and the Yankees.

At that point a mango sorbet arrived with a pot of green tea. The conversation switched to places they had visited or wanted to visit. Gen loved the south of France and had been there three times. Brad's travel experiences were limited to Mexico and Central America. Genovesa asked about the living conditions there and Brad launched into a speech about the need for medicine and clinicians.

"Oh, I'm sorry! I can be such a bore," said Brad.

"I find you anything but boring," said Gen. She took his hand in hers and gave it a gentle squeeze. "You're a compassionate man, with great dedication. And, I might add, you have very lovely eyes."

Brad blushed. He had not seen that coming. He wondered if Gen was always that forthright with people. Not knowing quite what to say, he said, "Would you call them hazel?"

"More green than hazel, but you're right: there are little specks of brown in there too."

"I suppose that's a matter of genetics," said Brad, trying to steer the conversation back to more neutral ground.

"Yes, but eye color is one of the most predictable features of a person's genetic code. There are very few Norwegians with brown eyes."

Brad signaled the waiter for the check. "You know, Genovesa, as fascinating as this is, I have a talk to give tomorrow, and I'd better get some sleep."

"Yes, I have a full day tomorrow too. Much less fun than this, though."

Brad paid the check.

"Thank you," said Gen. "I didn't intend…"

"Oh, forget about it," said Brad. "My treat."

They walked back slowly to their hotel, looking more than talking. When they arrived, walking to the elevator, Gen said, "Would you like to come up for a nightcap before you retire?"

No, Brad said to himself. Go get some sleep. But then Gen smiled at him, and Brad felt his willpower drain away. "Okay. Just a short one."

They went up to Gen's room and took out a half-bottle of white wine from the refrigerator of the mini-bar. Gen found some glasses while Brad popped the cork. Gen poured two glasses.

"To a successful convention," said Gen. They clinked glasses and drank. Gen's room had a lounge area with a sofa and chairs. Brad sat on the sofa. Gen slipped off her shoes and sat down next to him, turned sideways to face him.

Brad got out his phone and opened a photo. "Here's a picture of Olivia and the kids," he said.

"What a handsome family," said Gen earnestly.

"Thank you."

"I can see you in your kids," said Gen. She scooted closer to him on the couch. "Your good looks are hard to hide."

Brad smiled and looked at his watch. "I think I better go," he said, finishing his wine in a gulp.

"Don't go," said Gen, reaching for his hand. "It's not that late."

Brad was used to flirting, but not to being seduced. The temptation to stay was difficult to ignore. Gen leaned over and gently kissed him on the lips, holding her hands around his face. "Stay awhile," she said, pulling him towards her and kissing him again, this time lingering longer on his lips.

Brad could not deny the pleasure he felt in her kiss. It had been years since he had kissed anyone but Olivia. He found it exhilarating. Gen looked deeply into his eyes and kissed him again. This time Brad kissed her back. Gen kissed him on his cheeks and his neck while she unbuttoned his shirt. When Brad's shirt was open, Gen quickly slipped her blouse over her head.

"Will you unhook my bra?" she asked. Brad did so, all the time asking himself what he was doing, knowing full well that it could only lead to forbidden places where regret is the reigning emotion. Yet as his hands cupped her breasts, and she lay back against him, trembling slightly, he could think of little else besides the firmness of her breasts and the sweet smell of her hair. Gen's hand found his cock and squeezed it through his pants, giving off a little moan as she did so.

Gen turned and removed Brad's shoes, socks and shirt, then unbuckled his belt and pulled off his pants. Then she stood and took off her black dress pants, balancing on one shapely leg at a time, until she wore only black panties. She removed Brad's boxer shorts. While he was still sitting on the sofa, Gen kneeled, took Brad's erect member and put it in her mouth, running her tongue lightly around the tip. Brad groaned in pleasure. He pulled her panties off and felt her vagina which was wet and warm. She took his hand and led him to the bed. Brad lay down and Gen lowered herself gently, gasping quietly as he entered her.

Chapter Six

"Brad, mon," said Jasmine the week after the conference. "There's a man on the phone for you, someone named Briggs."

"Don't know the man."

"He's very insistent. Says it's of utmost importance. Maybe he be the one we been waitin' for."

"The million dollar benefactor."

"That one, yes. Line two."

Brad punched the button for line two. "Brad Collins," he said.

"Hello, Mr. Collins. Thank you for taking my call."

"Sure. How can I help?"

"My name is Briggs, Delmore Briggs, and I wanted to invite you to come to have coffee with me at your earliest convenience."

"What is it you want to discuss?" asked Brad.

"It's a private matter, Mr. Collins. Not something we should discuss over the phone or even at your office."

"A private matter? What are you talking about? Are you peddling graveplots? Do you have an irresistible time-share deal in Hawaii?"

"Very funny, Mr. Collins. I can see you have a quick wit. No, by 'private matter' I mean something to do with your family."

"My family? Who are you, Briggs?"

"I am a nobody. I am just a go-between. I have something for you."

"Like what?"

"Some documents."

"Documents? What the hell are you talking about?"

"I will explain it to you when we meet."

"Okay, okay. How about tomorrow at 10:00 at Paesano's?"

"Excellent. I will see you there."

"How will I know you?"

"I will recognize you, Mr. Collins. I'll watch for you tomorrow at ten." The caller hung up. Brad put his phone back in its cradle, thinking about their recent IRS audit. But surely Briggs would have introduced himself as an IRS agent, if that were the problem. Still, what else could it be? All their medical records were in order. His insurance was paid up. What the hell was this all about? Brad Collins did not sleep well that night.

At ten the next day in front of the restaurant, Brad was waiting for someone he didn't know, looking over the menu posted next to the door, shifting his weight from foot to foot.

"Mr. Collins?" said a voice behind him. "I am Delmore Briggs." Brad turned to face a short man who wore black-rimmed glasses and carried a briefcase. Briggs put out his fist. Brad hesitated, momentarily confused. Then he recovered and bumped knuckles with the man.

"Germs," Briggs explained. "No offence."

Briggs had a pencil-thin neck, and his head was shaped like a balloon. He looked like he might lift off at any moment. The briefcase seemed to tether him to the ground.

They were seated promptly and ordered coffee.

"Now, what's this all about, Mr. Briggs?" Brad demanded to know.

Briggs removed a manila envelope from his briefcase and handed it to Brad. Brad pulled out the contents: a series of photographs showing him having sex with Gen Phipps. The photos were detailed and highly erotic. "We also have footage from a surveillance camera," said Briggs.

"Oh, my God," Brad whispered. "Oh...my...God." His hands shook as he slid the photos back into the envelope. Without a word he opened his briefcase and extracted Gen Phipps's business card. He entered the number.

"Phoenix Orthopedics. May I help you?"

"Yes, may I speak to Dr. Genovesa Phipps please?"

"Phipps? I'm sorry, sir, we have no one on the staff by that name."

"Are you sure? She's a shoulder specialist. P-H-I-P-P-S."

"No, not at this clinic."

"Thank you," said Brad, ending the call. He glared at Briggs. "Blackmail?" he asked in a loud whisper. "You set me up to be black-mailed?"

"I don't like to use that word, but yes sir, we did. We sure as heck did."

"So what do you want?" he asked. "I am not a rich man. What do you want to destroy these? Are there other copies? Where are the origi-nals?"

"I appreciate a man who comes right to the point, Mr. Collins."

"Well?"

Briggs interlaced his fingers and put his hands on the table. "Mr. Collins, are you aware that there are secret passageways that go under the river between the U.S. and Mexico?"

"What the hell does that have to do with anything?" Brad asked a bit too loudly. A few heads turned in their direction.

"I assure you it is pertinent to your situation," Briggs said in a soft voice.

"All right. Tunnels. I've heard of them, sure."

"Yes. Now are you aware that there is one such tunnel that has its ingress and egress on your property?"

"No. There are no tunnels that I know of."

"Then it should interest you to know that there is one. Please allow me to show it to you." From his coat pocket, Briggs produced some snapshots of the yard and loading dock at Neighbors for Health. In one corner, in front of a cooler, a trap door stood open. Another shot showed a ladder descending into the darkness. Then there were shots of inside the tunnel and the exit in Nuevo Laredo.

"Holy shit!" said Brad. "And you say this crosses under the river to Mexico?"

"Yes, sir."

"Holy shit!" he said again.

"Now, in answer to your question, if we can gain unrestricted access to your tunnel, I can assure you that these photographs will not be seen by anyone else."

"I'm sure your word is good as gold, Briggs. What are you going to smuggle through the tunnel, anyway?"

"That is really none of your business, Mr. Collins."

"The hell it's not! It's my property."

"Frankly, for your own protection, it's better if you don't know how we plan to use the tunnel. To be blunt, Mr. D has his own private purposes."

"Mr. D? You're joking, right?" Briggs shook his head. "This is surreal. How do I get in touch with this crook?"

"You don't, frankly. I'll be your contact. And if I may give you a word of advice, the less you know the better. Your best hope is to work with us. The smoother it goes for us, the less incentive we have to show those photographs to anyone."

Brad looked around the room, scorching everything he saw with his eyes, coming to rest on the little man across the table from him. "You're a heartless bastard, Briggs. Do you even know what we do there?"

"Of course. I admire your good work, Mr. Collins. I can guarantee you that we will not interfere with your operation at all."

"A magnanimous gesture, you asshole."

Briggs went on unfazed. "We will work at night, between midnight and four a.m., so there should be no conflict between our work and yours. All we need is the code that unlocks the gate to the yard."

"That and a total lack of conscience."

"I don't give a darn about conscience," Briggs said lightly. "And given your little interlude with Dr. Phipps, I'm not sure you do either."

"It's people like you who drag us all down, Briggs. And, just to be clear: If I refuse—because it would probably involve me in a felony, not to mention the moral depravity of it—you will send the photos to my wife."

"Perhaps members of your board of directors will also receive copies."

"Jesus Christ," Brad muttered. He scowled sullenly at Briggs before he said, "All right, you son of a bitch. I'll give you the code."

"Good," said Briggs cheerfully. He pulled an index card from his pocket. "Please write it on this card."

Brad nodded. He restrained himself from punching Briggs in the face. He was angry at Briggs, but he was furious with himself. He wrote down the code. In exchange, Briggs shoved the manila envelope across the table to Brad.

"How do I know you don't have a copy of the photos or the video?" he asked.

"Well, I guess you won't, Mr. Collins. With digital technology I could easily keep copies of everything."

"And you probably have."

Briggs smiled. "What would you do if you were me?" he asked.

Brad said, "The cooler where we keep medicine and medical supplies is protected by heavy padlocks and a separate alarm system, so don't fuck with it."

"We have no interest in your medicine, Mr. Collins."

Thousands of Mexicans and Central Americans did have an interest in the medicine supplied by Neighbors for Health. Thousands more were fleeing the brutality and poverty of their own countries, hoping to start a new life in the United States. Some of them made it, and some of them died trying. Those that made it needed a job. Briggs planned to match the need for cheap labor in the U.S. with the immigrants' need for work. There were plenty of industries along the Gulf Coast willing to skirt the law by paying less than minimum wage to undocumented immigrants. And there were plenty of immigrants willing to take those jobs at five or six bucks an hour. Briggs knew a *coyote* in Monterrey who was able to supply him with fifteen or twenty able-bodied workers three times a week—for a fee, of course.

Briggs reasoned that the tunnel would give him an edge over other human traffickers, or "labor brokers," as he liked to call them. Going through the tunnel was safer and less visible than an overland crossing. He had the supply, he had a safe smuggling route, and he had clients in south Texas who needed what he was selling. All the pieces were in place.

Where Briggs grew up or why he landed in south Texas, no one knew. He was obviously not a native Texan. His lack of an accent betrayed that secret immediately. In fact, Briggs's accent would have befuddled a linguist. By all accounts his past was a mystery. He had worked at the pipe supply company until it closed, but before that? Briggs might have sold shoes or insurance. He might have painted landscapes or invested in stocks online. There were rumors that he had run Internet scams and fraudulent telephone schemes. But it was hard to know. Delmore Briggs didn't fit any standard profile. He dressed like a nerd from the 1980s, and he was polite to the point of deference. He didn't smoke, drink or swear, and he didn't seem to have any interest in sex. What did interest him was power—power and control. Since he didn't have an intimidating physical presence or a commanding personality, he learned how to attach himself to powerful people. He was willing—in fact, eager—to do the bidding of a man with vision. Wherever he went, he looked for those who were respected and recognized on the street, whether they were businessmen, politicians or gangsters. To them Briggs made himself useful.

If one thing was sure about Delmore Briggs, it was that he was educated. He spoke in full sentences, used correct grammar, and kept up with the news. He knew all sorts of seemingly random facts, such as the birthstone for November, the circumference of the earth in miles and kilometers, and Oscar winners going back to 1950. He could recite the prime numbers up to 233, and he quoted from Sun Tzu's *The Art of War*. He used this miscellaneous information to spice up a conversation, not to show off his intelligence. In fact, he downplayed his brains, saying that he had a good head for facts and figures but didn't have a mind that was strategic or creative.

After awhile his constant smiley-face demeanor got on people's nerves, but they put up with it because in the underworld where Briggs operated, every powerful person needed a go-between and sometimes a dog to kick. Briggs filled both roles.

Chapter Seven

Briggs knew a man named Mike Delaney—never mind how—who owned a bar in Brownsville called the Black Horse Saloon. The Black Horse sat on a corner lot in a seedy part of town. On one side three dusty and perennially parched papaya trees cast long thin shadows. A strip of dead grass ran along the other street. Behind the bar was a gravel parking lot. On the waterfront, a few blocks away, fishing boats unloaded their catch, and a salty tang rode the sea breeze past the Black Horse.

In the back room of his bar, Mike Delaney ran a sports gambling operation, which was illegal in Texas and in all states but Nevada. Briggs approached Delaney and explained to him about the tunnel. Delaney was intrigued.

"What are you proposing?" he asked Briggs.

"No one knows about the tunnel but us," Briggs replied. "We could set up a lucrative business, smuggling illegal workers through the tunnel. There is a labor shortage in the area, and there are always immigrants wanting to get into the United States. I know a *coyote* on the Mexican side who could corral the workers. It would be a good R.O.I."

"Why come to me when you could have the whole operation to yourself?"

"Excellent point, sir. But look at me, Mr. D. Do I look like the kind of guy who could pull this off?" Indeed, with his bow tie and glasses Briggs looked more like a high school math teacher than a trafficker in human lives. "We need some muscle to make this work. I figured you had the connections for that end of it. I surely don't."

Delaney grunted. "I got some guys. Mean sons-of-bitches too," he said. "But you know what? By itself it's not such a good "return on investment," as you say. To me it sounds like a lot of risk for a small payoff. I mean, how much could you charge an employer per worker? Four, five hundred bucks? A thousand tops." Briggs nodded his bobble-like head. "And how many workers could you bring in per week?"

"Maybe forty."

"So, worst case scenario, twenty thousand a week, less expenses. Hell, man, I make that in two good nights out of the back room. And your gig is seasonal too, right? What happens to the tunnel in the winter?"

Briggs shrugged. "I'm not sure, sir."

"What we need to do, Briggs, is to maximize our profits. We've got a tunnel; let's make the most of it."

"Very sensible, sir. What do you suggest?"

"How about drugs? We could use the workers as mules to carry the dope through the tunnel. Then we can make some real money."

"I don't know any drug dealers, Mr. D."

"I'll make some inquiries," said Delaney. "You go out and find some employers who need workers."

Although he was from Irish stock, Michael Todd Delaney was a south Texan, born and bred. His parents had moved to Houston from Boston before he was born and, a few years later, to Brownsville. He went to Mass alongside the Mexicans and Indians from mostly poor families and mostly devout, hard-working parents. Mike spoke with a south Texas drawl and had a smile that was as changeable as the weather. Sometimes it was friendly and other times it was wicked, a little crazy, even demonic. When he smiled, his blue eyes twinkled dangerously.

Mike Delaney did not strike one as a criminal. He was big but not menacing. He did not have a dark beard cross-hatched on his jaws. He did not wear a permanent scowl. He didn't even carry a gun. He looked more like the captain of a rugby team. His large oval head, bristling with closely cropped ginger hair, sat on a thick neck. He had thin lips and his eyes were set closely together. His ears were small and inconspicuous. Except for a set of buckled tea-stained teeth, he might have passed for handsome.

If crooks are made, not born, then Mike Delaney was a self-made crook. The son of a butcher, young Delaney became skilled with a cleaver, and took pride in his ability to separate joints and tendons from muscles with an economy of well-aimed blows. His father also taught him the value of pain—and the fear of pain—to elicit a confession or a promise. He came to fear the switch of a willow on his bare legs and the bed of rock salt in which he was made to kneel as a punishment. To balance the scales, he would venture out with his B.B. gun into the woods near his house, where he would pretend to be hiding from his tormentor. Birds and squirrels that felt the sting of his pellets were proxies for his father.

As a boy, Delaney was fascinated by criminals, especially the Western loners like Butch Cassidy, John Wesley Hardin and Billy the Kid. When he was a young man, out on his own, he began to consider a life of crime as a serious profession. He had tried his hand at several legitimate trades—construction, sales, electrician—but nothing clicked. He gave careful thought to becoming a criminal in a dispassionate and deliberate way. He looked at the pros and cons, the costs and rewards, the likelihood of success and the consequences of failure.

Delaney asked himself what sort of criminal he'd like to be. Like any businessman, his goal would be to make money, yet he knew that dirty money would attract violent characters, as surely as dead meat attracts flies. He had no doubt that he would have to use violence to assert his authority. Dissidents might lose a finger, an eye or a tongue. The most intractable might lose their lives. Delaney was not eager to employ violence, but he was willing to do so if necessary.

When he was upset by someone, Delaney presented his complaints to the offender in a calm voice, as if he were delivering a bit of friendly advice, no matter how egregious the error or how rude the insult. As he liked to say, he always made good on his promises—by which he meant threats. His threats were meant to instill fear and alarm in the offending party: the mess-maker, the big mouth, the brainless idiot seated before him.

Delaney studied the gangs in the area—the Dixie Mafia in Biloxi, the Tango Blast, the Texas Syndicate and the Matamoros cartel across the border. Most gang members were part of the prison culture and even on the outside they would hang with ex-cons and prison buddies. It was a kind of fraternity or club with a flexible and changeable hierarchy and plenty of room for individuals to commit crimes of their own choosing. Still, there were strong leaders, and some gangs were more organized than others. The larger gangs did business on both sides of the border, which was sometimes profitable but mostly was just a pain in the ass. The Mexican gangs were constantly encroaching onto Texas turf, creating a rift between the Mexicans and the Hispanic Texans. But the Texan gangs knew not to protest too much. The cartels were volatile and violent, and had no respect for territory or life.

Delaney noticed that the smaller gangs tended to cultivate the simpler crimes—robbery, burglary, auto theft—while the larger and more dangerous gangs concentrated on the riskier and more complex crimes of drugs, weapons, prostitution, human trafficking and murder.

What Delaney didn't see was any sports betting. Not in a full-service Las Vegas kind of way. This was the criminal niche that Delaney chose to fill, knowing that it was a minor but lucrative racket. Sports betting was unique among criminal activities, because it was a voluntary crime.

No one was hurt, hooked, robbed or exploited except as a consequence of their own independent, uncoerced actions.

The Black Horse Saloon was part of the plan from the beginning. At first, Delaney ran the Black Horse as a sports bar, nothing more. Yes, it catered to a rough and tumble bunch—often members of competing gangs—but it was all legit. Delaney made friends with the local police, and encouraged the cops to stop for a drop after their shift. The police liked having so many no-good tough guys all in one place; it was easier to keep track of them. It made for an odd dynamic, with the hoods hanging out drinking beer while a cop or two looked on. It was as cozy as a cell block.

One day Delaney was talking to police Sergeant Tom Logan, another Irish Texan, who was off-duty at the time.

"You know what I'd like to do?" asked Delaney.

"What's that?"

"The Super Bowl is coming up. I'd like to take a few backroom bets on it. Just for the fun of it."

"Oh, wouldja now? You'd have bettors wrapped around the block."

"All profits could go to charity. Perhaps to the Policemen's Widows Fund. Where's the harm in that?"

"No harm," said Logan. "Just that there's a law against it."

"So I've heard."

"Still and all," said Logan thoughtfully. "How much do you think you could raise for the Widows Fund? Theoretically speaking, I mean."

"Oh, I should think ten thousand dollars or so, wouldn't you?"

"That would make a nice contribution, indeed. I suppose if you limited the number of guests, so as not to draw attention to the event, we might have no need to check the back room at certain times."

And so the back room betting started. At first it was just the Super Bowl, but it soon expanded to other championship games and from there to regular season games. And once it started, the police began receiving a piece of the pie on a regular basis to the point where they couldn't investigate it even if they had wanted to because that would mean exposing their complicity.

News of the betting parlor spread quickly in the taverns, barber shops and pool halls of Brownsville. The police maintained a casual presence at the Black Horse, turning a blind eye to the traffic that came and went through the back door. No one was surprised at this, since political corruption was endemic in south Texas. The "*compadre* code," as it was called by longtime residents, was deeply rooted in the Rio Grande Valley. Mutual back-scratching made for unlikely alliances and cooperation between natural enemies. When prosecutors exposed corrupt practices and brought a case to trial, it was not unusual for their star witnesses to recant their testimony, or, more often, to be found dead in the sagebrush flats north of town before the day of the trial.

So the police knew Delaney was running an illegal sports betting empire at the Black Horse Saloon, but as long as the bribes kept coming, Delaney was above suspicion. And Mike Delaney stayed friendly with the cops even while his henchmen were breaking the fingers of gamblers who couldn't pay their debts.

What the police didn't know—and what surprised Delaney himself—is how successful the sports betting business would be. The cash came pouring in, like water through a breach in a levy. The more games and sports events Delaney added, the more money piled up. He filled one safe with bundles of bills and bought a bigger one. He parked some of the money in a bank in the Cayman Islands. Eventually, Delaney decided he needed to find a place to invest his profits, not because he wanted more money but because he lived in America where more is never enough. He considered several legitimate businesses—construction, high-tech start-ups, oil development—but none of these excited him. What made his heart beat faster was living on the edge, where deceit and corruption thrived and danger was a way of life. That's where the excitement was, and that's where the money was too. That's why Delaney opened the Black Horse, and that's why he was intrigued by Briggs's tunnel. It placed him where he liked to be: at the intersection of money and danger.

Chapter Eight

Henry Lucero had owned B.J.'s Shrimp Co. for thirty years, purchasing the little business for a song when it was in trouble, unable to compete with larger, well-established shrimp companies. A single man with no family responsibilities, Henry focused all his energy on the struggling enterprise and was determined to find a place in the shrimping industry for his small company. Although he had not mapped out a business plan, he plowed ahead with the confidence and resolve of an ambitious young man.

Thrifty and austere, Henry owned three suits off the rack—one dark brown, one light brown and one olive—that he wore in rotation. His half-dozen ties matched the color of all his suits. He owned ten identical white shirts, five of which were always at the cleaners. He kept his brown wingtips clean and shined. Henry didn't drink or smoke. For entertainment he watched sports on TV and read sports magazines. At night he watched the ten o'clock news, then read a chapter from a mystery novel before falling asleep. His only vice was gambling. He wished he could gamble on baseball and basketball games, but since that was illegal in Texas he made do with a few trips to Reno or Las Vegas each year.

Blessed with more common sense that most men, Henry was a natural bootstrap businessman. When he acquired B.J.'s, the first thing he did was to form alliances with some younger shrimpers who were looking to gain traction in the industry too. He promised to buy their entire catch for two cents a pound more than anyone else. Then he went looking for cheap, loyal labor. There was a small park near the waterfront where day laborers hung out waiting for work. They were mostly undocumented Mexicans willing to mow lawns and make cement and process seafood. There he met a man named Harris who said, "If you can offer steady work, I can get you good, reliable workers who will work cheap. I'll bring them right to your door." This was what Henry was looking for and he negotiated a price with Harris.

From Lucero's point of view, the U.S. government was doing all it could to stymie his efforts. He couldn't find enough good workers in Brownsville who would work for minimum wage. There were plenty of Mexicans who wanted work, but the government said no. Lucero was required to hire American workers first, regardless of their work ethic, which was lousy at best for this kind of work. Mexicans worked harder. They wanted the job more and would work for less money. But first he had to prove he couldn't find qualified American workers, and then he had to ask the government for permission to hire foreign workers, which would have required a mountain of paperwork and would have cost him dearly in fees. Plus, he had to supply housing and meals.

So Harris appeared as an angel from heaven. Screw the government, Lucero decided. He would do what he had to do to make his business competitive. He could have contrived some false employment documents—visas or IDs or I-9s or I-94s or H-2As—but if he was going to break the law, he decided, he might as well do it his way. He would fly under the radar. He would run a clean and safe operation, pass every inspection and comply with all the important regs. Except when it came to employment.

To the undocumented Mexicans who worked at B.J.'s, Henry offered less than minimum wage for the hard, repetitive work, but he did provide a clean place to live and three meals a day at a modest cost. He also offered basic health care—not insurance, but an in-house clinic—which no one else did at the time. This was not a magnanimous humanitarian gesture. It was plain business sense, because a healthy workforce is more productive than a sick one. Also, the more minor injuries that could be dealt with at B.J.'s clinic meant fewer trips to the ER and fewer reports to OSHA.

To compete with the big shrimpers, Lucero analyzed his processing system, coming up with simple ways to improve B.J.'s efficiency. When it came to distribution, he jumped over the middleman and sold direct to the customer, whether it be a grocery store, a restaurant chain or a barbeque joint. In all facets of his business, he emphasized freshness above everything else, forever tying the slogan "Fresh from the net" to B.J.'s Shrimp.

To his good fortune, these were banner years for the shrimping industry in America. Shrimp were plentiful, demand was growing, and prices were stable. Then in the early 2000s farmed shrimp from Southeast Asia began to flood the market, driving the price down and forcing small domestic companies out of business.

Henry managed to stay a step or two in front of his creditors, although his profits barely covered his costs. By selling direct and avoiding distributors, he made more profit, but he had to invest in a fleet of delivery trucks and drivers. B.J.'s Shrimp was perpetually balanced between success and failure. It was squeezed by large shrimping operations on one side and cheaper Asian imports on the other.

Henry never knew where his supply of labor came from, and he didn't ask, but for several years Harris kept him supplied with cheap illegal labor. During shrimping season, Harris called Henry regularly to take an order for laborers. But this year, as the season approached, Harris didn't call. When Henry tried to reach him, he found that Harris's phone was "out of service." No one at the labor pool knew what had happened to him—perhaps busted or killed, they said—but in any case it put Henry's labor force in jeopardy. That spring, when shrimping season began, Henry would be forced to hire legitimate labor at minimum wage plus overtime, which would play havoc with his bottom line. He was pondering what to do when he got a call from Delmore Briggs.

"Mr. Lucero," said Briggs. "I understand you have a labor shortage."

"Do I know you?" Lucero asked.

"No, sir. Not from Adam. My name is Delmore Briggs and I am a labor broker."

The two men set up a meeting at a diner in Brownsville. It was a long and narrow room with booths down one side and a soda fountain bar down the other, fronted by stools covered in a shiny turquoise vinyl. They sat in a booth. Henry ordered coffee and Briggs asked for a strawberry shake. Each booth had a jukebox selector, and Briggs leafed through the song choices.

"Most of these songs are fifty years old," he remarked. "The Everly Brothers, Marty Robbins, Patti Page…." Their orders arrived.

"Mr. Briggs," said Lucero impatiently, "do you have a proposal for me?"

"Yes, sir, I do," said Briggs turning away from the juke box. "I can deliver to you as many workers as you need, when you need them. They're all illegals, but they want to work. They want the ching-ching." He rubbed his fingers against his thumb. "As you know, most illegals will work for less than minimum wage. But how much less, that's up to you."

"And how much do you charge per worker?"

"One thousand dollars delivered to your plant."

"A thousand? I used to pay five hundred."

"Maybe so, but we have our expenses and we undertake the risk. Our price is one thousand per worker."

Henry nodded, doing the math in his head. If he had to pay minimum wage for a forty-hour week plus overtime for twenty more hours, a week's wages would be over five hundred bucks—not counting Social

Security and all that crap. On the other hand, he normally paid illegal workers four hundred for a sixty-hour week, so he'd recover his cost of Briggs's fee in four or five weeks. Henry kept adding more workers until the season peaked, when he began to lay them off, and by then he'd have no broker's fee at all. Besides, it was getting harder and harder to find American workers who would work shrimp at all, even for minimum wage. And *legal* "guest workers?" The paperwork alone was prohibitive. Maybe a large shrimp processor could afford it, but not a small outfit like his.

"Tell me, Briggs," he said. "Until this season I had a reliable source for workers through a man named Harris. This year he seems to have dropped out of sight. Do you know what happened to him?"

"I never knew Harris, but I heard he died in a fire," Briggs improvised.

"I'm sorry to hear that," said Lucero. "I trusted that man. And trust is a valuable asset in this sort of agreement."

"I hope to earn your trust too, Mr. Lucero."

"You know, Briggs, they say there is honor among thieves, and I would have to hope that it is true. Because I do not know you, and—let's be blunt—we are discussing a serious violation of the law. How do I know you're not a federal agent trying to set up some kind of sting that would shut me down?"

"To be honest, Mr. Lucero, your operation is too small for the feds to worry about. You could say they have bigger fish to fry."

A rare smile passed over Lucero's face. "Yes, I suppose that's true," he said. "Briggs, I'm the kind of man who believes in deeds more than words. So I'll give it a shot, and we'll see what happens."

"Fair enough, Mr. Lucero. You won't be disappointed."

"Shrimping season is about to begin, so how soon can we start?"

"Right away. I supply labor for other clients as well—sugar cane processors, fertilizer manufacturers, motels—so I have a constant stream of workers coming in. It'll be just like it was before."

"Good."

As they were leaving, a Johnny Cash song was playing on the juke box.

"I'm stuck in Folsom Prison
And time keeps dragging on.
But that train keeps a-rollin'
On down to San Antone.

When I was a baby,
My mama told me, 'Son,
Always be a good boy,
Don't ever play with guns.'
But I shot a man in Reno,
Just to watch him die.
When I hear the whistle blowing,
I hang my head and cry."

"That boy needs a geography lesson," said Briggs.

"What ?" Henry asked, lost in his own thoughts.

"If he shot a man in Reno, which is in Nevada, why is he in Folsom State Prison, which is in California? Neither of them is close to San Antonio."

"What are you talking about?" said Henry, mystified.

"Never mind," said Briggs.

Chapter Nine

"El Flaco" (or "Slim") was a curious nickname, since the man was not tall. "El Chapo" ("Shorty") would have been more apt, but that name was already taken by another cartel boss. The name "Flaco" referred, almost derisively, to his thin, even scrawny frame, which he tried to stretch with high-heeled cowboy boots and a Stetson hat. He had a propensity for pastel-colored snap-button shirts with elaborate embroidery on the shoulders and yoke. His long, skinny neck stuck up above the collar, and his Adam's apple protruded out so far that kids stared at it. When he got excited or angry, his voice turned shrill and his ropey arms looped through the air like lassos. He had a Mexican's dark skin and thick black hair. On his narrow upper lip, he wore a pencil moustache, thin as a knife blade.

Despite his clownish appearance, El Flaco was a powerful and dangerous man. It was well known that he had a merciless mean streak probably acquired from being pushed around and beaten up as a child. He lost every fist fight he was in, and he finally turned to using weapons to defend himself. He schooled himself in the use of brass knuckles, knives, guns, whips and crude weapons, such as cattle prods and electric drills.

El Flaco eliminated his enemies ruthlessly and efficiently. He never lashed out at them impulsively and rarely hit them the same way twice. Some of his methods for murder were original and grotesque, such as forcing splintered glass down an adversary's throat through a feeding tube. Once, he put an enemy in a small stall with an angry bull, and let the bull trample the man to death, hoisting him on his horns and flinging him to the ground. Police found the murder weapon snorting and slamming himself against the walls of the stall, the gory victim limp and lifeless beneath its bloody hooves.

El Flaco's world was black and white, perhaps more *negro* than *blanco*. He divided people into two classes, *amigos* and *enemigos*. Anyone else, *es nadie*. From his underlings, El Flaco expected absolute loyalty, and he did not tolerate insubordination.

"Briggs, your Spanish is pretty good, right?" asked Mike Delaney.

"It's adequate."

"I want you to get in touch with El Flaco for me."

"Sir?"

"El Flaco, the Mexican bandit. I want to talk to him. But first I want *you* to talk to his chief lieutenant, second in command or whatever. His captain."

Briggs was agitated by the thought. "Mr. D, El Flaco is a dangerous man. Don't you think we should stay under his radar?"

"Whatsamatter, Briggs? Afraid of a beaner?" Delaney laughed. "Everybody thinks Flaco is a tough customer. I think he's a friggin' phony. Just a greaseball in a fancy shirt. He cuts off a guy's nuts because he's afraid someone will do it to him. I say…" Delaney finished the sentence by spitting on the floor. Looking at Briggs's wide-eyed face, he said, "Don't worry, Briggs. I'll be nice. I think he can help us."

Briggs was not convinced. "El Flaco is a violent thug. He's unpredictable and has no respect for anything, even himself. Why would we want to draw attention to ourselves, Mr. D?"

"Because Flaco sells drugs, and he's *el jefe* down there. Make some phone calls, Briggs. See who you can get on the phone. Someone in Flaco's inner circle."

"What should I say?"

"Say that I have a proposition for him, something that will benefit both of us. A bilateral proposal."

Briggs did have one connection with a gang member in Mexico. He had helped him locate a fugitive who had tried to assassinate El Flaco. All the other would-be assassins from that band of renegades had been killed. The sole survivor had been hiding out in Brownsville. Briggs found out where he was holed up and led the Mexican gunmen to the motel where the wanted man was hiding. Flaco's man unleashed a bloodbath of bullets and fled back to Mexico.

Briggs reached this killer and asked him to relay a message to El Flaco: that Mike Delaney of Texas had some mutually beneficial business to discuss with him, worth millions of dollars a year.

El Flaco considered the message thoughtfully. He did not know this Mike Delaney. Maybe he had heard his name once or twice. He was told that Delaney was a small-time operator in Brownsville who ran a sports book. Flaco could not imagine why such a man would interest him. What did interest him was Texas. It would be quite a coup if he could add some of Texas to his territory. A base in Texas would provide a foothold to expand his operation. Meeting this Mike Delaney in Brownsville would give him a chance to survey the situation from the inside.

Delaney also wanted to have the meeting in Brownsville. He was sure that Flaco had far superior muscle and fire-power, and he thought being on his own turf would help to level the odds. He wanted Flaco to feel inferior and out of place.

They worked out the details over the phone. It would have been easier and much less risky for them to have the meeting in Mexico, where Flaco could remain hidden. His face was well-known to guards at the border crossings, and using a false passport or hiding him in a truck were dicey propositions. Even bribes were not foolproof. Delaney had been waiting for these objections.

"There is an alternative travel route," he said to Flaco. "I have a tunnel under the Rio Grande." Flaco suddenly sensed a greater opportunity at hand. A tunnel would offer him a safer way to smuggle goods. Perhaps they could work out a deal to share the tunnel. He could always seize it outright by force, but that would only lead to sabotage and subterfuge.

"Where is the tunnel?" he asked.

"On your side it's just outside Nuevo Laredo. On my side it comes out in a locked parking lot. I can arrange to take you there and pick you up on the other side.

"Is it watched?" Flaco asked.

"I think not. We use it three times a week. It is safe."

"*Bueno.*" El Flaco realized this must be the tunnel he had heard about but had been unable to locate.

A date and time were arranged for El Flaco to meet Delaney at the Black Horse Saloon. On a cloudless night, shortly before midnight, a shiny black Hummer bumped across the wasteland on the outskirts of Nuevo Laredo to the tunnel entrance. Flaco had brought a confidante and two bodyguards. He was given kneepads and gloves. With one guard in front of him and one behind, both with beaming flashlights, he crawled through the cement pipe, almost retching at the stench. Outside the gate of Neighbors for Health, they were met by a Marathon Coach that slept four and were whisked away down the road to Brownsville. El Flaco went to bed. They pulled up to the Black Horse at four a.m. and parked behind the bar, out of sight from the road.

Flaco slept until nine, then showered and shaved in the coach's compact but well-appointed restroom. He put on a lavender cowboy shirt and gray slacks. He decided not to wear a bolo tie as he often did.

Briggs escorted him to the upstairs office where Delaney was waiting. Two bouncers from Delaney's saloon stood by; their muscles popped out of black polo shirts. Flaco was flanked by his two bodyguards: thuggish men in suits, although their suit jackets did not hide the guns in their shoulder holsters.

"*Buenos dias*, Señor Flaco," said Delaney, rising to shake Flaco's hand. "Welcome to the Black Horse. May I offer you some coffee?"

"Coffee is a good idea," Flaco said. "I will practice *mi inglés* with you, okay, Mr. Delaney?" He had trouble with "Delaney."

"Call me Mike, Mr. Flaco. Have a seat, *por favor*. How was your trip?"

"I sleep like the baby."

"That's quite a bus, ain't it?"

"Yes, Mr. Mike. Is good. El Flaco is first class all the way."

"I am always delighted to meet classy folks."

"Is not necessary to have delight, Mr. Mike."

"No? How should I feel?"

"Nervous."

"I'm not the nervous type, Mr. Flaco. How 'bout a doughnut?"

Delaney held out a plateful of doughnuts and El Flaco selected one with chocolate frosting. Delaney gave him a paper plate and a small paper napkin.

"How are things in Matamoros, Mr. Flaco? Having any trouble with the police?"

"No, no trouble. We come and we go, no problem. People know El Flaco is *el jefe*."

"Good. That's good to hear. You are the man I want to talk to."

"About what you do want to talk, Mr. Mike?"

"About money. Money and drugs."

"Okay. We are, *como se dice, cuándo la página es el mismo?*"

"That's right. We're on the same page, hombre. On the same page. Here's the deal, Mr. Flaco. I have a little gambling business here. People bet on sports events: football, basketball, NASCAR, tennis, whatever. I'm making pretty good money, and I want to invest it in another profitable enterprise. You with me so far?"

"*Sí*, I am very with you."

"We both know there is a market for drugs here, especially cocaine and heroin. Now I understand that you sell cocaine and heroin, am I right?"

"*Sí*, you are right exactly."

"I would like to become a regular customer of yours, Mr. Flaco. Every week I get drugs from you, and every week you get money from me. Fair enough?"

"I forget what is 'fair'?"

"*Justo*," said Briggs, who was sitting inconspicuously in a corner of the room.

"Ah, *sí*. *Es justo* if the price *es justo*."

"Of course, of course," said Delaney. "We'd have to agree on the price, just like it was coffee beans or oil or something else."

"The price, it change," said Flaco. "Is one price now, *y* next week is *un otre*."

"Sure. Supply and demand. Good old *capitalismo*, right, Mr. Flaco? But if I am a good customer and always pay my bill on time, then I should get your best price, don't you agree?"

Flaco stood up suddenly. His half-eaten doughnut fell to the floor and his styrofoam cup of coffee went flying, spilling its contents on one of his stooges. Flaco's face turned dark and his eyes flashed wildly.

"*Yo decido el preció. Yo! Y tu lo pagas*!" he squealed. His fists were balled up so tightly that his knuckles turned white. His arms looped through the air.

"Chill, Mr. Flaco," said Delaney calmly. "I'm not trying to cheat you here. I'm just sayin' good customers should get good treatment. I'm gonna be your best customer. Maybe not your biggest customer, but your most reliable."

Flaco unclenched his fists, relaxed his shoulders and sat down again. He took out a handkerchief to wipe the saliva off his lips. "I am chill now," he said as his face regained its normal color. He reached up to tighten his bolo tie, but then realized he wasn't wearing one and tugged on his collar instead.

By the time they parted, Delaney and El Flaco had come to an agreement. Delaney would continue to smuggle illegal workers through the tunnel, and would buy as many as twenty bricks of heroin per week from El Flaco, using the workers to carry the drugs across the border. The driver on the U.S. side would pay cash for the heroin.

While not considered an honorable practice, smuggling was nothing new in the Rio Grande Valley. It dated back at least to the Civil War, when unscrupulous traders smuggled Confederate cotton south into Mexico. From there the cotton went north by boat to the textile mills of New Hampshire where it was turned into uniforms for the Union Army. Delaney and El Flaco joined a long line of local smugglers. Some of them got away with it. Of those who didn't, some went to prison, and some were shot or hung by the neck.

Chapter Ten

After the phone call from Brad, Eddie Maez stretched out on the dock and watched the colors fade in the sky. He wondered what could be so important that Brad wouldn't discuss it on the phone. As night came, the horizon disappeared, and it became impossible to tell the sky from the water. The stars reflected off the Gulf, making the fusion complete. Eddie packed up his fishing gear and beer bottles and walked back to his cottage. The next day he piled all his luggage into his car and drove up to San Antonio where he booked a room at the Havana Hotel, a classic haunt where he liked to stay if someone else was paying for his room.

The two men had been friends for five years, ever since Brad had suggested that Eddie investigate the legitimacy of some shadowy pharmaceutical companies. Brad supplied him with names and technical assistance. Eventually Eddie nailed a fraudulent outfit that was trying to pass off inert chemicals as life-saving vaccines. Eddie's snooping provided enough evidence to shut down the company and send its top officers to prison. Eddie won an award for investigative journalism, and Brad was named Non-Profit Executive of the Year.

After a restful night at the Havana and a hearty breakfast, Eddie headed over to Brad's office. A cold front was moving through, but they braved a chilly wind and ambled along the River Walk, out of downtown, past the flour mill and the century-old mansions with their high fences and manicured grounds. Brad knew Eddie would be discreet, so he told him the whole story: about the tunnel, about how he was set up and how he was being blackmailed, and about what would happen if he refused to play along.

"Whoa, you got yourself in deep, bro. What do you want me to do?"

"Find out what you can about their smuggling operation and find out about Delmore Briggs; find out who the mysterious Mr. D is. Whatever you can dig up. I've got to figure out how to put them out of business. I don't want anyone to see those photos."

"Why not just call the feds?"

"You think they'll be discreet? 'Please don't tell my Board. Please don't tell the press.' Hell, the whole world is going to find out if I go to the feds. And need I say, not a word of this to anyone. Remember you're working for me, not the paper."

"You're playing with fire, Brad."

"That's why I called you. What the hell am I going to do now?"

"You looking for advice? I'll give you some. Don't fight it alone. Tell your Board. Tell ICE. This thing is too big for you to tackle by yourself. Brad Collins vs. a Mexican drug cartel? My money's on the cartel."

"Thanks for the vote of confidence. But don't you see? If this comes out publicly, I could lose everything."

"Not necessarily. You're a victim, man."

Brad turned his jacket collar up against the wind.

"You tell Olivia you're being blackmailed?" Eddie asked. "You tell her about the photos?"

Brad shook his head. "I've been trying to figure out how to do that without dire consequences."

"Like being kicked out of the house on your cheating ass?"

"Yeah, like that."

"Look, man, you got to talk to her. That's the number one thing you got to do."

Brad looked tired and depressed. "I know, I know. I've been wrestling with how to tell Olivia. I don't want to lose her, Eddie." His eyes welled with tears that rolled down his cheeks when he blinked. "I'm probably going to lose my job, and I don't want to lose her too. And, god help me, the kids."

"Dude, if she loves you, she won't dump you, but you gotta be straight with her. You don't want her to hear about it by reading about it in the paper."

Brad bristled and looked at his friend. "What do you know about women?" he asked. "You never even go out on dates."

"I'm aware of that, but the point is…."

Brad interrupted. "I get your point," he said.

Chapter Eleven

Olivia had her book club that night. Brad got dinner, helped the kids with their homework and got them to bed by 9:00. For the next hour-and-a-half, Brad walked nervously around the house. The TV was on, and he watched it now and then, running down the menu of choices, switching between sports, news and sitcom reruns. He decided that coffee would just make him more jumpy, and he didn't want to start drinking, although he had put a bottle of white wine in the refrigerator just in case. He wasn't expecting a celebration; that was just wishful thinking. He tried to read an editorial about Palestine and Israel, but he couldn't get past the second paragraph.

Brad practiced what he was going to say, looking at himself in the bathroom mirror, trying to look apologetic—yet loving, honest, sincere. He tried out hand gestures and postures. He experimented with compliments on her hair, questions about her book club, something about the kids being helpful with the dishes.

He decided to escort Olivia to the living room. He didn't want this discussion to take place in the kitchen, among the hanging pots, a shelf full of cups to throw, and, God forbid, knives at hand.

Eventually Brad heard Olivia's car drive up, followed by the familiar sounds of a garage door opening and closing. He turned off the television, picked up the editorial about Israel and Gaza and took it into the living room. He heard the door open from the garage to the kitchen.

"In here, honey," Brad called out. He could hear her taking off her jacket, changing shoes and brushing her hair briefly into place. She went to the living room.

"Hi, sweetie," Olivia said, giving Brad a kiss on the cheek. "How were the kids tonight? Everything fine?"

"Yeah, no problems. We had a nice dinner, talking about, you know, their friends, their teachers, girlfriends, boyfriends…. Then they did their homework and went to bed. Easy peasy."

"They're such good kids. We are so lucky. We don't have the problems some families have, with kids sneaking out at night, talking back…forget homework!" Olivia put her arm around her husband's head, hugging it.

"You're right," he said. "We *are* lucky, and I really love our family. I feel privileged to be part of it."

"Oh, Brad. What a sweet thing to say." She reflected a moment and then said, "What's wrong? Something's wrong, isn't there?"

"No, no. I just…."

"You just what?"

"Olivia, could you sit down a minute. We need to talk."

Olivia sat down. "Did something happen with the kids? What's going on?"

"No, the kids are fine. It's me. I have to tell you something, Olivia."

"What? Tell me what?"

"I think it would be best if I told you the whole story."

"The whole story? What is this about?"

"Okay. Well. This happened shortly after I got back from San Francisco a few weeks ago, okay? I was approached by a man, guy by the name of Delmore Briggs, who, it turns out, is a criminal. But I didn't know that at first. He asked me if I knew that there is a trap door on our loading dock at Laredo that leads to a tunnel underneath the Rio Grande."

"Are you serious? A tunnel?"

"Yeah. And this guy Briggs, he wants to use the tunnel for…well, he didn't say what for. Smuggling something, I assume. Drugs, undocumented immigrants, guns, I don't know."

"Oh my god, Brad! What did you say?"

"I would have said 'no,' of course, but he had something on me."

"You mean a gun? My god! He had a gun?"

"No, he didn't have a gun. He had some…pictures. Photographs."

"Okay, you lost me there. Just tell me what the fuck is going on, Brad."

"Well, while I was at the World Health Congress conference last month, I met this woman."

"This woman? What woman? Are you telling me you're having an affair?"

"No, no. No, I am not having an affair. I don't know where this woman lives. I don't even know her real name."

"What the hell are you saying?"

"She said she was a doctor, gave me her card even. We talked about medicine. Olivia, she seemed legit."

"Legit? What, legit enough to fuck?"

"No—she was, I guess you'd say, a call girl."

Olivia got up from her cushioned chair, walked over to Brad and slapped him on the face as hard as she could. Brad felt it all the way down his spine.

"Wait, wait!" he said. "I didn't go looking for her. I didn't pay her money."

"You didn't even pay her?" She slapped him again.

"I mean, she seduced me, Olivia."

Olivia laughed wildly. "You mean she seduced your cock because you couldn't keep it in your pants. Like you had no part in it."

"I guess you could say that. But she had criminal intent."

"Oh, that's rich. You just had sex, but she had sex with criminal intent."

Olivia picked up a glass figurine on the coffee table and threw it at Brad. The figurine smashed into a wall, scattering fragments of glass all over the living room.

"Olivia, I'm so sorry! Believe me! I'm not sure how it happened. She took me by surprise. She came on to me, and she was very sexy, and…."

"And you just couldn't help yourself."

Brad started to say something, but then just shrugged his shoulders in silence. After awhile, he said, "I'm sorry, Olivia. It was a terrible mistake."

"It was a decision, not a mistake!"

"Okay, it was a terrible decision. Please forgive me," he begged. "It won't happen again."

"God, you are pathetic." There was silence in the room, and then Olivia said, "So what does all this have to do with what's-his-name and the tunnel?"

"Briggs. His name is Briggs."

"And?"

"Well. Shortly after the convention, I got a call from Briggs, and he says he has something to show me. So we meet, and he's got an envelope full of photos of me and Gen—or whatever her name is—you know, having sex, and…."

Olivia crossed the room and began beating Brad with her fists, yelling, "Brad, Brad, how could you? I hate you!"

"Olivia, please! You've got to listen to me." He grabbed her wrists so she would stop hitting him. When he let go, she collapsed on the sofa.

Olivia lay on her back and put her arm over her eyes. "Go on," she said.

Brad let out a heavy sigh. "So Briggs says that he wants to use the tunnel that comes up in our yard, and if I don't let him, he's going to send these photos to you and the press and my Board. So you see, he had paid this woman to seduce me in order to get the pictures to black-mail me with."

"Well, you certainly did your best to help him out."

"I was duped. I was set up."

"If you'd kept your cock in your pants, you wouldn't be…. God-damn it, Brad! So what happened after you saw the pictures?"

"I told him he could use the tunnel if he would destroy the photos."

"So now you have smugglers—like, dangerous criminals—working out of Neighbors for Health. Brad, I can't believe this. You are such an idiot! Don't you think he kept copies of the pictures?"

"Probably. But at least I've bought myself some time to figure out what to do."

"There's only one thing to do, and that's to go to the authorities."

"I know that, and I will. But first I'd like to know more about their operation. I hired Eddie Maez to check it out. He's going down to La-redo tomorrow."

"Jesus, Brad."

"I know. It's fucked up." Silence settled in the room. Both Brad and Olivia were wrapped up in their own thoughts, trying to work through it all and somehow understand the consequences of what they might do next.

"The most important thing I want to say," said Brad. "Is 'I love you, I love our kids, our life…more than anything…and I'm sorry for what I did. I hope you can forgive me.'"

There, he said it. And it was heartfelt and true.

Olivia looked him in the eye and knew that he meant it, every word, and she believed him. Still, she felt angry and betrayed. She fumed in silence, feeling her heart thumping, her muscles suddenly weak. Finally she took a deep breath and let it out slowly.

"I love you too, Brad. But I would appreciate it if you would sleep on the couch tonight. This isn't an easy 'hug and make up.' I need to be with it by myself for a while. I'll see you in the morning." She gathered her purse and tote bag and headed for the bedroom.

Brad rustled around in the linen cabinet until he found a blanket and a pillow. He poured himself a shot of bourbon but left it sitting on the bar, untouched. He felt shaky but good about their conversation. He thought she would stick by him, even if the pictures did surface in public. Olivia taught middle school, where there was sure to be a flurry of rumors and questions and whisperings once Brad went to the cops—that is, if the story made the papers, which of course it would. But Olivia could handle it, Brad thought, and what's more, she *would*, despite the indignities she would have to endure. Still, it would be best if the photos never came to light. Yet the photos, he realized, did not only document his marital infidelities but also provided proof against the blackmailers. The photos proved he was being set up. They weren't just fodder for someone's divorce, they were evidence of a criminal act. Brad took off his shoes and crawled under the blanket. His thoughts became increasingly abstruse and their pathways took odd turns until he finally fell asleep.

In the bedroom, Olivia changed into her nightgown, put on face cream and hand lotion. She got into bed and turned out the light. For a long time she lay in bed, unmoving, her eyes wide open staring into the darkness. Her thoughts had no structure, but moved from memory to memory: with the kids on the coast, a family reunion at her parents' house, Christmas at home, a Little League game, their wedding…. They had a good life, she thought, even if it was a bit conventional. But they were happy and comfortable, a paragon of the modern family. Not any more, she mused. Now they were down in the muck with everyone else.

She sighed. Life is messy. Fat tears formed in her eyes and spilled over onto her pillow. They came for a long time, and she let them run.

Chapter Twelve

Eddie Maez drove the three hours from San Antonio to Laredo. It was, he was convinced, one of the most boring drives in America: flat as plywood, straight as a nail. On the night air, the smell of mesquite blew in through the open windows. When he got to Laredo he left his car a few blocks away and entered the yard just before midnight.

Brad had briefed him on the layout of the yard, and he stationed himself in a shadowy corner, with a view of the trap door. He wanted a cigarette, even though he had given them up years ago. He popped a stick of gum into his mouth. At two a.m. a cargo truck arrived and entered the yard, and two men got out. The driver watched his partner open the trap door with a crowbar. A short while later a man climbed out of the shaft onto the loading dock. He wore simple clothes and a small backpack, and was directed to climb into the back of the truck. Others followed, twenty-two in all, both men and women. Although it was hard to see their features in the darkness, they appeared to be Latinos, mostly teenagers and young adults. When the last one emerged and was herded into the truck, the driver pulled down the roll-up door. He drove out of the yard. His partner locked the gate, climbed into the cab, and they drove away.

Eddie went back to his car to get a headlamp and a pair of knee pads. Then he approached the underground entryway and opened the trap door. He unwrapped a fresh piece of gum before he descended into the depths with a small camera in his pocket and an automatic pistol in his shoulder holster. He took a deep breath and closed the trap door above him. After all these years, tunnels still gave him the willies. Although he was a short man, Eddie had to crawl through the pipe. It was only four or five feet in diameter, and he was too old to duck-walk hunched over. Hell, even the tunnels in Nam were bigger than this one. What a crazy thing to do for a no-good cause. "Stupid friggin' war," he whispered. He shook his head and chewed his gum. Above him he could hear the river flowing: a rolling, hissing sound. A snake slithered through a crack and disappeared in the darkness ahead. Where water trickled down the side, a mossy slime was growing. The water on the bottom of the pipe was dark with sediment and smelled of sewage. He snapped a few photos.

The tunnel ended at another ladder. Eddie climbed up. He nudged the trap door open, very carefully and slowly. No one was there. He came out in a thicket of stunted mesquite trees surrounded by a landscape of prickly pear cactus and rocky soil. Ragged piñons struggled to survive. A few broken-down cars sat beside abandoned tin-roofed shacks. The wind rattled the metal roofs and blew dust into Eddie's eyes. A swath of thick bushes grew along the river, but beyond that there was nothing but sagebrush and cactus. He placed a small GPS device in the midst of a cactus patch near the trap door. Then he returned through the tunnel to the Neighbors for Health facility. The sky was beginning to lighten.

Eddie continued his surveillance for four nights. To pass the time, he brought his iPod and listened to selections from his vast blues collection. He liked Albert Collins, Stevie Ray Vaughn, and Freddy Fender. Sometimes he'd throw in some classic sides of Lydia Mendoza or a few Tex-Mex bands like Los Lonely Boys and the Texas Tornadoes. When he saw the lights of a truck approaching the yard, he turned off the music and blended in with the building.

The second night the truck didn't come. It returned on the third night. Some immigrants came up through the tunnel with brown bricks shrink-wrapped to their chests. Before the migrants climbed into the truck, the driver's partner cut off the parcels with a pair of scissors and stashed them in grapefruit boxes. Eddie counted ten bricks concealed in boxes labeled Ruby Red. The driver and his helper loaded the boxes into the truck. They also handed over a bulky backpack from a compartment on the truck to a third man who disappeared back down the tunnel. They closed the trap door, covered it with dirt, tamped it down, and drove away.

The last night Eddie parked across the street where he had a view of the yard. As usual the truck arrived at two a.m. "Very punctual operation," noted Eddie. He slouched down in the darkness. When the truck pulled out of the yard, he gave it a block's head start and then pulled out behind it.

The truck got onto Highway 83 and headed southeast. It was a good road and not busy at three a.m., so it was easy for Eddie to follow the truck.

They came to a checkpoint.

It was one of those temporary checkpoints that the Border Patrol set up in remote areas to deter smuggling—of goods or people—a kind of guerilla tactic dreamed up in Washington that was more bother than it was worth. A singlewide trailer, borrowed from the Parks Dept., provided an office, an interrogation room and two jail cells. At night, bright spotlights lit up the little operation, giving the misapprehension that it was bigger and tougher than it actually was. At 3:30 on a weekday night, it was staffed by two cops, one of each gender. The male cop was an old veteran whose face was severely wrinkled from heavy smoking, just putting in his time and counting the days until he could retire with a pension. The female was a young woman who wore black lipstick and heavy mascara. Eddie thought it was strange that the two truckers would not try to avoid the checkpoint. Surely they knew about it. There were bumpy back roads that skirted the checkpoint, unnamed roads the farmers used to transport soy beans, okra, sugar cane—and farm work-ers, both legal and illegal.

The female cop was on duty for westbound traffic; the male had the eastbound side. The truck slowed down and the officer came out to meet it. Eddie pulled up as far as he could, hoping he could hear the conver-sation.

"IDs please," said the grizzled cop. The driver handed over their driver's licenses. The cop looked at the IDs, then back to the truckers. "Proof of citizenship," he said.

The driver had a passport and his buddy had a birth certificate. The cop studied them briefly.

"What are you hauling?" he asked.

"Mostly grapefruit. Some sugar cane." The old cop nodded, but he didn't open up the roll-up door that covered the back of the truck.

Eddie didn't get it until he saw a flash of green change hands from the driver to the cop. "Of course," he thought. "I'm an idiot."

"Drive safe," said the cop as he waved the truck through. The cops then gave Eddie's empty car a cursory look and sent him on his way.

On the outskirts of Brownsville, the truck stopped at a shrimp pro-cessing plant called B.J.'s Shrimp Co. There was a guardpost at the gate. The security guard pushed a button to open the electric gate. Then the truck disappeared around towards the back and the gate slid closed. It was 6:30 a.m.

Before he hit the road back to San Antonio, Eddie found a diner where he scarfed down some griddlecakes and fried eggs and fortified himself with lots of black coffee.

Although the day was bright and the coffee had been strong, Eddie had trouble staying awake for the four-hour drive to San Antonio. He put on some kick-ass Cajun music, shoved some fresh gum in his mouth and kept driving. When he finally got back, in the early afternoon, he checked back into the Havana, pulled off his shoes, lay down on the bed and fell asleep.

When he awoke it was dark out. The clock radio said 9:47. Eddie got up, dressed for bed and ordered some fried chicken and potato salad from room service. After he watched the 10:00 news, he climbed into bed and slept another eight hours.

In the morning, feeling refreshed, he called Brad and suggested they meet for lunch. Eddie named a popular diner on Lasoya Street. The Mexican polkas pumping through the sound system were loud enough to cover their conversation. Some people in a back corner booth were leaving, and Eddie grabbed the relatively quiet spot. A boy bussed the table, and gave them menus.

"So I assume you have something for me," Brad said.

"Yeah, I do. There's some bad shit happening at your warehouse, Brad. You're not going to believe this. First of all, they're bringing in what appear to be Mexican illegals, presumably to do shit jobs, but I can't be sure about that. I was there four nights, and every night but one I saw the same thing. At 2 a.m. a truck arrives. A guy gets out and opens the gate for the truck to drive into the yard. Then he opens the trap door you told me about, and about twenty Mexicans come up—including teenaged boys and girls. They all get in the back of the truck and drive away. The next night, the truck never came. The *third* night, same thing as the first night, except this time some of them have these packages attached to their chests with shrink wrap. Bricks of something wrapped in brown paper. I'm guessing heroin, but it could have been cocaine or something else entirely. Stolen jewels, who knows? The truck driver cuts off all the parcels with a pair of scissors and stashes them in Ruby Red Grapefruit boxes."

"Hold on a minute. Grapefruit boxes?"

"Ruby Reds. Crazy, huh?"

"Okay, then what?"

"Then everybody piles into the truck and they're off. The fourth night I park across the street and wait there in my car. Two a.m., just like clockwork, the truck arrives. The Mexicans come up the ladder out of the tunnel—I say Mexicans, but they could have been Guatemalan, Honduran, Salvadoran, something like that. Anyway, they come up, no brown bricks this time. They get in the truck and take off. I follow them. They drive south on 83 all the way to Brownsville. Four fuckin' hours to a place called B.J.'s Shrimp Co. They have a guard there who opens the gate for them. The truck drives in and the gate slides closed. That's it. End of the line for me."

Brad didn't say anything for a minute. They gave the waiter their orders. Brad swallowed some water. "Fuckin' A," he said. "Did you check out the tunnel?"

"Oh, yeah, there's that! The first night after they left, I went down into the tunnel—stinky, slimy place. Concrete pipe, four feet in diameter. Had a miner's light on my head and knee pads. I carried a gun, just in case. I didn't run into anyone, but it's pretty creepy crawling through there. Here," he said handing Brad some snapshots. "I took a few pictures. It comes out in this deserted area, covered with cactus and trash. There was nothing around—a few shacks and abandoned trailers. I saw cars moving on a road about half a mile away, I'd say. I planted a GPS device in a patch of prickly pear. If you ever want to know where the tunnel goes on the Mexican side, we can find it."

Brad nodded thoughtfully. "Nice work, Eddie." He toyed with his enchilada. "Grapefruit boxes," he murmured to himself.

Chapter Thirteen

A gathering of whitewashed huts, made of mud and straw, stand on stilts, windows open to the outside. The thatched roofs are nearly three feet thick. A large porch aprons two sides, hammocks hanging still as a photograph in the heavy, breathless air. Parrots call through the tropical trees. A hot sun beams in the blue sky of Honduras.

Campesinos live here. Subsistence farmers. They grow corn and beans for themselves and coffee for the cooperative. They live in the hills and build terraces for their crops. Once in a while, a hurricane comes through with fierce winds and heavy rains. The people rebuild their homes, repair the terraces and begin farming again. No one knows how old the village is, as no written records exist. Stories passed down over the ages tell how their ancestors survived not only hurricanes but marauding tribes, disease and wild beasts. Like their stories, their religious traditions and the ancient knowledge of farming and weaving have been passed down from one generation to the next.

Carlos Cruz and Sofia Guzman had been friends from beyond their memory. They grew up together in neighboring families in their village carved out of the forest. To say they fell in love and got married would be misleading. "Love" was a concept they did not recognize, except as something they'd seen in movie magazines and comic books. They simply felt that their destinies were intertwined and that they were meant to be together.

One thing they both knew is that farming is hard work, especially with nothing but hand tools. There were no gas motors to help pump the water and no tractors to till the tiers of land, only oxen and plow. Some people would leave the village—for the sake of the family—to find work in a city doing mind-numbing factory work, but with real wages—

enough to send back home where they needed money for the necessities, and maybe, someday, a generator.

But Carlos and Sofia had bigger dreams. Carlos dreamed of being a teacher or perhaps an engineer, and Sofia wanted to be a doctor. They wanted to help their people. Thanks to the Catholic mission school three miles from their village, both Carlos and Sofia had an eighth grade education. They could read and write and do basic math. They felt capable of reaching their goals, but they knew it would never happen in rural Honduras. Nor would it happen in Tegucigalpa, the capital city, a crowded and dangerous place with the highest murder rate in the Americas. Besides, only wealthy Hondurans could afford to go to college, and Carlos and Sofia were dirt poor.

When they went to the U.S. Consulate to see about getting a visa to work in the U.S., they were confronted with a staggering set of requirements and a thick pile of paperwork. Bottom line: To get a worker's visa they had to have a job waiting for them in the States. Getting a visitor's visa was even more daunting. They needed to own property, to have money in the bank, and to be currently employed. A third way into the U.S. was to be granted political asylum. For that they needed to prove that they lived in "credible fear" of persecution.

The only other way to get into the United States was the most common: cross the border illegally.

The young couple had heard the stories of illegal migrants trying to get into the United States. They had heard about the high cost, the risk, the consequences of getting caught or, worse, dying while trying to cross the hot and barren borderlands. But if you made it, the possibilities were limitless—so they had heard. If you worked hard enough, it was said, you could start your own business, become a professional or maybe even a movie star. At worst you could learn plumbing or landscaping or car repair and still make more money than you ever could at home in

Honduras. You could live in a house with indoor toilets and hot water and have enough left over each month to send money home to your family.

It was not a cheap journey. Gangs extorted money, *coyotes* demanded fees, and border guards took bribes. It cost thousands of dollars to sneak across the border, and then you could still get caught and sent back at any time. Carlos and Sofia needed $5000 each. Despite the costs and the dangers, thousands crossed over to *la otra ladra* every month. Many of them believed that, if caught, the U.S. would grant them asylum as political refugees, but this was not the case. Most of those apprehended were sent back to Honduras.

Carlos and Sofia knew all this, but they wanted to go anyway. They believed they would find a way to fulfill their dreams.

They were young, just married, not even twenty. They considered going to the city, getting jobs in a garment factory, but they knew it would only provide a life of drudgery. Not only that, but in the cities, gangs were in control now. The murder rate was sky high, and the police were killed or bought off. No, Carlos and Sofia wanted to go to the United States, where they believed it was safer, and they could make plenty of money, two or three times what they could make at a factory— or so they had heard.

A *coyote* lived in the area, a man who would take them there, for a fee of $3000 each. There were twenty people, ranging in age from fourteen to forty, who wanted to leave, including Carlos and Sofia. These people had borrowed money wherever they could, and they saved every coin. Some promised their land to the *coyote* if his fee was not paid off on time. Carlos and Sofia were determined to go, and their families stood with them.

The difficult and frightening trip required crossing three borders: from Honduras into Guatemala, from there to Mexico and finally into the United States. The first was not hard—it only took a large enough bribe to the Guatemalan immigration official and another for the Honduran gang member who threatened to rape Sofia if they didn't give him $300. They didn't argue.

They traveled through Guatemala in an old army truck that had once been used to transport troops. It was large enough for all twenty passengers. A green canvas tarp was tied to an overhead rack, to keep off the sun and the rain. At first—going down the mountainside—the road was rocky and rutted, and progress was slow. But once they reached the lowlands, where the pavement began, the ride smoothed out, except for the butt-busting, spine-jolting potholes. They drove through a flat jungle with crops on both sides of the road: bananas, pineapples, avocados and guavas. Alongside the road, a farmer led an ox that pulled a cartful of coconuts. When they passed through small towns, the road narrowed and they drove by a few blocks of houses and shops, dodging chickens and dogs. Now and then they stopped to fill the tank with gas. Before going on, the *coyote* would collect another fee of $200 per person.

After two days of driving through mountains and desert, rugged jungles and desolate plains, they stopped near the Suchiate River, the boundary between Guatemala and Mexico. At the dock, several crude rafts—made of wooden platforms and inflated inner-tubes from large trucks—waited for them. This trip was cheap—five dollars per person—and the couple was dropped off at a trading post in Chiapas, Mexico.

They planned to take the infamous train, known as *La Bestia*, or The Beast, from Arriaga to Nuevo Laredo, with several stops along the way. The main freight of this train was commodities such as cement, scrap metal, fertilizer and diesel fuel. Sitting on top of the train cars, or standing in between them, was the human freight, bound for the United States. The train looked festive, with scores of people lining the top, dressed in bright colors. But most were nervous about the journey. They had heard the stories of people falling off the train, or being pushed off, of severed limbs, of robberies, rapes and kidnappings.

A fellow traveler advised Carlos and Sofia on how to board the train. "Wait at the front of a freight car," he said. "When the train starts, run alongside at the same speed as the train, grab the ladder and pull yourself up. Don't try to get on from the back end of a car because if you slip and fall, the wheels of the next car will cut off your legs. It's true! I've seen it happen."

It took them nearly two weeks to get to Nuevo Laredo. Along the way, when the train stopped, the young couple would buy a little food. At a few stops they were able to stay in a safe house where they got a meal and a good night's sleep without having to worry about being harassed. Sometimes they bought cigarettes to give away in exchange for safety and protection. On cold nights they would smoke some of the cigarettes to help them stay warm.

When the train arrived at its destination in *Nuevo Laredo*, they climbed down, and the *coyote* put them on another military transport truck. They were told they were going to cross the Rio Grande through an underground tunnel, and that they would emerge in a U.S. warehouse in Texas. From there, they would board another truck and be driven to a camp where they would live and work.

At the entrance to the tunnel, they were each given a flashlight— cheap but strong enough to pierce three feet into the darkness. The *peóns* crawled through the pipe in silence, their hearts thumping. When they emerged into the yard on the U.S. side, they climbed into the back of a tractor-trailer. It was a common metal trailer with a roll up door. When the door was closed it was pitch black inside the truck. The metal trailer kept out the rain and hid its human cargo from sight, but on a hot sunny day it could become an oven with scorching temperatures and poor circulation. Luckily, they traveled at night.

B.J.'s Shrimp Co. was on the southern tip of Texas, not far from the Gulf of Mexico. The truck arrived as the dark watery horizon was just beginning to brighten. Inside a fenced compound—"For your safety and security," said the sign—there were two long wooden buildings with beds and bare mattresses. There was a thin blanket at the end of each bed. Carlos and Sofia climbed down from the truck with their one canvas bag. They looked into the bunkhouses and realized that one was for men, the other for women. A white man with a big belly said to pick a bed and get some sleep. Work would begin in a few hours. He did not say what the work would be. Reluctantly, Carlos and Sofia separated and tried to sleep.

A few hours later the man was back. For a big man, with impressive girth and upper body strength, he was surprisingly nimble and quick. The Bossman, as he was called, was almost bald, which made him look older than his 40 years. Still, his days as a Longhorn lineman were well in the past.

"*Holá*, everyone!" he shouted from outside the bunkhouses. "*Buenos diás*! Everybody out! Come outside, *por favor*."

Another man was standing next to the big man, translating his words into Spanish. The immigrants emerged disheveled from their journey, squint-eyed and hazy from lack of sleep.

"*Bienvenidos*!" said the big man. "Welcome to B.J.'s Shrimp Company. *Mi nombre es* Chester McPherson, *pero me puedes llamar* Bossman. We're going to do a quick orientation here. My Spanish ain't so good, so I have a translator here. Okay? Okay, here we go. We sell shrimp."

"*Vendemos camarónes*," said the translator.

"Your job is to process the shrimp. *Comprende*?

"*Tu vas processar los camarónes.*"

"They come here from a boat, packed in ice, okay? The first thing you do is get 'em out of the ice and into the cooker."

"*Los pescaderos ponen los camarónes en hielo. Lo sacas del hielo y lo pones agua caliente.*"

"*Agua calor, muy calor*, right? So be careful around those boilers, okay?"

"*Cuidado. El agua esta muy caliente.*"

"The shrimp boils a few minutes, just long enough to kill it. Then it goes back in the ice to chill it down as fast as possible. The quicker the better."

"*Los camarónes ebullian para pocos minutes y despues regressán al hielo.*"

"*Entonces*, you'll take the head off"—the Bossman made a twisting motion with his hands—"and toss it in a pile; the heads are used for cat food."

"*Despues tu quitas las cabezas y lo tiras con los restos. Ellós van en la comida de gata.*"

The Bossman surveyed the faces before him. All he got back were expressions of confusion, regret, fear. That was normal. It was the angry faces he had to watch for. "Okay, then the shrimp go onto a series of conveyor belts to be peeled, sized and cleaned again.

The translator translated.

"Now, the shrimping season is coming on strong now, and we're going to need you to work long hours. We've got about four months of good shrimping left, so this is where you make your money. That's why you're here, ain't it? *Dinero*?" He held up his hand and rubbed his thumb against his other fingers. "You can make a lot of money in the next few months."

The translator translated this speech word for word. He even included the hand motion to emphasize the money. While he was translating, the Bossman paced back and forth. He continued to pace for a moment after the translator had finished.

"Okay, food," he went on. "We have a cantina and a little grocery store down that way. I recommend the cantina for lunch because Anna makes a good burrito and because you only get a half hour for lunch. You don't really have time to go out for lunch. If you have to, though, there is a McDonald's about two blocks down that way." The Bossman pointed toward the main gate.

"Basically, for meals you're on your own. There's a stove in each bunkhouse, so you can cook breakfast, dinner, whatever. There's a Walmart about four blocks away. We also carry some basics in the cantina, including sandwiches and sodas." The translator explained about meals.

"Let's talk about gettin' paid. You get paid once a week, on Saturday, in cash. You're making $6.00 an hour less forty bucks a week for your housing. Now again, you don't have to live here, but there ain't anywhere else nearby, and most places are more expensive anyways, if they'll rent to you at all. That forty bucks includes your bed and your utilities, with hot showers.

"Now I'm gonna split you up and put you with more experienced workers so you can learn what to do. Don't worry; it ain't hard. *No hay problema.* You just got to work fast."

"*No es difícil,*" said the translator. "*Pero necessito trabajo rápido. Muy rápido.* Okay?"

"One more thing. Each of you will have your own locker where you can keep your money and your personal possessions. If you're worried about your money being safe—and you should be—then you might want to use our little bank. For five bucks a week, we'll store your money for you. For ten we'll wire it home for you, if you're set up for that. So think about that." The translator repeated this in Spanish.

"Now Charlie here" (indicating the translator) "is going to walk you through the plant and explain things. But first, here's a pile of work clothes. Pick out some that fit and keep them clean. The washing machines are free."

They all put on blue work clothes with hairnets, thin blue gloves, rubber aprons and boots. Charlie explained that the gloves and hairnets were required and were for sale in *la tiendita*. He briefly explained what the workers were doing, and then assigned them each a job and a buddy to show them what to do. The astringent smell of ammonia mixed with the briny smell of fish made it hard to breathe.

The first week was hell for Carlos and Sofia. They had to work a 60-hour week, six days of 10-hour shifts. By the end of the week, they could barely stand up. They had each made $360, after subtracting forty bucks for their room. They hadn't had time to do anything besides work and sleep, so they hadn't been to Walmart yet. Instead, they ate out of the cantina, which brought their earnings down to almost $300 each. It was much more than they could make at home, but Carlos had to wonder if it was worth it.

Chapter Fourteen

Brad sent Eddie back to Brownsville to see what he could find out about B.J.'s Shrimp Co.: living conditions, wages, use of child labor, and whatever else he could dig up before turning the case over to the feds. He had a bundle of business cards printed up that said, *Eduardo Maez, Investigator*, and gave his cell phone number. The next Sunday Eddie drove down to Brownsville, hoping to talk to some of the workers. He knew B.J.'s was closed on Sunday and guessed that the workers would sleep a little late. So he had arrived at noon, and parked near the facility.

After a while he saw a young couple come out of the plant, holding hands, walking down the block looking tired and dejected. After two weeks Carlos and Sofia were miserable. They were constantly exhausted. Their muscles ached, they were homesick and blue. The only time they had together was Sunday when the plant was closed. That is when they went to Walmart together to buy food for the week. Their only solace was that they were making more money than they thought possible. When the shrimping season was over, they could pay off their debts, buy new shoes for everyone in their families, and still have enough to feed them all for months.

They were at Walmart in the peanut butter aisle when an older man came up beside them, picked a jar of peanut butter off the shelf and examined the label.

"*Ustedes jovenes trabajan en B.J.'s?*" he asked, not turning his head, as if talking to the peanut butter jar.

"*Sí?*" said Carlos.

"Processing shrimp, right? *Con camarónes?*" Eddie's Spanish was rough.

"*Sí.*"

"Are they treating you okay? I mean, *qué tal el trabajo?*"

Carlos and Sofia looked at each other, wondering who this guy was. "Okay*, pero necesitamos trabajar muchas horas. Sesenta o mas a semain.*"

"You know that is illegal, right? You do not have to do that," the man continued in Spanish. "You are probably undocumented, so if you ever want to talk, call me." He pulled a business card out of his shirt pocket and handed it to Carlos. "I am not a cop, but I could help you if you need it." The man put the jar of peanut butter back on the shelf and walked away. Aware of a surveillance camera, Carlos and Sofia put a jar of peanut butter in their cart and moved on down the aisle in the other direction.

When Carlos and Sofia finished their shopping, they walked back to B.J.'s with their bags of groceries and talked about their encounter at the store. For Carlos and Sofia, it had been a puzzling moment. Meeting the stranger named Eduardo Maez was puzzling because, as Sofia said in Spanish, "He seemed to know all about us. Do you think he was from Immigration?"

"Nah," said Carlos. "If he was ICE he would have asked for our papers."

"He did not even ask our names."

"He seemed like an okay guy," said Carlos. "But I hope we do not need his help."

"He knew we are illegals. And what we are doing is illegal."

"We are outlaws, man. We're Bonnie and Clyde." Carlos laughed.

"You know how that ended," said Sofia.

They had been at B.J.'s for more than two weeks now, and it was maddening and diabolic that they could not sleep together. At least they could cook together and spend time together in the kitchen. They were too tired to do anything else anyway. They didn't linger over dinner because they had to get some sleep before it all started over at 2:00 a.m. So they cleaned up the kitchen and went to bed, with a longing good-night kiss.

As for the work, it was tolerable despite the long hours. Carlos and Sofia liked most of their co-workers, who came from all over Mexico and Central America, and after two weeks they felt a bond growing among them. They compared experiences and told stories about life in their home countries. They learned about each other's families and re-alized they had much in common. They all came from poverty and had stories about drug dealers, gang activity, corrupt cops, and the disap-pearance of family members. They realized that violence and random deaths were facts of life all over Central America, something they all had to cope with.

Eddie spent the rest of the day trying to engage people to talk about the working conditions at B.J.'s. He had a fistful of business cards in his hand, and he gave one to whoever would take it. "They're free," Eddie said. "Take one. Call me if you want to talk about your job at B.J.'s. I could help with that."

People took a card like they'd take an advertising flyer: not really wanting it, but taking it anyway, without breaking stride or making eye contact. Some people would stuff it in their pocket or purse; others would toss it in a trash can or drop it on the ground. One woman carried it with her for awhile, as she herded her kids along the street. She threw it at a trash can as she walked by, but she missed and Eddie's card flut-tered to the ground.

The next day, at 8:00 on Monday morning, a new black Buick pulled into a parking place at B.J.'s Shrimp Co. in front of a sign that said, "Reserved for Henry Lucero." The driver got out of his car and swept his eyes over the grounds in front of his business. Henry Lucero liked to keep his entryway clean and tidy, but on Monday mornings he usually found some litter tossed away by thoughtless Sunday shoppers. He picked up a white burger bag, a Nintendo wrapper and a Sunday shopping supplement. He crumpled them all together in a wad and stuffed it into a trash can. He noticed a business card on the ground by the trash can and picked that up, too. He frowned when he read it, and put it in his pocket.

Chapter Fifteen

When BJ's owner Henry Lucero was eight, a friend asked him to join a baseball team with him. Henry agreed, even though he didn't own a glove. But he liked it and got good at it. He was a bit bigger than his teammates. He could play outfield or first, and he ran like a hound dog, lickety split, legs flying, arms flailing. When his family moved to Brownsville, he joined the high school team and became a local star, making the South Texas All Stars in his senior year. He grew up a fan of the San Antonio Missions in the Texas League, and frequently fell asleep listening to Cardinals games on the powerful KMOX radio station in St. Louis. Henry didn't play after high school, but he followed the game, read the box scores, and kept up with the trades and up-and-coming minor leaguers. He also coached a Little League team that had earned a reputation for having sound fundamentals. Henry knew baseball. It was his grand passion.

His love of baseball led to a deep interest in other sports. Gradually, Henry became a hardcore sports nut. He pored over box scores, league standings, and poll results. He tracked individual statistics of key players. He knew who was injured and who was likely to be traded or released. He spent a good part of every weekend channel-surfing between various games or contests. He watched football, baseball, basketball, golf, hockey, tennis, track, you name it.

Like many sports fans, Henry liked to gamble. Those two ingredients, sports and gambling, make a potent cocktail. And when the customer believes he knows enough to beat the odds, as Henry did, you've got the makings for a serious hangover.

Computerized bookmakers were based in other countries and were commonly used by U.S. citizens who lived outside Nevada and wanted to gamble on sports. Henry dabbled in online betting, but he found it too impersonal. He thought he could beat the odds in many games, but he wanted to do it with a real person, with real money changing hands, not with a computer and a wire transfer. When he mentioned this to Delmore Briggs, Briggs suggested he visit the Black Horse Saloon.

Henry had been in more dive bars than he could remember, but he would never forget his first time at the Black Horse Saloon. The bar was a dim room on a dark street just off the waterfront. It was a low-ceilinged, rough-hewn men's club where the drinks were strong and cheap—no spendy single-malt Scotches here. Weapons were against the rules, but that rule was routinely disregarded. The photos on the walls were an homage to tough guys and crooks—boxers, NFL linemen, men in combat, James Cagney in *Public Enemy,* Brando on his bike. Instead of music there were a dozen televisions tuned to different games, creating a cacophony of sports broadcasting.

The Black Horse had its whores and its hookers, its bag men and hit men. It was a hang-out for a subculture of violence, threats, bribes and lies. But the real action took place in the back.

"What'll you have?" asked the barkeeper.

"Briggs said I might find some action here," Henry said, putting a twenty dollar bill on the bar.

The barkeeper pocketed the twenty. "Yeah, through that door." He inclined his head to a door on a side wall.

"Thanks," said Henry. He worked his way through the tables to the side door. He passed an empty stage and a dance floor where two men, a white guy and a black guy, were arm wrestling. Their arms were straight as a flagpole, but they must have been at it awhile because they were dripping sweat, and the veins were popping out on their heads. Their wrists were as thick as baseball bats and just as strong. The face of the white guy was Alabama red and the black guy's face was dark as chocolate. A circle of onlookers were yelling out their comments and cracks, and someone was taking bets with pencil and paper.

Going in the door, Henry found himself in a cubicle with another door that led to the actual betting parlor. There were two security men there, a Mexican and a cowboy. "You got any guns or drugs on you?" asked the cowboy, while the Mexican patted him down.

"No."

"You ever been here before?"

"No."

"Okay. Welcome to the Black Horse. Now, besides no guns or drugs, we got two other rules. Which is, don't start nothin' or we'll kick your ass out. If you have a dispute with somebody, you two settle it outside. Got it?"

"Sure," said Henry. "What's the other rule?"

"Cash only with the bookies. You wanna use a credit card, you can go home and get online. All right?"

"Fine by me. Mind if I ask you something?"

"Shoot."

"The cops ever raid this place?"

"Once in a while. Mostly they just come into the bar and don't come back here. We have an arrangement. Okay?"

Henry nodded and the Mexican opened the other door. "Have a good night," he said.

Henry was immediately immersed in a noisy, bustling scene. A dozen men, and a few women, were seated at computer terminals checking scores, line-ups, injury reports, point spreads and who-knows-what else in sports match-ups around the world. Others were watching sports contests on one of several televisions mounted on the walls. They were yelling encouragement, cheering, and booing the refs, just like in any sports bar.

High on the walls were electronic boards that listed all the betting opportunities at that time—games, fights, races—along with the odds. One wall was for professional sports, one for college and one for high school football in Texas. If there were too many events to list at once, they kept flashing back and forth, like flights on an airport monitor. The boards were hooked up via satellite directly to a sportsbook in Las Vegas where the oddsmakers did their work.

In a separate room behind a facade of bulletproof glass, three bookies were taking bets, collecting money, issuing betting tickets and paying out cash to winners.

Henry felt at home here. He watched the scene with a big grin on his face, like a kid in the stands who had just caught a foul ball. The Spurs were playing the Heat, and Henry noticed that the Heat was a two-point favorite. But he knew that their point guard had been fighting the flu, so he found a bookie and made a bet on the Spurs. He won. From that night on, Henry was a regular at the Black Horse Saloon.

Chapter Sixteen

The smuggling operation was going smoothly, but distribution was proving difficult. They were selling all the smack to one main distributor in Houston who then sold it to middlemen around the state. Delaney said they could increase their profits if they could distribute the drugs directly to the next level.

Briggs thought of a possible solution, but it required the cooperation of Henry Lucero.

Briggs had found a small chain of twenty fish shops, Little Saigon Fish Co., conveniently located along the Gulf Coast in Texas and Louisiana. Shrimp tacos were their specialty. Most of the outlets were in strip malls and were really little more than over-sized food trucks. But the fish shops were struggling and the owner was willing to sell. Briggs's idea was to use the fish shops as drop spots for the contraband drugs. The beauty of the plan was that B.J.'s could deliver the drugs disguised as a fish product. It would slot right into the system.

"Perfect!" said Mike Delaney when Briggs first explained the plan to him.

Once a week Briggs dropped by Henry's office to collect the money for that week's new workers. As usual the receptionist buzzed Henry to say that Delmore Briggs was there to see him, and Henry said to send him on back.

Henry Lucero was a tall broad-shouldered man whose long nose, large ears and sagging cheeks gave him the look of a basset hound. His neatly trimmed fringe of dark hair framed his bald brown dome handsomely. He moved slowly and deliberately in all matters. Nothing seemed to startle him or delight him. He exuded a calm control that was sometimes mistaken for honesty, even kindness or caring. His years of hard work and the constant struggle to keep his business afloat had worn away his enjoyment of life.

Henry was sitting behind a large wooden desk that had neat stacks of paper around the edges. In the middle were some documents he was working on and to his left was a smaller desk for a computer. His chair was an old-fashioned wooden swivel chair that tilted back. His brown suit coat was hanging from the back of the chair.

"Hello, Briggs," said Henry, leaning back with his arms behind his head.

"Good morning, Mr. Lucero. How are your new workers doing?"

"So far, so good, Briggs. Everything has been going smoothly." He swiveled around to open the safe behind his desk and extracted $6,000 in hundreds. "I got six new workers this week," he said, handing the money to Briggs.

"The shrimp catch must be pretty good this year."

"I can't complain."

The two men chatted about items of no consequence for a few minutes. Lucero fidgeted with his tie pin and straightened up some papers on his desk that didn't need straightening.

Briggs said, "Well, I'll let you get back to work, Mr. Lucero. But first there is something I want to show you."

Opening his briefcase, Briggs placed the money in it and pulled out a parcel about the size of a Russian novel. It was wrapped in brown paper and again in plastic wrap.

He said, "This is a kilo of heroin," laying the package on Henry's desk. "It's worth $40,000 wholesale, $100,000 on the street."

Henry brought the chair down hard and put his fists on the desk. "What's this got to do with me?" he asked belligerently. He had nothing but distaste for drug users and contempt for drug dealers.

"I could use your help, sir."

"For what?" Henry growled.

"Distribution," Briggs answered. "And money laundering. You see, my boss is bringing in ten to twenty kilos of cocaine or heroin each week with the workers."

"You're doing *what*? You're smuggling dope in with the workers?"

"Yes."

"You bastard!" Henry said with an uncommon show of emotion. "If I had known that I wouldn't be doing business with you. Drugs are ruining this country! I want no part in it."

Briggs stayed calm. "This is a new enterprise for us, Mr. Lucero, and I'm afraid you're already a part of it."

"Like hell I am! I signed on for workers, not drugs."

"That's fine, Mr. Lucero. You don't have to participate. I just saw an opportunity for you and thought you might want to take advantage of it."

"What are you talking about? Opportunity for what?"

"Well," said Briggs, "you're shipping shrimp to dozens of restaurants and grocery stores and fish markets. I have the opportunity to obtain a chain of small fish markets that would be an ideal front for the drug operation. The chain will buy your shrimp, but your drivers would also deliver the heroin to us on the same truck. It would show up on the manifest as a phony product. You get paid market price for it, to keep your books straight, but you get paid a lot more from me—in cash, of course. The dope is smuggled in with the workers. We repackage it, and you deliver it. As I said, you get your cut in cash."

Henry shook his head, his mind whirling at the idea being thrown at him. He knew that he was already engaged in criminal activities—labor law violations, false tax reports—but it had gotten to the point where he believed there was nothing wrong with what he was doing. In his mind, he was helping pull people out of poverty. He was doing his workers a service. It shouldn't be illegal, he believed, to set his own pay scale, as long as the workers weren't coerced. They weren't slaves, after all, and he wasn't a slave owner. But drugs? That was another matter. He had always been anti-drug. He'd even volunteered to be on a task force to address the drug problem on the Texas Gulf Coast.

"No deal, Briggs. Drugs are the scourge of our time. It's a violent, dirty business. I want nothing to do with it."

"Mr. Lucero, the dope is coming in one way or another. You might as well get your share."

"Drugs ruin lives. I don't want a share of that."

"I forgot to mention what your cut would be, Mr. Lucero," Briggs said, as if he had not heard Henry. "Five percent of wholesale. At ten kilos a week, that would amount to about $20,000 a week, about a million per year. It could go directly into an off-shore bank account."

"I said no, Briggs. Now, get your ass out of here before I lose my temper."

Briggs replaced the heroin into his briefcase and got up. "Whatever you say, Mr. Lucero. I just wanted to offer you the opportunity to make some easy money."

"There's no such thing as easy money, Briggs. You always got to pay for it in the end."

Later that day Briggs went to the Black Horse. "We have a problem," Briggs told Delaney.

"Yeah? What's that?"

"Lucero doesn't want to get involved, even though I offered him a lucrative piece of the action."

"Why not?"

"He's anti-drug."

"Anti-drug? What a chump. Well, he's not anti-gambling. He's down here three or four times a week betting on games, mostly baseball.

And he bets big too. He's been winning, but that won't last. We just have to be patient. His luck is going to run out, and he'll start losing. He's not going to quit gambling. He's going to keep on gambling because he thinks he's got it all figured out. But he doesn't, and so he'll keep on losing. And when he gets desperate, you offer to cover his losses—if he'll play ball with us. And he will."

Delaney invited the owner of the Little Saigon Fish Co. to come over and discuss a buy-out.

"I'll pay you $10,000 per store," Delaney said to the owner. "$200,000 total."

"$275,000," said the owner of the chain—not a Vietnamese man at all, but a beefy red-necked cracker with a network of drinker's veins mapped on his jowls like red and blue highways on a map.

"Two hundred thou," said Delaney. He reached behind his desk, pulled out a hard shell briefcase and placed it on the desk. He opened the latches and raised the lid. "There it is. You'd be a fool not to take it. My next offer will be lower."

Delaney opened a drawer and took out a bolt cutter, nearly three feet long. "Ever see one of these things before?" he asked.

"A bolt cutter? Sure," said the cracker.

Delaney nodded. "Great for cutting locks. They work on fingers too," he said, squeezing the handles together. Delaney looked at the cracker's fingers. "Woo, that's a nice ring you got. I hope it fits on a different finger. Of course, if it don't, you can always get it resized." He looked the cracker in the eye as he played with the bolt cutter.

"You tryin'a threaten me, Delaney? 'Cause I don't react well to threats."

Delaney pushed a button mounted on the side of the desk. One of his bouncers opened the door, slid in and quietly closed the door behind him. Standing in front of the door, he spread his feet and crossed his arms.

The cracker looked at the bouncer. "So this is how it is, huh? I have a long memory, Delaney." He fingered the diamond-studded ring.

"Yes, I'm sure you'd remember me every time you felt for your ring," Delaney replied.

The cracker stood up and snapped the briefcase shut. Without another word, he picked it up and walked out of the room, followed by Delaney's lackey.

Chapter Seventeen

Henry became a familiar face at the Black Horse Saloon. The barmen and bouncers addressed him as "Mr. Lucero." Most of the habitual gamblers called him "B.J.," because of his business. The only person who consistently called him "Henry" was the owner, Mike Delaney.

"Hello, Henry," said Mike one summer night when Henry walked in. The barkeeper immediately poured him a club soda with lemon and ice. "The horses been treatin' you all right?"

"Oh, I don't play the ponies anymore, Mike. It's baseball season now. On any given night, I got fifteen games to choose from. You a baseball fan, Mike?"

"Nope. Baseball's too complicated for me. Too many players, too many teams, batting averages, ERAs, what he done with two strikes on him and a runner on third.... Know what I mean? Who can remember all that stuff? No, I'll stick with Texas Hold 'Em. Eye-to-eye bluffing. That's my game."

Any fan would agree that knowing a sport doesn't mean you can predict the outcome of games. One of the attractive things about a sport is its unpredictability. A great pitcher has his off nights, players get injured, good batters go into unexplainable slumps, an average player will have a superlative year, streaks come and go. Henry certainly knew this, yet he still felt his knowledge and insight into the game should give him an edge, and so he began betting heavily on baseball games.

On the field, baseball is the same as it always was. If Babe Ruth or Satchel Paige walked through the cornfield of the past onto today's baseball diamond, they would fit right in. The rules are the same, and the dimensions of the field have not changed. They still take infield, shag flies, and throw the ball around the horn after an out. But behind the scenes, on the business side of baseball, it's a whole new ballgame. Due to the collection and manipulation of statistics—so-called Sabermetrics—the people in "the front office" draw conclusions that lead to investing millions of dollars into players, ballparks, advertising and a roster of other expenses. It works just like any big business does.

Henry tended to rely on the old-time statistics: the box score, ERA, number of strikeouts, number of errors. His knowledge of these things and a few others, including injuries and the weather, added up to something he called "baseball sense." It thrilled Henry to ponder the evidence and then try to beat the odds. He spent more and more time at his desk looking at different match-ups, trying to outguess the oddsmakers. He developed his own method for predicting games. For a while he did well, meaning he won over half the time. Then, like a hitter coming off a hot streak, his luck changed. It seemed like he couldn't pick a winner to save his life. He resorted to doing more research, spending entire mornings analyzing the games of the day. He read up on probability and, in desperation, even looked at occult practices as a means of predicting the outcomes of games. After a two-week slide, Henry had to dip into the company cash reserve to pay off some of his debt. Hoping to recoup his losses, Henry gambled more money on more games, and lost more money. One evening at the saloon, Delaney took note and passed the word on to Briggs.

The next day Henry got a visit from Delmore Briggs. After some small talk Briggs came to the point.

"Mr. Lucero, I heard through the grapevine that you could use some cash."

"Who told you that?" Henry immediately felt perspiration on his upper lip.

"I've got my sources, and they're usually right."

"Well, there's no use denying it, Briggs. I've been betting on base-ball games, and lately I've been losing." Henry loosened his tie.

"How far down are you, if you don't mind me asking?"

"About a hundred grand."

"That's not so bad. How much time do you have?"

"A week. Well, six days now. I can make the vig on it, but that's just digging myself in deeper the way I see it."

"You see it right. Say, Mr. Lucero," Briggs said as if it had just oc-curred to him, "remember that deal I spoke to you about?"

"To distribute dope? Yeah, I remember." He took out a handkerchief and daubed his lip, then passed it over his bald head.

"Well, the offer's still good. You could make that hundred grand in a month. I'll even front you the dough so you can take care of your debt now, all at once. Normally I would never agree to a proposition such as this, but I'll make an exception for you, Mr. Lucero, because you're almost like part of the family."

Henry didn't say a word. He hated the idea and didn't want to have anything to do with it. But where else could he get that kind of money in a hurry? Henry had come to trust Briggs. His ever-cheerful disposi-tion irritated Henry because it seemed false, yet he always kept his word.

Briggs waited patiently while Henry thought about it. When he fi-nally spoke, his voice was barely audible. "Okay. I'll do it."

"That's terrific, Mr. Lucero. How about I come by tomorrow after-noon to set up the details. I'll bring the money with me."

"All right," said Henry, feeling depressed and defeated.

The next evening, when Henry climbed the stairs to Mike Delaney's office above the bar to pay off his debt, no one asked him where he got the money, which Briggs had taken out of Delaney's safe that morning. Now it went back in.

Briggs told Henry that they needed a better way to conceal the dope. He explained that they had been using grapefruit boxes to transport the blocks of heroin, dropping them off at the distributor in Houston. "But if your drivers are going to make the deliveries, we need better packaging, something that looks like it belongs in B.J.'s product line," Briggs said.

Henry said, "Work it out with the Bossman. I don't want to know about it."

"That's probably smart," Briggs agreed.

Henry called the Bossman into his office, introduced him to Briggs and explained that they were adding an item to their product line, to be sold exclusively to the Little Saigon chain. "You two can work out the details," he said and left the room.

Briggs explained the set-up and the need to develop a better way to disguise the dope.

"What's in it for me?" asked the Bossman. He didn't seem the least bit bothered by becoming part of a drug ring—as long as he got a piece of the action, which he would, of course.

Briggs and the Bossman hit on the idea of creating a special package to disguise the drugs. B.J.'s already sold blocks of fishcake, made of fish brought in with the shrimp catch, wrapped in plastic bags simply labeled "Fishcake," in blue lettering, that they sold primarily to restaurants. They designed a similar bag, large enough to hold a block of heroin, labeled "Premium Fishcake" in red lettering. The Bossman would take the grapefruit boxes off the truck and repackage the heroin as Premium Fishcake.

The drug distribution system worked without a kink. Henry was making more money than he dreamed was possible. He paid back Briggs ten grand at a time. When his debt was paid off, Henry started gambling again, and winning again, like magic. Now when Henry watched a game in which he had a stake, he hung on every pitch and pounded the table. It felt great to be back in the game.

Chapter Eighteen

No workers on the waterfront had responded to Eddie's business cards. None of the workers at B.J.'s wanted to talk to him any more than to the immigration authorities, and he really couldn't blame them. Eddie could have given up right there, but seeing the faces of the workers coming out of the tunnel—scared yet brave—had moved him. They reminded him of faces he had seen in Vietnam, on both sides. And knowing the evil power of the drugs taped to their chests also took him back to Vietnam, where too many of his buddies got hooked on heroin to avoid the physical and mental pain of the war. He knew it would poison lives and families, and that made him angry. Why should the drug lords, he asked himself, profit from the desperation of others?

This motivated him to do more, maybe even make a difference. Brad hadn't asked Eddie to do any more spywork, but Eddie felt like it was his job to see it through. He wanted to know what went on inside of B.J.'s. The reporter in him demanded to know what happened after they passed through the gate. There was something else too. It wasn't so much that he wanted to right a wrong; it was that he was enjoying the work. Maybe he wasn't ready to retire yet, after all.

It was not about proving himself. He'd had a good run. He felt comfortable in his skin and a gun still felt comfortable in his hand. It was not about money nor, if he was honest, was it purely altruistic. Sure, he didn't like what he had witnessed in Laredo, but he wasn't a crusader in the drug war or an advocate of immigration reform. No, the truth was, he was enjoying the thrill of it. He craved tension and danger the way some people crave sex. There was always a tipping point in his investigations where the rush of adrenaline became as important as the story itself.

He thought about telling Brad what he was going to do, but he didn't want to defend himself to Brad. He would tell him afterwards. He didn't need Brad's approval. All he needed was grit and a steady hand.

Eddie could not say whether his wartime exploits in Vietnam were the origin of his steely nerves, or rather a demonstration of them. All he knew was that he had them. Of course, when the action was over and the danger was gone, when the adrenaline drained away, Eddie would break out in a heavy sweat and his legs would fold like hot wax. But in the heat of action he was unflappable.

Eddie knew he could find the trap door on the Mexican side of the river because of the locator he'd planted there. And he knew what time of night they would come. What he didn't know was exactly how he would blend in with the immigrants without being noticed. He would have to camp out there and wait.

The next day Eddie drove to Brownsville and left his car in a long-term parking lot near B.J.'s Shrimp. Then he took a bus to Laredo and walked across the bridge into Mexico, using his passport to get in. From there, while the sun was sliding down under the horizon, Eddie took a cab to the general vicinity of the tunnel entrance. In the desolate area on the outskirts of town, the cab driver looked puzzled but didn't say anything. Eddie used the locator to lead him to the tunnel's entrance. He recognized the cluster of trees that surrounded the trap door. He hid behind a disabled Oldsmobile, stripped to the bones by scavengers, except for the tail fins that were intact and provided enough cover, especially in the dark. Eddie turned off the locator and settled in to wait for the truck.

It was pleasant lying there in the Mexican dust, looking up at the stars. Unlike mega-cities such as Phoenix or L.A., the lights from the twin cities of Laredo and Nuevo Laredo only slightly dimmed the stars. The towns were both too small and too poor to blot out the stars entirely.

Eddie had used his knife to clear an area of cactus and burrs, and had pulled up the most bothersome rocks. The ground was still warm from a day in the sun. The air was stirring—not quite enough to call it a breeze.

Eddie wore a dark baseball cap and jeans, broken in but not worn out. He wore a white peasant blouse that was smudged with dirt. His old Nikes were beginning to split at the seams. He hadn't bathed or shaved in two days. He carried a few belongings in a backpack—a toothbrush, a half-bar of soap and a towel, two T-shirts, a second pair of underwear, a double-edged razor—a bottle of water and some food. Dirt was caked underneath his fingernails and accentuated the lines in his face.

The truck arrived at 1:30 a.m., as dependable as a British train. Moments earlier Eddie had seen the headlights bouncing across the desert and tucked himself behind the fins of the Olds. When the truck arrived, the driver told everyone to get out. He pointed at two men to come lift the trap door open. The driver's co-pilot watched the workers file off the truck and directed them to gather near the trap door. Eddie slipped through the darkness to join the others as the group was forming. A few people stared at him, trying to remember his face, but most were oblivious to there being a new man among them, or too frightened to care.

When it came time to descend the ladder to the tunnel, Eddie took a place in the middle of the line, pulled his cap down and went down the ladder without a second glance from the driver, who handed him a dim flashlight as he prepared to descend the ladder. Ten men were selected to carry a kilo of heroin each, but Eddie was not one of them. The chosen ones had the heroin strapped to their chest with plastic shrink wrap.

The second half of the handler team—the stateside driver and his helper—was there in the supply yard, waiting for the workers. The relay truck was backed up and ready to load. After the drugs-for-money exchange, the group immediately got into the waiting truck and soon they were on their way down Hwy. 83. Eddie sat in the truck bed and tried to get some rest, if not sleep, relaxing into the hum of wheels on the highway. He let the white noise lull him into a meditative state, unaware of anything but the hum of rubber on the road. When they arrived at their destination, Eddie snapped to attention. He discovered that they had not stopped at B.J.'s, but at a hog rendering plant. The smell was awful, almost more than Eddie could take. Some workers looked pale and sickly. This was not in Eddie's plan.

The driver's assistant got down from the truck cab and went to the back of the truck. "*Necessito diez hombres aqui.*" He began to point at people who didn't look like they were about to puke—and called out "*Uno, dos, tres, cuatro, cinco, seis, sieta, ocho, nueve, diez. Adelante!*" Eddie kept his head down and was passed over. The chosen ten picked up their rucksacks and travel bags and climbed out of the truck. Eddie had almost been hoisted on his own petard, as his C.O. used to say. But the next stop was B.J.'s, where Eddie and the rest of the group disembarked.

The new arrivals went into the yard by the barracks, where the Bossman and Charlie, the translator, were waiting for them. The Bossman went through the instructions and rules again, repeating almost word for word what he had said to Carlos and Sofia's group. Each of the new workers was issued a set of work clothes. Then he told them to get some sleep because their training shift would start in a few hours.

After some restless sleep on the hard mattresses, the new workers were awakened by the Bossman. "Half an hour until your first shift," he shouted. "Get your blues on." Eddie put on his uniform and grabbed a cup of coffee and a roll from the cantina. He ate quietly and mindlessly. He was worried he would stick out among the workers because of his age. He had dyed his hair black to cover up the gray, but there was no way to hide the lines in his face.

116

Eddie needn't have worried. In their uniforms, the workers almost looked identical. Age disappeared. Judging from their attire, they could have been working at a nuclear reactor. Head to toe, they were covered in sky blue uniforms: Everyone wore a hair net and a white face mask, topped with a baseball cap featuring the company logo; a snug-fitting long-sleeved top underneath a yellow rubber apron, loose pants stuffed inside rubber boots, and disposable latex gloves.

They assembled outside the barracks. A veteran worker led the way to the work floor. In a large room dozens of workers stood side by side in front of conveyor belts. At different work stations, the shrimp were cleaned, graded for size, peeled, deveined and cleaned again. Then they were placed in plastic totes—color-coded for size—covered with ice and placed in a refrigerated room. Next to the cooler was a freezer where some shrimp were frozen, set aside to sell in the off-season.

The conveyors hummed and rattled, the peeler clanked at uneven intervals, and water flowed constantly to clean the shrimp and wash away detritus. No one talked. Eddie's first job was at the cull table. As the shrimp passed by on the conveyor, he and the others removed any unwanted material, such as shells, broken shrimp and stray heads, leaving only perfect shrimp. It was fatiguing, mind-numbing work, standing for hours at a time sliding shells and shrimp pieces off of a conveyor belt that never stopped or even slowed down. At the end of his shift, Eddie went back to the barracks and collapsed into a deep sleep.

The next few days Eddie kept his ears open for any kind of labor violations—verbal abuse, harassment, threats—but observed nothing. The Bossman was loud and demanding but he stopped short of bullying or intimidation. On his third day the Bossman told Eddie to break down some cardboard boxes and put them in the cardboard crusher. Eddie was halfway through the stack of discarded cartons when he came upon a few boxes labeled Ruby Red Grapefruit. Surely these had been used to transport the blocks of heroin, he thought, hidden underneath a layer of grapefruits. A few days later, when the next truckful of workers arrived, Eddie was watching. A few workers got off, and then the driver pulled three grapefruit boxes from the truck and carried them up to the Boss-man's office. While the Bossman was giving his usual spiel to the new workers, Eddie wanted to creep up the stairs and look in the boxes but decided it was too risky.

On Sundays the plant was closed and the Bossman was off-duty. So the next Sunday Eddie snuck up the stairs to the Bossman's office. It was locked. An old-fashioned transom window lay above the doorframe to the office, and it was open. Eddie found a chair at the end of the hall and placed it beneath the transom. He climbed onto the chair, but still couldn't see into the window. Eddie had noticed a pile of cinder blocks in a corner of the work floor. He hurried down the stairs, hoisted a ce-ment block and climbed laboriously back up to the second floor. Laying the cinder block across the seat of the chair, he climbed on top of the block. *God, I'm too old for this shit,* he thought.

Perched on the cinder block, standing on his toes, grasping the tran-som and pulling himself up, Eddie could peek over the transom. Around the edges of the room were boxes full of reports, record books, tools and machine parts. In the middle was a large table, on which sat three Ruby Red Grapefruit boxes. The boxes were open but Eddie couldn't see over the sides. At the end of the table there was a stack of plastic bags the size of a block of heroin. It was hard for Eddie to make out the label, but the letters were red, and he gradually pieced them into the words "Premium Fishcake."

A gull swooped down through the open-air front of the work area.

"Awk! Awk!" it squalled.

Eddie thought he heard a car's engine just outside the gate. He put the chair back at the end of the hall and put the cinder block underneath it. A breeze was rattling through the ropes and nets. With that sound for cover, Eddie rushed down the stairs. When he turned the corner toward the barracks he almost ran into Henry Lucero.

"Looking for something?" asked Lucero.

"I, uh, I thought I heard some music," Eddie stammered. "Sounded like someone was playing a flute, but I guess I was wrong. Must have been the wind."

"Uh huh. Do you work here?"

"Yes, sir."

"The work area is off-limits when you're not working."

"Sorry, sir," Eddie said as he turned toward the workers' quarters.

"Hold on a minute," said Lucero, freezing Eddie in his attempted escape. "You're not talking Mexican."

"No, sir. Born and raised in San Antonio. My family moved to Mexico when I was twelve."

"Name?"

"Aguilar. Tomás Aguilar."

"Doesn't ring a bell. You must be new."

"Yes, sir. This is my first week."

"Well, in the future don't populate the floor unless you're working. It's a safety hazard. If something happened to you, I'd be liable."

"Yes, sir. Sorry, sir."

Eddie hurried away. Henry stood there wondering about this fellow. He seemed older than most of his workers. What was he doing here? He could be on the lam, wanted for something or another. What if he was? What could Henry do about it? Turn him in and he might sing like a bird, squawk like a gull about B.J.'s wage and hour violations. He had better talk to Briggs.

Chapter Nineteen

That evening Lucero was unconsciously humming *Folsom Prison Blues* when he happened to find Eddie's card in his coat pocket. It made him wonder if this Maez had been snooping around B.J.'s. He knew that labor agitators had been working the Gulf Coast recently, circulating a petition for shorter hours and better pay. There were rumors of a strike, but he hadn't any reason to think his employees were talking strike. They were just happy to have the work, as far as Lucero could tell. Besides, they were here illegally, and if they started making demands, they would have to go public, which could only lead to deportation. Henry wasn't worried. Yet he was still curious what this Eduardo Maez was up to.

Lucero did a Google search on Eduardo Maez and found out he had been a hot-shot reporter in Houston until his recent retirement. He had been a private investigator before he became a reporter, and in the Army before that. There was a picture of him, too: a sturdy man in his thirties with curly black hair—square-jawed and muscular—wearing a dark suit and holding an award, smiling broadly. Lucero did a double take as he realized that he was looking at the same man he had encountered wandering around the plant that afternoon, only he was years younger in the picture. He had called himself Aguilar, not Maez, but Henry was sure it was the same man. Lucero ran off a copy of the photo and put it in his pocket.

Once or twice a day, Henry would make a circuit through the work floor, spreading around words of praise and encouragement to the workers, being friendly, and showing that he cared. He hoped his daily visits built morale among the workers, or at least introduced the fear that they could be fired if they didn't measure up. On Monday, Henry made one of his daily tours during Eddie's shift. Eddie was working on the peeling machine, but even with a hairnet and a face mask Henry recognized the man he knew as Tomás Aguilar. Take twenty years of worry lines off his face and it was also the reporter for the Houston paper, Eddie Maez, supposedly retired. Henry caught his eye as he strolled by.

"Hello, Tomás," he said.

"Sir," said Eddie.

Back in his office, Lucero called Delmore Briggs, and put him on speakerphone.

"Briggs, we got a problem," he said brusquely, pacing the room.

"What's that?"

"One of the workers you sent me is a spy, a saboteur." Lucero picked up a newspaper, rolled it up and began slapping it against his leg.

"How do you know that?"

"For one thing, he goes by two names. For another, he's American. I found him out on the floor yesterday, alone. I don't trust him."

"So fire him. I'll absorb the cost."

"It's not quite that simple, Briggs."

Briggs suspected it probably *was* that simple, but he humored Henry. "Why not?" he asked.

Henry threw the newspaper on his desk and picked up the phone. "I think maybe he's a newspaper reporter looking to expose me, or a whistleblower, or a union organizer. I don't know what he's up to, but I smell a rat. I can't just fire him and turn him loose. That might be just what he wants."

"How about I put a couple of guys on his tail. Make it obvious he's being followed. Maybe threaten him, instill a little fear in him. How's that sound?"

"That might help."

"What's he look like?"

"Stocky man, about 5'10", strong-looking." He pulled Eddie's picture from his pocket and studied it. "Half-breed, probably: broad face, dark reddish skin, clean-shaven, curly hair, brown eyes...."

"Name?" asked Briggs.

"Eduardo Maez."

"Age?"

"Hard to tell. Maybe 50? 55?"

"Fifty?" exclaimed Briggs. "I don't send you anyone over thirty, Mr. Lucero. You sure he's one of ours?"

"I ain't hired anyone else."

"All right. You fire him tomorrow morning, and I'll have two guys waiting for him at the gate. Hopefully he'll think twice about blowing the whistle on B.J.'s."

"Okay, Briggs. I'll tell the Bossman to pull him off the morning shift and let him go."

The next day, in the middle of Eddie's shift, the Bossman told Eddie to follow him to his office. Eddie followed him up the wooden staircase to the glassed-in office overlooking the work floor. The Bossman went to his desk and lowered his bulk into the office chair. He sighed.

"You're fired, mister, effective immediately. Here's your last pay envelope. I want you off the premises. Now. So pack up whatever you brought with you and say 'Adios' to anyone who might care."

"May I ask why you're firing me? I do a good job."

"You do okay, pardner, but Mr. Lucero don't trust you, and that's the only reason that really matters. We know who you are, Mr. Maez. An old newspaper man, sticking your nose in here hoping you'll find somethin' to write about. Somethin' shocking. Somethin' that'll sell papers. But you ain't gonna find anything. Clean and safe working conditions, stamp of approval from Agriculture, free medical care, cheap meals. Nobody's complainin'.

"So clear out. If you ask any more questions, it's liable to make me angry, and you don't want that, trust me." He slapped his hand on the desk with a loud thwack. "Go!" he yelled.

Eddie turned and went. He felt angry and relieved at the same time. He went to the barracks and stuffed his gear in his backpack.

"*A dónde vas*?" asked the young man who slept in a bed nearby. It was Carlos, with whom he had spoken in Walmart a few weeks earlier. Since Eddie's arrival they had worked side by side a few times. Carlos was surprised that Eddie was working at B.J.'s. For one thing, he was much older than the other workers. For another, he was obviously an American—the only one on the floor. But it was not his business, and he said nothing.

"*No se. Me botarón*," answered Eddie. "I got fired."

"*Porque?*"

Eddie shrugged. "*Escucha*," he said. "Wouldn't you like to help me screw these bastards?"

"*Si, pero necesito dinero*. I need the money."

"I'll help you find a better job," Eddie said in Spanish.

"If you can find a better job, then why do you not have one yourself?"

Eddie laughed. "Good point. We need to talk. What time does your shift end?"

"Six o'clock."

"Okay. Meet me at Walmart when you get off. Sporting goods department. Okay?"

Carlos hesitated but nodded and whispered, "Okay."

Chapter Twenty

Eddie shouldered his backpack and walked out into the heat of the day. He walked up the hill toward the long-term parking lot where he had left his car. Half-a-block away two men were following Eddie, making no effort to hide themselves. As a licensed Private Investigator, Eddie had a permit to carry a gun, which was loaded and lying on the floor underneath the front seat of his car. He could grab it quickly if he needed to, but he didn't want to use it.

When he reached the car lot, the two men stopped and waited across the street. One man slapped a billy-club into his palm, easily and idly. The other was smoking a cigarette. Eddie paid the attendant. While he was waiting for the gopher to get his car, Eddie gave the two thugs a careful look. The man with the club was the shorter, about 5'10" and muscled up. He was under thirty but already balding. The taller man was a bit older. He wore a straw cowboy hat, tilted back, and Eddie could see that his face was pockmarked with acne scars. The tips of his cowboy boots were covered with a shiny silver metal. He had a load of something in his jacket pocket.

Eddie drove away slowly. He watched the thugs in his rearview mirror. They didn't move. They just stood insolently watching the car go out of sight, a clear warning not to return.

But Eddie was in no hurry to leave. For one thing, he wanted to talk to Carlos. For another, being fired and warned off only made him more curious. He already knew B.J.'s was paying less than minimum wage and no overtime. Shifts were unpredictable and sometimes unlawfully long. And of course, most of the workers were there illegally. The smugglers were bringing in dope as well as workers. Eddie wondered who was behind it all. Who was calling the shots? His investigative antennae were up, and he wanted to know more.

Eddie had a few hours to kill before six o'clock. He drove aimlessly through the streets of Brownsville—past the high school, past used car dealers and pawn shops, past the Old Morgue, until finally in the warehouse district he saw a corner bar called the Black Horse Saloon.

Eddie knew of the Black Horse Saloon. It was known as a sports bar patronized by outlaws and ex-cons, gamblers and drug dealers, toughs and goons. Rumor had it that there was a full-fledged sports gambling operation in a back room. More than once, Eddie had asked his editor at the newspaper if he could look into the Black Horse. He knew there was a story there, but his editor always said no. "Whattaya, crazy? I'm not gonna be responsible for you getting shot at or knifed for no good reason. That place isn't worth writing about. It's just a bunch of low-lifes and losers." This was the standard line, but Eddie couldn't understand why it was okay for him to be threatened and shot at for a story about corporate crime, but not okay for a story about the Black Horse Saloon. He suspected his editor placed bets with a bookie there.

Despite all Eddie had heard about the Black Horse he had never been inside the joint. He wanted to go in now, but it was nearly six o'clock. He decided to come back later.

Just before six, Eddie squeezed between two behemoth SUVs in the Walmart parking lot and went to the sporting goods department. He stood around looking at the fishing gear for fifteen minutes before he saw Carlos loitering in the next aisle, trying on baseball gloves and hitting them in the pocket with his fist. Carlos remembered a time not so long ago when he played baseball with other kids from the neighborhood. They had fielded balls barehanded because no one could afford a glove. The new glove felt good on Carlos's hand. The leather was stiff and smelled sweet and exotic like cinnamon.

Eddie came over and joined him. He grabbed a mitt and started doing the same thing, slapping his fist into the pocket.

"Nice glove, *que no*? You would not miss any fly balls with this baby." He mimicked catching a fly ball, saying, "It's back, back, back, and," he slammed his fist into the glove, "caught at the wall."

Carlos didn't like working at B.J.'s. He didn't like the long hours, the meager existence, and always working tired. But he was young and strong. He was also desperate for money, so he put up with the working conditions, worked hard and kept his mouth shut.

"So Carlos," Eddie said in broken Spanish, "B.J.'s is breaking a number of laws. You are not supposed to work so many hours. You are supposed to get paid more, and even more when you work overtime. I would like to go to the feds and blow the whistle of these bastards, but I cannot do it alone. I need more people who will come with me and force them to investigate."

"No, Señor Maez," replied Carlos. "You do not understand. We do not want to shut it down. We want the money. We want the feds to stay away."

Eddie reflected on this. "What about the brown packages they bring in? Do you know what is in those packages?"

"Drugs, I suppose."

"Right, which will end up on the street, making junkies out of kids your age."

"Not my problem. Drugs are bad, but muling that shit over, well, that is the price of the job."

"That and several hundred dollars. Why should you pay someone to bring you here?"

"Because they are getting me a job."

"But you are being exploited, used and then discarded."

Carlos shrugged. "No, that is not the way I see it. I am on a mission, you know. I am helping my family, *mi hermano, mi abuela*...."

"How about the drugs? If anyone got caught, they would go to prison. Should you not get paid for being the mule?"

"Of course. I will mention that to the Bossman," Carlos said with a teasing look. Then with a serious face, he said, "I cannot help you, hombre. I must go." Carlos turned to walk away.

"Wait!" Eddie said. "Do you still have my card?"

"Yes. It's in the bottom of my pack."

"Good. Call me if you need help."

"Thank you, Señor Maez."

When Eddie got back to his car, it was still sandwiched between the two SUVs, but its wheels were sitting on the pavement with the tires slashed. Little shards of glass and pieces of red plastic littered the asphalt where someone had smashed in the headlights and taillights. In next row over, the two thugs who had followed him to his car leaned casually against a pick-up truck. The shorter muscled man twirled his billy club while the tall cowboy with the acne scars cleaned his fingernails with a six-inch knife.

The two goons had been buddies ever since grade school when they had spent time in juvenile detention together for vandalism and petty theft. The shorter one, named Billy Bonner, had crude tattoos on his forearm from a stint in prison. One tattoo was supposed to be an eagle but looked more like a turkey. The taller man was named Axel Rodd, a cruel joke his parents had played on him. As adults they eked out a living doing dirty work for the likes of Mike Delaney.

Billy and Axel sauntered over to Eddie.

Before anyone could say a word, one of the SUVs beeped as the doors were unlocked remotely. A Mexican family—a man, woman and two kids—approached pushing a cartful of groceries.

"His tires are flat," whispered one of the kids to the other, loud enough for everyone to hear.

The cowboy folded his knife and put in the front pocket of his jeans. "Watch out for the glass," he said to the kids.

"*Montar el carro!*" said the father to the kids sternly. The family climbed into the van while the father made haste to unload the bags of groceries into the back. Then he got in the van and drove away.

"You ain't welcome around here no more," said Billy to Eddie.

Eddie leaned against his car and faced the men squarely. He wasn't afraid of them—not on a Sunday afternoon at a busy store. He thought about bringing out his gun, but he didn't want to escalate the situation. So he said, "Tell me something, fellas. Do they sell tires in there?" Eddie gestured at Walmart.

"Yeah, they do," said Axel, just as Billy said, "No, you need a tire store."

The two thugs looked at each other. "No, man, Walmart sells tires," said Axel to his buddy. "They even put 'em on for you."

"For real?"

"Yeah, no lie, man."

"Well, there you go," said Billy, turning back to Eddie. He was embarrassed at being wrong, but he feigned indifference. "Lucky for you they sell tires here."

Eddie said, "Yeah, this is my lucky day."

"So buy yourself some new tires, and then drive away and don't come back."

"Why would I want to come back?" asked Eddie with a shrug of innocence.

"Because you're a trouble-maker," Axel said. "Why else would a P.I. take a job at B.J.'s Shrimp in the first place? Yeah, mister, we know who you are." He reached in his shirt pocket and pulled out one of

129

Eddie's business cards. "Eduardo Maez," he read. "Investigator." He looked at Eddie and put the card back into his pocket. "For a P.I. you're not very cautious, are you, Mr. Maez?"

"I don't know what you're talking about."

"Is that right? What I'm talking about is that the Bossman don't like spies."

"Everyone is happy here," interjected Billy. "We don't need nobody stirring up trouble."

"If we see you around here again, we might break your fingers," the cowboy said, nodding towards the billy club.

"So get lost," said Billy. "Let's go, Axel."

The two men gave Eddie a last look of warning, then walked slowly away.

Eddie went to the automotive department and talked them into pushing his car to Walmart's garage where he bought four new tires.

He drove back to the Black Horse Saloon. The place was moderately busy, with the TVs showing highlights while sports analysts blathered on about injuries, possible trades and late-breaking rumors. Eddie took a seat at the bar and ordered a beer.

He swiveled around to face the room and scanned the crowd. It was a mix of whites and Hispanics, sitting at separate booths, mostly men with scars, tattoos or rotten teeth. Sometimes all three. At one booth the two bozos who slit his tires were drinking beer. Eddie turned away from them. Towards the back of the room there was a wooden staircase leading up to the second floor where a tinted window overlooked the saloon. A few minutes later, a man came down the stairs, wearing glasses and a bow-tie, carrying a briefcase. *Short-sleeve dress shirt and a bow-tie?* Eddie marveled to himself. *Is that a pocket protector? Good grief!*

With his fingers the man with the briefcase beckoned the two thugs who got up and followed him to the door. Eddie twisted away, trying to hide his face. "Good night, Jack," said the man to the bartender without a glance.

"Good night, Mr. Briggs." Eddie almost choked on his beer.

He waited half an hour and had another beer. When he left the Black Horse, it was dark outside, and he didn't see the blow coming. Billy Bonner struck him viciously from behind with his billy club, hitting the hollow between the neck and shoulder. A jolt of pain shot through Eddie's arm. His gun was in his shoulder holster, but he couldn't lift his arm that high. The blow deadened his arm but didn't knock him to the ground. A smack behind his knees took care of that. It wasn't a hard smack, but the club was hard.

"You fellas work for Briggs?" Eddie managed to ask.

In response the cowboy kicked him in the ribs with his steel-toed boot.

"Thought we told you to clear out," said Axel.

"Did you mean now?" Eddie gasped.

"Smart ass. We told you, and we told you nice, but you didn't listen, did you?" The club came down on his kidneys. "You hear us now?"

"Yeah, I'm getting the message."

"Good," said Axel, taking out a switchblade and flipping it open. "Next time I'll let my knife do the talking." He gave Eddie another kick to the ribs and walked away.

After the beating, Eddie decided he'd had enough. On the drive back to San Antonio he determined he didn't need corroboration from other workers. He had enough information to trigger a raid or an investigation. The authorities could do the rest of the work. His body ached from the beating. Why should he risk a broken hand—or worse? He didn't have to prove himself to anyone.

Before calling in the posse, though, Eddie wanted to talk to Brad. His name would have to come up. The feds would interview him. They would want to know if he was involved, and Brad needed to know how he would answer that question. But before he called Brad, Eddie wanted to know who owned the Black Horse Saloon. He checked the Texas Registry of Corporations online and found the bar was owned by a sole proprietor named Delaney. Michael Todd Delaney. Next he called a friend of his with the Houston Police and asked him to check to see if Michael Todd Delaney had a criminal record. Then he called Brad to set up a time to meet the next day.

They met at the Havana and sat under the palm trees. Eddie told Brad what he'd been up to: about going through the tunnel with other immigrants, about working at B.J.'s for a few days—"until they got wise and fired my ass"—about trying in vain to find someone to go on the record about labor violations at B.J.'s, and about the thugs who beat him up. "I want to take my story to the feds and let them bust this operation wide open," Eddie said.

"Whoa, not so fast. There are still some big holes to fill in."

"Like what?"

"Like who is Briggs and who does he work for?"

"Tell me, Brad. Does this Briggs character look like a nerd? Very white, almost albino, with thinning hair. Short, maybe five-five? Has a round head and a scrawny neck? Wears glasses with black frames? Kind of looks like Truman Capote?"

"Yeah," said Brad, surprised at the accuracy of the description. "He's about forty, forty-five. Favors a bow tie with a short-sleeved shirt. Do you know him?"

"No, but I saw him at a bar in Brownsville, the Black Horse Saloon. Word is, the place is a front for an illegal sports betting operation run by an Irishman named Delaney. Michael Todd Delaney."

"Ah. The secretive Mr. D."

"Right. Briggs was coming out of his office when I saw him. Bartender called him Mr. Briggs."

"Why would Briggs be meeting with Delaney?"

"I don't know. Maybe he works for him. Maybe Briggs is Delaney's messenger, his mouthpiece."

"Wait. You're saying the Black Horse is a front for a sports gambling enterprise, which is itself a front for a smuggling operation?"

Eddie shrugged. "Why not?"

"And Delaney owns the Black Horse?"

"The Irish mob meets the Mexican mafia. Look, I asked a buddy of mine in the Houston PD to check up on Delaney. He has no record. A couple of arrests for assault, but the charges didn't stick. He walked. But I'll give you ten-to-one that some of the fine patrons of his bar have arrest records that stretch from here to Florida. Some of them did time no doubt. When they get out, they go right to the Black Horse. It's a nice place to take a date."

Brad nodded. "So Delaney has, what? A network of *coyotes* in Mexico bringing in workers illegally?"

"Yeah, and they come bringing drugs."

"Which get distributed through B.J.'s Shrimp. Man, this is fuckin' crazy!"

"There's only one problem," Eddie said.

"Yeah, what is that?"

"Lack of evidence. We can allege there is smuggling going on because I saw it. And you can tie Briggs to the smugglers through the blackmail scheme. But we can't tie Briggs to Delaney, at least in any criminal way, and therefore we can't tie Delaney to the smugglers."

"Don't you watch TV?" asked Brad. "The cops arrest Briggs and charge him with all sorts of crimes, then they offer to drop some of the charges if he gives up Delaney."

"What about the lawyers?"

"What lawyers?"

"The ones Delaney will have at his side at all times. Briggs may have a few too."

"Hmm," Brad opined.

Part Two

Chapter Twenty-One

"Raelynn, stop it! I mean it! You throw another pea, I'll smack you. You *know* I will," said the fat lady in lavender tights. She took a pull from the vodka bottle on the table.

Ten-year-old Raelynn bounced a pea off her mother's forehead, laughing and putting her arms up for self-protection. Clumsily, her mother swung the palm of her hand, aiming for Raelynn's head. Whap! The slap slid harmlessly off her elbow.

"Why do you have to be this way, Raelynn? Now pick up that pea." She lit a menthol cigarette.

Raelynn shook her head firmly and tossed another pea at her mother.

"Okay, that's it, young lady." She put her cigarette in the ashtray. "You're going to bed. Get up!"

Raelynn's mother heaved her own bloated body to a standing position. She grabbed Raelynn by a wrist and tried to pull her up, but Raelynn slumped like a rag doll, and her mother had to drag her across the kitchen floor and down the hall, gathering dust and dirt all the way into the girl's bedroom. It was a hurricane of a room—a cyclone of dirty clothes, half-empty plates of food and a few toys. Raelynn's mother shoved her into the room. The skinny-bodied girl sprawled across the bed in a tumult of grimy sheets. She lay there glaring at her mother.

"As long as you're gonna be there all night, you might as well clean it up," said the fat lady, sweeping her bulbous arms out to indicate the grand scale of the mess. "I'm sure as hell not gonna to do it for you. You wanna live in a pigsty, that's your business." Bulging out of tight-fitting stretchwear in every direction, her mother slammed the door and locked it.

"The laundry-mat is open 'til ten." She was yelling to make sure Raelynn could hear her through the door. "So you wanna go down there, just bang on the door and I'll let you out. I'll go with you even. And you wanna know why?" she yelled. "Sure as hell not because you're being a little angel. It's because I'm afraid you'll run off again. I gotta keep my eyes on you all the time." She went back to the kitchen and retrieved her cigarette. Then she said in a softer voice, "Except when you're in school; then you're *their* problem." She took another swig from the vodka bottle.

Raelynn Weeks had been conceived one hot night in a motel near Ft. Hood. Her mother, Patti Weeks, had been drinking all evening at various bars near the base. Along the way she hooked up with a soldier who was about to be shipped out to Germany. Patti remembered that he was tall and bony, and he had a tattoo on his left shoulder depicting two serpents spiraling around a sword. She had no idea what the symbol meant, but she decided that the two snakes were her and the soldier. The sword was the Army, which brought them together and split them apart. Patti wasn't sure of the soldier's name. Maybe he never told her. Or maybe he gave her a false name. She referred to him as "Wiley" because he wore a Wiley Coyote T-shirt that night.

When Patti woke up the next morning, Wiley was gone without a trace. Patti was disappointed. She was still horny from the drunken sex they had enjoyed, and she had hoped for a good-bye fuck. But she wasn't sad or even surprised. Just disappointed. She began to play with herself, quickly bringing herself to orgasm. She let the feeling fade and then began again, getting more and more excited until she came in one long orgasmic shudder. She didn't have sex with a man again for more than two months, by which time she knew she was pregnant.

Whether Patti Weeks was a poster child for poor white women in Texas was a legitimate question, for she was certainly qualified for the position. She lived in a moss-covered trailer home in Corpus Christi. She worked at Walmart restocking shelves and putting away returns. Her schedule changed every week and she was afraid to ask for a regular schedule because she needed the job and didn't want to make waves. Her boss was a prick who could make an employee's life miserable. Besides this, Patti was fat, closing in on obese, and she had a wart on her neck with black hair growing out of it. Fat people are known to be jolly, but Patti was a dour, depressed woman who had so little joy in her life that, sad to say, she gave birth to Raelynn in large part to give meaning and purpose to her own life. She thought that having a child would give her direction without realizing that it was she who should be giving direction to the child, not the other way around.

It's true that Patti Weeks did not have a stellar childhood herself. She grew up in a series of foster homes where she was frequently teased and taunted, wearing hand-me-down clothes and coats that smelled like mothballs. She had one toy of her own, a rag doll named Wanda that was never out of her hand. Wanda was the only one who understood, and Patti loved her more than anything. If Wanda had been lost or stolen, Patti would have been devastated, but luckily no one coveted the doll, as it was dirty, crusty and torn.

Emotionally bereft, tolerated rather than loved, Patti was never encouraged to apply herself in school. On the contrary, she was scolded for not understanding the lessons and considered "retarded" by adults. She went into high school barely able to read and incapable of doing even long division. She dropped out a few months later.

Given her shortcomings, she should not have become a mother, and indeed Patti considered having an abortion. But by the time she went to the abortion clinic for a consultation, she was in her third trimester. By then abortion was out of the question and she had to carry the baby to term. Patti did not regret this turn of events. The rest of her life was so barren, she convinced herself that having a baby around would improve her outlook on life. Perhaps it did, but that did not make Patti a good mother. She endured long bouts of Raelynn's crying fits by shutting the door and turning up the television. She let the baby lie on her mattress in soiled diapers for hours at a time. She fed Raelynn when she needed to express milk from her giant breasts, not when Raelynn was hungry.

Patti couldn't find anyone to watch Raelynn while she went to work, at least not anyone she could afford. She ended up quitting her job and going on public assistance to pay her food bills, her rent, and her utilities. Sometimes she did laundry and ironing in her trailer home to afford necessities like vodka and cigarettes. Finally, Patti answered an ad for someone to do phone sex for six dollars an hour. Patti interviewed for the job over the phone and was hired. Her voice was low and smooth; it had a sultry sexiness to it that men liked. She also was able to convince men that she was dying to suck their cock or take it up the ass, or whatever turned them on. Sometimes she would rub her vagina to enhance the experience for herself, giving a certain real texture to her moans and pleas. Patti was pleased. She had finally found something she was good at that she could do at home by herself on her own time.

Raelynn Weeks grew up wild, nearly feral. It's a wonder that she was born without any mental or physical defects, given her mother's daily alcohol intake. Raelynn's obese mother was dismally incompetent, herself a case of chronic neglect. When Raelynn was three, a caseworker from Child Protective Services discovered that she was not potty-trained and barely spoke. No surprise, Raelynn became a ward of the state.

For a few years, like her mother before her, Raelynn was moved from one foster home to another, never lasting longer than six months with any one family. She was angry, disobedient and prone to violent behavior. When Raelynn was seven, she was awarded back to her mother, on the condition that Patti attend parenting classes. She did this but used the sessions to complain about Raelynn's outrageous antics.

School was a blessing for both mother and daughter. It gave each of them several hours a day apart from one another. Thanks to a couple of observant and encouraging teachers, Raelynn became a good student, especially in math. Basic concepts of mathematics she understood easily, and by third grade she was helping other students figure out the mysteries of multiplication and division. Raelynn liked the neatness of mathematics. She liked the way each number had one immutable meaning, and that in equations both sides had to agree. It was so contrary to life itself, where nothing balanced and nothing was fair.

The years passed. Raelynn and Patti didn't like each other, but they settled into a pattern that allowed them to survive. It consisted of noncompliance on Raelynn's part, and of neglect and verbal abuse on Patti's part. In middle school Raelynn was tagged for what she was: a poor kid from the wrong side of the tracks. Her clothes were from Goodwill, and her face and hands were often smudged with dirt. Patti kept Raelynn's hair tied back in a ponytail, only it wasn't ever quite long enough to be held securely by the rubber band. So Raelynn's face was ringed with a halo of hairs, strands sticking out every which way. It was one of those intentionally mean things that Raelynn's mother would do: keeping Raelynn's hair at an impossible length, just a snip too short for a successful ponytail. Raelynn got into the habit of brushing the wild hairs back from her face with one hand or the other, a habit that stuck with her even when her hair was cut short and her face was free from stray hairs.

Threats—and outlandish promises—were routinely made but never carried out or fulfilled. At age thirteen Raelynn ran away again and Patti didn't even bother to report it. Raelynn lived on the streets for a few days—long enough to know that life on the streets was even worse than living at home. So she went home, unsure what fate awaited her there.

"Hah!" snorted her mother when Raelynn walked in the door. Her mouth was almost lost in the folds of fat surrounding it. She was heating up some canned ravioli, stirring it with one hand and holding a cigarette with the other. "I knew you'd come crawling back when you got hungry."

"I'm not crawling, and there's never anything good to eat around here anyway."

"Why'd you come back then?"

"Ma, you would not believe the mean kids out there. Some of them are nice, but the others just want to take your money and try to mess with you."

"I told you, didn't I? You didn't get knocked up, did you?"

"No, I didn't get knocked up. Jesus. I'm not as stupid as you are."

"Fuck you! You prolly took some drug and don't even remember what happened."

"*This place* is what I was trying to forget about. You're such a pig."

"Just go to your room, young lady. I don't even want you around. You aggravate me, you really do." She took a last drag on her cigarette and crushed it in the ashtray. Then she scraped the ravioli onto a plate.

"You're gonna eat that slop?" asked Raelynn.

"Shut up and go to your room like I said."

"Gladly."

Raelynn was small, compact and thick of muscle. As a young child she was seen as a fat butterball, but after a few growth spurts she stretched out and developed muscles in place of fat. By the time she reached high school, Raelynn had the physique of a boxer or a gymnast. Contrary to her mother, as in so many other ways, Raelynn liked to use her body. She enjoyed running and lifting weights. By a stroke of luck, Raelynn's high school offered Taekwondo, which Raelynn found empowering. She liked being strong and quick. It counterbalanced her mother's total indolence and sloth, and it also meant she could protect herself if she ever had to fend off a psycho or a desperate man.

Despite her physicality, Raelynn did not participate in popular sports. She was a subversive, not a jock. In high school Raelynn hung out with a group of outsiders, drop-outs, mavericks and other misfits. She didn't look like a rebel—she didn't have tattoos or studs, and she didn't wear black lipstick. She stayed out of trouble and never got caught shoplifting or smoking pot. Her crowd hated country music and football. That and her physique stamped her as a "lesbo" in the eyes of her more popular peers. But they knew she was smart, and Raelynn earned a reputation as a computer whiz. Some of her outlaw friends wound up dead or in prison, but Raelynn made it through to graduation. She even had good enough grades to get in to Texas A & M, Corpus Christi campus, with a tuition waiver.

"So you gonna move out now that you're goin' to college, Miss Smartypants?" asked her mother.

"You're supposed to be happy for me."

"I'll be happy when you start payin' me rent."

"Ma, you're a piece of work. I'd love to go live on my own, or in a dorm room, but I can't afford it. My scholarship pays for tuition, but that's all. I have to come up with room and board and all the fees and shit. So you're stuck with me for now. Believe me, I'll get out of here as fast as I can." That turned out to be three-and-a-half years. Raelynn took some classes in the summer to speed things up.

Her main goal was to live a lifestyle as different from her mother's as possible: to live in a clean house with flowers on the table and food in the fridge. When she was fifteen or sixteen, Raelynn started taking responsibility for herself. Her room was clean. She washed her own clothes She cooked meals for herself. As much as possible she steered clear of her mother, leaving her to smoke her cigarettes and drink her vodka in front of the TV. Raelynn took care of herself and left her mom alone.

College was a revelation. Raelynn's isolated worldview splintered and broke apart as she became aware of history, politics, science and other disciplines. She became a good researcher and an independent thinker. In an economics class the students were asked to write a paper suggesting a solution to the problem of illegal immigration from Mexico. Raelynn advocated for relaxing the border between the U.S. and Mexico, using it for voting and tax purposes only.

"This country was built on hard work and ingenuity, not on sloth and laziness," Raelynn wrote. "Everyone should have a chance to come here and live the American Dream if they want to. If they've got the guts to follow their passion for freedom, then we should have the heart to welcome them."

The professor selected some of the papers, including Raelynn's, to be discussed by the whole class. He asked Raelynn to state her thesis.

"If there are jobs available that no American citizen or lawful permanent resident wants to do," said Raelynn, "then why not give them to people who *do* want to do them? How many Americans employ undocumented workers to clean their houses, tend their yards, walk their dogs, even care for their children? We don't even know because they are undocumented. How do they get paid? In cash. Is this money reported to the IRS? No. With open immigration at least we would know who lives in the United States and how big the underground economy is."

Another student spoke up. "This is an insidious and dangerous idea. What would become of U.S. citizens who are unemployed or underemployed? They would be forced out of the labor market simply because they are American citizens, because as American citizens they must be paid minimum wage. But how many employers are going to hire someone at $7.25 an hour when they can get the work done for five? Unemployed citizens would have to rely on unemployment insurance, which would bankrupt our system and cause economic chaos."

Raelynn responded: "You're saying that capitalism and free choice result in economic chaos?" The debate went on a few minutes longer until the professor interrupted and moved on to discuss another student's paper. The discussion crystallized a new feeling that had been growing in Raelynn. She could think for herself and earn the respect of her peers. After years of being put down and criticized by her mother, Raelynn finally felt good about herself.

Chapter Twenty-Two

Despite her new-found self-respect, Raelynn knew that in order to pull herself out of her mother's pigpen, she needed to make money. As she made her way through her first year of college, she asked herself what course of study would provide opportunities to earn a solid wage. She decided to major in computer science and minor in bookkeeping and accounting. As graduation approached, Raelynn started to look for work, preferably in a different city. She looked online, scoured the want-ads in newspapers all over the state, and became a regular at the college's job placement office. Most of the job postings required more experience than she had, which was none. Finally she spotted a newspaper want-ad for a bookkeeper for a "thriving shrimp business" in Brownsville that, perhaps because it was in such an unglamorous place, had no requirements other than a thorough grounding in bookkeeping. She applied for the job and was called for an interview at a business called B.J.'s Shrimp Co.

Raelynn was shown into the owner's office by the receptionist. The tall brown man behind a desk rose from his swivel chair and gave Raelynn a quick forced smile. "I'm Henry Lucero," he said, gesturing for her to sit down.

"Raelynn Weeks," she said. For awhile Henry just studied Raelynn's resume without saying anything.

"Why do you want to work here?" he finally asked, looking up.

"I'm not sure I do," replied Raelynn, trying to sound self-confident. "I'd like to know more about the job first."

Henry stared at her over the top of his reading glasses, as if Raelynn were a work of modern art that he didn't understand. Finally, he smiled and said, "Okay. You'd be responsible for keeping the books, communicating with the IRS, providing me with weekly sales and expense reports.... That sort of thing."

"Do you have a written job description?"

"No."

"Okay. Why is your current bookkeeper leaving?"

"What difference does that make?"

"I'm just trying to get a sense of the job, Mr. Lucero."

"Hmm. Do you know anything about the shrimping business, Raelynn?"

"Nope. But I'm a quick study and my college coursework has convinced me that businesses have more similarities than differences, at least from a financial point of view." Henry looked at Raelynn eye to eye, over the tops of his glasses. Raelynn looked back with a small smile on her face that made Henry wonder if she was concealing something.

"Then you're familiar with tax accounting."

"Oh, yes, although I'm not a licensed accountant."

"Tell me, Raelynn, do you find that businesses tend to cheat on their taxes? Of course, there are legal loopholes, but I'm talking about misreporting certain data, specifically wages and hours worked."

"I would have no way to know whether the numbers are accurate or not. I have to assume they are."

"Yes, of course."

"That would mean also misreporting Social Security, FICA.... Everything would be affected."

"Yes."

"I wouldn't want to hide anything. Errors are better than lies." Raelynn was suspicious of this line of inquiry. "Mr. Lucero, is this some kind of test?" she asked. "Why are we talking about defrauding the IRS?"

"Would you report an irregularity, a suspicion or a questionable number to the IRS?"

"Not if the books balanced. I only see the numbers, Mr. Lucero, not the workers' time cards."

Henry leaned back in his chair and put his hands behind his head. Raelynn could hear the workers down below shouting to one another in Spanish, giving orders, passing on information, making jokes. Then he asked, "Raelynn, what is your opinion on immigration?"

The question hung in the air like a cloud of cigarette smoke.

"Immigration?" She cleared her throat. "Well, sir, I think the laws should be more lenient. I don't believe in keeping people out. I believe in letting them in. Sometimes people just need a chance."

Henry smiled. "Raelynn, you've got no previous job experience, no knowledge of the shrimping industry, a pretty slim resume, but as you say, sometimes people just need a chance."

So Raelynn wound up working for Henry Lucero at B.J.'s Shrimp Co. She was the best bookkeeper he'd ever had. She was a wizard with numbers, developing better ways to track B.J.'s costs, liquidity, liabilities, assets and profits.

Raelynn realized early on that Henry was violating the law. He hired undocumented workers, he paid less than minimum wage, he didn't pay overtime, he didn't provide mandated breaks, and when the season was over, he fired his workers without so much as a bus ticket out of town. On the other hand, he didn't cheat anyone out of their earnings, and workers could quit at any time with no questions asked. Raelynn did not have to doctor the books to cover up the violations, because the time and wage sheets were already prepared, the hours totaled, and the form signed by the employee. This part of Raelynn's job was simple and straightforward. It was also so meticulous that the IRS never questioned it. The workers could complain to the Dept. of Labor, but then they would lose their jobs and be deported, so they didn't complain to anyone but each other.

To his credit, Henry provided a safe and clean workplace. This, naturally, made good business sense because he couldn't afford to be shut down for safety violations. All the equipment was properly cleaned and maintained, all the temperatures were at or below regulation, everyone wore the proper attire and followed the safety regs rigorously. USDA and OSHA inspectors came by without prior notification, but they always had a hard time finding any violations to write up at B.J.'s.

Although Raelynn knew that what she was doing was illegal, it didn't bother her. She rather relished the opportunity to outwit the IRS and the immigration officials. Besides, she didn't consider this job her final destination. She would save enough money to make a move, and then head off to Los Angeles, Chicago, Denver or Portland. She would live in a nice house with a garden in back, she would have a bright office with a view of the city, she might even have a husband.

Raelynn's memories of living in her mother's musty trailer were still all too vivid. Mice built nests in the walls and moss grew along the bottom of the metal siding. The so-called mobile home sat on cinder blocks and at one time had been bright yellow with chrome trim. But over time it had changed to the color and texture of curdled cream. The chrome looked dull and leaden. Strewn around the ground nearby were failed flower pots, a small bicycle on its side, and a deflated swimming pool.

This was the poverty of pocketbook and soul that Raelynn yearned to get away from. She knew she was tagged as trailer trash by some, and she couldn't disagree, which is why she wanted out. She also knew that Brownsville was a pit, although no worse than Corpus Christi, but she didn't care. Brownsville was 160 miles away from her mother, and since her mother rarely left the trailer, Raelynn might as well have been in China.

B.J.'s Shrimp was a different kettle of fish. Without saying so directly, Henry had asked Raelynn to cook the books, break the law, lie to the IRS. She got paid well for doing this. She imagined herself taking trips to New York and New Orleans, maybe Europe. For the first time she could conceive of living somewhere other than south Texas. She wanted out, and Henry Lucero was going to provide her a means of escape.

Chapter Twenty-Three

After braving the tunnels of Cu Chi, Eddie's platoon was rewarded for their daring with a three-day pass to Saigon during the celebration of the New Year. They rented private rooms with running water and their own toilets. It was February, and the days were cool and dry. The nights were alive with twelve-foot paper dragons, bands of strolling musicians and the aroma of grilled meats. Eddie and his buddies wandered the streets, passing a bottle of rice wine. The sparklers and fireworks were unnerving to everyone because the war was raging not far from the city.

At midnight, at the peak of the festival, Eddie found himself dancing with a young woman called Kim who was thin and graceful as a pussy willow. Soul music set the mood with its exuberant love songs and funky background horn riffs. An hour later they were still dancing, but slower now, her arms around his neck, their foreheads touching, both of them a bit drunk.

"Come back to my room with me," said Eddie. Kim didn't speak English and looked at him uncomprehendingly. "You." Eddie pointed at Kim. "And me." He touched his own chest. "Go." He pointed to the door. He took Kim's hand and led her toward the door. She didn't resist.

They walked through the streets together holding hands, laughing at the masks and costumes, the face paint and pantomimes—though Eddie was also constantly looking for signs of danger. When they reached Eddie's place, they walked up to the second floor and flung open the window shutters to let in the night air and the sounds of celebration.

Nguyen Kim was 20 years old. New to Saigon, fleeing the bombs and mortar attacks on her country village, she was alone and homeless. She had been sleeping in a boarding house with other single women, and she desperately wanted out of there. She missed the forest, with its bird song and the cool stream that flowed nearby. She missed her family. Amidst the throngs of people in Saigon, Kim was lonely. She was happy to have the companionship of the nice American soldier named Eddie.

Like most other men his age, 21, Eddie was horny and hungry most of the time. The war focused his energy elsewhere, but in Saigon, relieved of his soldierly duties, his natural feelings returned. He found Kim incredibly sexy and desirable. He didn't think much further than that.

They made love more than once that night, then slept late into the day. When Eddie awoke, Kim was combing her hair by the window and singing. Eddie lay in bed listening until she stopped and turned around.

"You have a lovely voice," he said, and she smiled.

Many young women forced by the war to move from the countryside to the cities turned to prostitution to survive. But Kim cleaned houses and at night she sang in bars for tips. The next time Eddie came to Saigon he searched for Kim and found her in a small bar, singing, accompanied by a man playing acoustic guitar. Eddie found a seat and listened to Kim sing. The music seemed sad and had a yearning quality that captivated him. (Later he found out they were popular love songs.) After a while, when the duo took a break, he approached Kim.

"Remember me?" he asked.

Kim flung her arms around his neck. "Eddie!" she squealed.

"Your singing is beautiful," he said as they hugged tightly. Kim didn't understand what he said, but she was obviously happy to see him. From then on, Eddie went to Saigon whenever he could. He would seek out Kim and would usually find her singing in a bar or café. When she was finished performing for the night, they would spend the rest of the night together making love.

Then on one visit, Kim said, "I am pray-na."

"You're what?"

"Pray-na."

"Pregnant? You're pregnant?" Kim nodded. "You're going to have a baby?" He mimed cradling a baby in his arms, and she nodded again. "Oh, God, you can't have a baby now, not in the middle of a war. You're pregnant? Are you sure? For fuck's sake!" Actually, there was a part of Eddie that was thrilled by the news. Under normal circumstances, he might have welcomed the idea of being a father. He liked Kim. Maybe even loved her. They had fun together. They could have a baby together. But not here, not now. Eddie's tour of duty in Nam would be over in three months, and he wanted the fuck out of there. If only he could bring Kim back with him, he would. But, of course, that was not allowed. Eddie gave his military address to Kim and made sure she understood that she needed to keep in touch with him. He didn't want to lose contact with her. He would investigate ways to bring Kim and the baby to the States. He wouldn't abandon them.

On his last weekend in Saigon before he returned home, Eddie tried to express this to Kim. "I will come back," he said, "when the war is over. I will find you. Send me post cards with your address." He mimed his words as well as he could. He showed her a post card, saying, "I send to you. You send to me." He hoped she understood, but he couldn't be sure.

Eddie had saved much of his Army pay while in Vietnam. There wasn't a lot to spend money on other than booze, and that was cheap. He gave most of his savings to Kim. "For you and the baby," he explained. Kim hugged him like there was no tomorrow. As they both knew, there might not be one.

A few months after his return to the States, Eddie received a note in rough English handwriting that said, "Baby come. Girl name An." Soon thereafter Eddie was discharged in California. He wanted to go look for Kim and An, but the war prevented it.

When he moved back to Texas, he sent a note to Kim giving her his new address. He didn't hear back. After the war ended in 1975, the Communists dealt with thousands of displaced people by sending them to re-education camps in the country, where they were put to work farming. He didn't know what had happened to Kim and An, and he feared the worst.

Like many veterans, Eddie was scarred by the war—by what he'd seen happen to civilians, children and soldiers on both sides. Over time, the anger and guilt and horror he felt receded but never entirely went away. His experiences returned in dreams and flashbacks, whisking him back to the war in a way so realistic that he could smell the burning flesh and feel the warm blood ooze from a wounded soldier. But more than anything, he felt haunted by Kim and An, anguished by their unknown fate.

This is probably why Eddie threw himself into working as an investigator and later into the job as a reporter for the Houston daily paper. He didn't want to think about Kim and An. He went into the work headlong, taking on all manner of fraud and public deceit. He exposed an illegal land swap that would have turned public land into a private development for pennies on the dollar. He uncovered a plastics factory that was dumping its toxic waste into the Brazos River, and he fingered an oil company that was bribing inspectors to look the other way on structural defects in a tanker—until the tanker sprang a leak and bled oil into the Gulf. Eddie let his job consume him, in part so that he wouldn't have time for a personal relationship with anyone. His investigations left no time for a social life, and the few flings he did have ended abruptly after a short time.

Eddie's hesitancy, or perhaps inability, to form a bond with anyone may have stemmed from his forced abandonment of Kim and An. He would not discuss it, so he was the only one who knew the truth. And the truth, when he dared to face it, was that he was a father, yet he was unable to care for his child, unable to be part of her childhood, and worst of all, unable to really love her. A million times over the years Eddie thought of returning to Vietnam to look for Kim and An. But he convinced himself that it was an impossible task, because he didn't know where they lived, what they looked like, or even if they were still alive.

Eddie's secret left a gaping hole in his heart, bleeding like a gunshot wound, except that it could not be sutured up, nor could it heal because Eddie did his best to ignore it.

One night Eddie was at home pounding out a story when he hit a wall. He couldn't write another word. He couldn't concentrate on the facts, and what he had just written didn't make much sense. He had been drinking cup after cup of coffee to fuel his work, but now he shoved aside his coffee cup and poured himself two fingers of rye whiskey. He drank it in three swallows and poured himself another. He began thinking about his one-dimensional life, and his mind drifted to Kim and An.

Why do I continue to obsess about Kim and An? he asked himself. *That was 40 years ago. Why can't I leave it behind? For God's sake, why does it torment me so relentlessly? I never married, never had kids, never even had a steady girlfriend. And why? Maybe I use Kim and An as an excuse for not having a life of my own. It may be too late, but I need to move on. I need to give myself a chance to develop relationships with other people—and not just people I'm interviewing for a story.*

That was the moment Eddie knew he had to leave the newspaper and try to construct a new life. Eddie convinced himself that he needed to act now before he started to make excuses for not doing anything. It had happened before. But what to do? He was too old for the bar scene and not interested in attending a church group or a yoga class. He didn't know the answer. He only knew he had to make a change. The next day he handed in his resignation.

The newspaper didn't want Eddie to go. He had been a rock-solid reporter for years, and they didn't want to lose him. They offered him an extended vacation, a pay raise, even a temporary transfer to a less stressful department, but Eddie turned down all offers. His mind was made up. After he left, in March, he fled to Padre Island to decompress and decide how he would go about enriching his life. But then Brad had called, and Eddie had been pulled back in. Now here it was late summer and he still had done nothing to fill the void that he felt in his soul.

One night on an impulse he Googled "online dating services," and got back 23.4 million results in 0.3 seconds. *"One of these sites ought to help,"* he joked with grim sarcasm. After browsing the top twenty, including a few for seniors or people "over 50" or "young at heart," he chose a site and registered there. He proceeded to fill out a long questionnaire about himself and what sort of person he was looking for.

The questions went on and on, delving into Eddie's tastes and dislikes. How did he feel about dogs, fragrances, traveling, religion, diet, politics, race, sports, etcetera, all of which Eddie could answer promptly...until he came to a section called "Accomplishments and Regrets." The accomplishment part of it was easy. Eddie had won plenty of awards for reporting that he could fall back on, but how could he explain, on a one to five scale, how he regretted having lived such a lopsided life? How could he quantify his feelings about fatherhood, intimacy and love? He had only idealized notions of these topics because he had spent his life avoiding them.

Another part of the questionnaire quizzed Eddie on what sort of person he was seeking. Eddie poured himself a shot of rye to help him think about that one. The questions were not frivolous and yet they were questions he rarely thought about, not consciously anyway. On the question of age, he hesitated to rule anyone out. Younger women appealed to him sexually, but older women might be wiser and more stable—how could he know? He ended up checking the "No preference" box. About his own age he was tempted to lie—to go with 55, since he did look good for 62—but decided that lying about his age would not be the best way to start a relationship.

It was late when Eddie finished the questionnaire. The arrow from his mouse hovered over the "Submit" button. In a moment of fear and rationality, he thought about saving it to read in the light of day when his head was not fogged by whiskey. But then his finger twitched, clicking on "Submit." And it was sent.

Chapter Twenty-Four

Raelynn knew a lot about spreadsheets and balance sheets but nothing about shrimp. In one sense, she realized, B.J.'s could be selling toys or light bulbs and her job would be much the same. But she wanted to know more about the industry she was working in. It would be good for customer relations, she told Mr. Lucero, and he agreed. Raelynn gave herself a crash course in shrimp.

She began with the basics: biology, life cycle, varieties, habitat. She learned how humans fit into the chain through trawling, processing and sales. She came to realize that there were basically two kinds of shrimp: bay shrimp and Gulf shrimp. Bay shrimp were juvenile Gulf shrimp that lived in the bays, estuaries and rivers within 10 miles of the Gulf coast. They were brought in to a processor fresh every day. Gulf shrimp, the adults, were much larger than the juveniles and lived in the deep waters of the Gulf far from land. The shrimpers who fished for Gulf shrimp were often at sea for weeks at a time and kept their catch frozen until they returned to port. So shrimpers were divided into two competing camps: the Gulf shrimpers who said that the bay shrimpers caught too many of the young shrimp before they could mature, and bay shrimpers who said that the Gulf shrimpers caught too many mama shrimp before they could spawn. B.J.'s processed both types of shrimp, depending on the season.

All shrimpers agreed that they were being undermined by shrimp farmers, who raised shrimp in huge land-based plantations. Most of these shrimp farmers were Asian, who froze their shrimp, shipped it to the U.S. and sold it for less than American producers.

Raelynn pored over statistics that revealed an industry in crisis. For a medley of reasons—environmental, economic, social—the number of shrimp was declining. The state was issuing fewer licenses to fish for shrimp and the shrimping season was shorter. The number of shrimp boats on the Gulf was dwindling. Shrimpers squabbled amongst themselves over fewer shrimp. Meanwhile, Americans were buying more shrimp than ever, most of which was coming from Asia.

Raelynn wondered what she had gotten herself into. Maybe she should have tried harder to land a job with one of the new high-tech businesses in Austin, but instead she was in a backwater town working in a dying industry for a fraudulent owner.

On top of this shocking realization, Raelynn felt a hollow place inside her. She was so glad to be away from her mother and on her own that she didn't notice it right away, but gradually she became aware of an empty place in her gut, as real as hunger pangs. She wanted more out of life, but she wasn't sure exactly what. Her own business maybe, travel, or a family…something just out of reach and out of focus. She wanted something to soothe away the loneliness that she felt when she walked into her apartment after work, silent but for the humming of the refrigerator, and saw, once again, a red zero on her answering machine. Likewise, her cell phone was disturbingly quiet.

Of course Raelynn realized that she was unlikely to get any calls from friends of either gender when she never made any calls herself. But whom would she call? She didn't know anyone in Brownsville, other than a few shrimpers and business associates. Even online, with the entire world at her fingertips, she had disturbingly few friends or connections. She kept in touch with some friends from college, but none of them lived anywhere near Brownsville. Raelynn felt that using social media to find friends online would be an admission of failure in the real world. Eventually though, one Saturday night, feeling foolish and desperate, Raelynn went online and registered with a couple of online dating services. Within a few days, a landslide of possible matches came back to her, and the sheer volume of responses boosted her self-esteem. *"I am desirable,"* she said to herself. *"At least online."* She spent hours scrutinizing them, trying to get a sense of who was on the other end of each "loveline," as one site called it. She analyzed the data looking for the right equation, the perfect proof, a formula for love. Her calculations cancelled out all but three candidates.

Two of the finalists were white men in their late twenties. The similarities didn't end there. Neither had kids or other entanglements; neither man smoked, and both described themselves as "fit." Neither was very religious and both had college degrees. One owned a chain of Jiffy Lubes and the other was the business manager for a non-profit in Austin. Raelynn didn't know what they looked like, as exchanging photos came a bit later in the process. But she knew that one was born in Texas and the other came from St. Louis. Raelynn tried to make sense of this fragmented data, but the two men seemed alarmingly alike. One was allergic to cats.

The third man declined to give his age, but from other bits of information, Raelynn deduced that he was older. Yet he seemed like an interesting man. He was a prize-winning journalist and formerly worked as a private investigator. A member of both the NRA and the ACLU. Born and raised in San Antonio. Mother and father both deceased. He was not married but had one adult child, "whereabouts unknown." This man seemed more worldly than the other two. He had more life experience and more mystery. *Maybe he's too old for me,* thought Raelynn, *but at least he's got some character.*

Raelynn took the next step, contacting the older man through the website, which kept a cautious distance between them. His name was Eddie. He posted a photo on the website: Eddie at work at a computer in a cubicle. Magazines, papers and Post-its were strewn around like flower petals at a wedding. Eddie, wearing a white shirt with his sleeves rolled up, was turning in his chair to look up at the camera, smiling. His face was broad and dark, his black hair thick and wavy. He was nice-looking, but Raelynn wondered how old the photo was.

Eddie didn't even look at his dating sites for a few weeks. For one thing he was busy; for another he was afraid he wouldn't get any bites. When he finally did look, he was not surprised. He got only a few replies and wasn't wowed by any of them. Only one was a woman under 40, a bookkeeper at a business in Brownsville. A bookkeeper? Sounded dull to Eddie. *She's probably given up on the under-forty guys and isn't much to look at. Or she's a golddigger.* Still, he kept thinking about one thing the bookkeeper had said. Under a section called "Self-reflections," she had written: *I have an outsider's point of view. If not for some good teachers I had in grade school, I might have become an outlaw—not a violent criminal but maybe a cat burglar or a cyber-thief. I might have done some time.*

Eddie found this revelation candid, and slightly titillating, but also puzzling. Why did she volunteer this information? He wanted to meet the person who would mention this to a stranger. He wondered if she had tattoos or piercings. He replied to her posting: *Do you want to get off this website and correspond directly?* He gave her his email address. A few days later he received an email from her.

Hello Eddie,

This is Raelynn. We met online. Thanks for responding to my post. So, this is awkward, isn't it? You sound like an interesting man. I'm curious about your child. You don't know where she lives, or what? Is she sailing around the world or trekking through Mongolia? (Just kidding.) How old is she? For that matter, how old are you? I'm 24. I'm not sure how much age matters, but it means something. I have my *favorite music and TV shows and all the stuff I grew up with, which is probably different from what you grew up with. How far back do you go? Cosby? M*A*S*H? Gilligan's Island? Sorry. Sometimes I measure time by sitcoms. I'm not completely shallow though. Have you read Camus? He's amazing. I remember one scene where the hero (or anti-hero) gets thrown in prison. He's a chain smoker but they won't let him have any cigarettes, so he sucks on splinters of wood. Poor bastard. I don't smoke, probably because my mother is a chain smoker and I learned to hate it. I hate her too, most of the time. I mean, she's my mother, so I care about her a little bit, but mostly I can't stand her. She's a cretin. But she's the only family I've got, since my father took off before I was even born. I suppose my mother is responsible for who I am because I'm pretty much the opposite of her. She's fat and I'm not, she's a slob and I'm a neatnik, she likes country music and I prefer the aching void. (I stole that last bit from some composer who hates Musak, as do I. Even more than country.) Let's see, what else? I guess you know from my profile that I work as a bookkeeper. It's a good job, as far as pay goes, but I want to do more with my life than balance the books. I don't know what yet. Something more exciting and worthy of doing. I mean, our time on Earth is finite, and it seems to me that we should take advantage of it, not just get by.*

So what's next? You could write me back if you want. I'd like that.

Sincerely yours,

Raelynn Weeks

Eddie knew right away that this would never work out as a romantic relationship. The age difference was too great. Nothing could replace life experience, and Raelynn hadn't had enough of it yet. But he found her fresh and funny, not at all jaded, as he was. He decided he would at least like to meet her.

Hi Raelynn,

I really enjoyed your email. Thanks for being so forthcoming about your life. In answer to your questions, I am 62. I recently retired from the newspaper business. My daughter would be 40 years old now, which blows my mind. She was conceived and born during the war in Vietnam while I was in the Army. Sadly, I lost track of her and her mother during the last years of the war and the chaotic situation of the post-war years. I think you're right that age makes a difference in a relationship. There is probably too great a gap in our ages for romance, but I would like to meet you anyway. Would you have dinner with me sometime soon? I will come to Brownsville. You can pick out a nice restaurant for us. As Humphrey Bogart says at the end of Casablanca, "This could be the beginning of a beautiful friendship."

Eddie Maez

This was not what Raelynn had in mind when she looked online, but it was better than another night home alone. In a few short emails, they decided on a date, time and place. Eddie offered to pick her up, and Raelynn accepted, even though it made her uneasy.

Chapter Twenty-Five

Eddie arrived at Raelynn's second-floor apartment with flowers. He rang the bell and held the bouquet behind his back. Raelynn opened the door, wearing a dark purple dress and beaded earrings. She had grown her hair out when she moved to Brownsville and dyed it with henna, giving it a red tinge. Eddie was relieved to see that Raelynn was a few inches shorter than he was.

"Raelynn, I presume?"

"Eddie?"

"You look exquisite." He presented the flowers with a flourish. "These are for you."

"Wow. Thanks! I'm not used to getting flowers."

"I'm not used to giving them."

"Why don't you come in a minute so I can put these in a vase. Then we can go."

Eddie came in and closed the door. Out of habit he surveyed Raelynn's apartment: sparsely furnished in the Ikea mode with a few posters and prints on white walls, a medium-sized television, and a hallway leading to other rooms. He had to suppress the urge to write it all down in a notebook. Raelynn put water in a vase for the flowers. She removed some magazines from a glass-topped coffee table and placed the flowers there.

"Nice," she said. "Thanks."

Eddie stepped out into the hallway, and Raelynn locked the door. They circled down the cement steps holding onto the spiral handrail and got into Eddie's Honda Accord. The car was clean and had a full tank.

Raelynn had picked out a good restaurant: not fancy but with good food. She apologized for its being in a strip mall.

"That's okay," said Eddie. "At least I don't have to tip the valet."

Once they had been seated, they ordered their drinks, a chardonnay for Raelynn and a vodka martini for Eddie. He asked what he thought was an innocent question. "You're a bookkeeper, is that right? What kind of business is it?"

"It's a seafood processor called B.J.'s Shrimp Co."

Eddie's glass was halfway to his mouth, but he set it down slowly.

"Is something wrong?" asked Raelynn. "You look...startled."

"It's just that...I know someone who worked at B.J.'s—as a floor worker."

"And?"

"And he didn't like it much. Hard work, long hours, not much fun."

"Fun? No, that's not a word I would use to describe processing shrimp. Mr. Lucero, the owner, runs a tight ship, you could say. The employee's manual is about this thick." She held her thumb and fore-finger an inch apart. "Not that anyone reads it. It's all in English any-way."

"Most of the workers speak Spanish?"

"All of them, seems like."

Eddie's mind raced ahead, wondering how he should proceed. How was this possible? The one date he had had in months turns out to be an employee of B.J.'s Shrimp! He didn't want to lie to Raelynn or hide the truth from her, but neither did he want to spill all the details of her em-ployer's illegal activities. What did she know? Where did she stand? He took a step sideways.

"And Mr. Lucero? He's a good boss?"

"We get along fine. He's very...down to business, you know? Like, he doesn't make small talk or flirt with me or joke around. He's all about the numbers. Which is fine. He hired me to work, and he treats me pro-fessionally. It pays good." She shrugged. "What more can I ask?"

Eddie nodded and looked into Raelynn's eyes, still trying to decide which way to go with the conversation. What would she do if he told her what he knew about B.J.'s?

"The smell doesn't bother you?" he stalled.

"No, not really. I'm in the office where it's not so bad. You get used to it."

Yeah, right, Eddie thought.

"What about you?" Raelynn asked. "Your profile said you write for a newspaper?"

Eddie felt like he'd been thrown a lifeline. "Yes. That is, I did for a long time. I retired recently. From the newspaper business, anyway."

"Like, what did you write about? Business? Sports?"

"No, I was on the crime beat for several years, then politics for several more. Not that there's much difference."

Raelynn laughed. "That's funny," she said. "You should get paid double if you're writing about a criminal politician."

"Yeah, it's a two-fer."

"So what was one of the best crimes you covered?" She laughed and made air quotes. "'Best crimes.' I mean, one of the most interesting."

"Well, let's see. A few years back there was a sheriff who had his deputies crack down on speeders. They would give the driver a ticket, unless he or she wanted to donate to the county's fund for youth education. If they donated fifty bucks cash, the cop would overlook the traffic violation."

"And people paid the fine?"

"Oh, yeah, if they had the cash. Nobody wants a speeding violation on their record. Plus the hassle of it."

"What happened to the money?"

"Well, guess what? There was no county fund for youth education, and the money went into a special account everyone called 'The Sheriff's Account.'"

"Which was used for what?"

"All sorts of things. Staff parties, junkets to nice vacation spots, football tickets…. The Sheriff's new pickup truck.

"Wild! I would probably book the income as Contributions, strictly speaking, and the expenses as, let's see, Department Functions, and break that out into Entertainment and Bribes." Raelynn giggled at the thought. "Of course, if it's cash, I wouldn't have to book it at all."

"Exactly. And what's funny is that the sheriff didn't want the money to show up anywhere, so instead of putting it in the bank, they just kept it in the safe. Thousands of dollars at any given time."

"Wow, that's crazy."

"That's Texas." Eddie decided to test the water. "So how many people work at the shrimp company?"

"Oh, about a hundred during the peak season. In the off-season there are only a few. More of us in the office than on the floor."

"That's quite a swing. Where do the seasonal workers come from?"

"Not my department. But I'd guess Mexico or Central America."

"Illegals?"

Raelynn locked eyes with him for a moment. "Sounds like you've got your reporter's hat on."

"Sorry. Force of habit, I guess."

"Do you have something against immigrant workers?"

"Not if they're legal."

"And if they're not?"

"Then they tend to get exploited. Paid less than minimum wage, not given the proper break time…. That sort of thing."

Raelynn toyed with her food. "The minimum wage is a bad idea," she said. "Should be abolished."

"Why do you say that?"

"Hey. If someone is willing to work for five dollars an hour, why should an employer be forced to pay more? It's none of the government's business."

"Raelynn, have you ever heard of *Das Kapital*?"

"Karl Marx. The workers own the means of production? That's bullshit. Excuse my French, Eddie, but the *owners* own the means of production, and they should be able to buy labor off the open market, just like any other commodity."

"Pure, unfettered capitalism."

"What's wrong with that?"

"Well, mainly that it doesn't protect the rights of the workers. They should be protected from abuse, working unreasonably long shifts, wage gouging...."

"Did I hear an opinion there? I thought reporters were supposed to be objective."

Raelynn smiled and Eddie chuckled.

"Well, I'm not a reporter any more, just a citizen with opinions."

They stopped talking and looked at one another with open faces, each taking in the other's face and demeanor fully for the first time. The smile stayed in Raelynn's eyes but her lips slid into an ironic slant. "You really are old, you know," she said. "Old enough to be my father."

"I know, I know. But I'm enjoying myself anyway. I hope you are too."

"'This could be the start of a beautiful friendship,'" said Raelynn, trying to match Bogie's tone.

"Pretty good. You've seen the movie?"

"I rented it after getting your email. I like black and white films. They're relics from another age, like listening to old scratchy records."

"Hey, don't put me on the shelf with the other antiques quite yet. *Casablanca* was made before I was born."

"Well, still. You're analog and I'm digital."

The waitress came to take their plates.

"You have a daughter, right?" Raelynn asked after the table was cleared.

"I guess so. I've never seen her."

"Well, I never saw my father, so we're even."

"Yeah, in a way. Do you know his name?"

"No. My ma always called him Wiley. After Wiley Coyote. But she never mentioned him, except to put me down. As in, 'You're a worthless piece of shit, Raelynn, just like Wiley.'"

"Really? I'm sorry. Does your mother live in Brownsville?"

"No, thank God. Corpus Christi. I haven't seen her for over a year. For all I know, she's drunk herself to death by now."

Eddie couldn't think of anything to say to that. Whatever he said would be either patronizing or inappropriate. He let a silence hang between them. Finally, he said, "Congratulations on surviving a wretched childhood, Raelynn."

"Yeah, thanks."

They sat there comfortably quiet, each lost in thought.

Raelynn finally broke the spell. "What happened to your daughter's mother?" she asked in a voice soft with sympathy.

Eddie bit his lip to fight back tears.

"I don't know. It was during the war. I had to leave her in Vietnam."

"What was her name?"

"Kim." It had been years since he had said her name out loud. His chest felt like someone had hit it with a brick.

172

"Did you love her?"

Eddie looked into Raelynn's eyes. "I don't know," he said. "I didn't think about love in those days."

"What did you think about?"

"Death."

Chapter Twenty-Six

Eddie stayed at a motel that night and drove back to Houston the next day. He had returned to Houston from San Antonio a few weeks earlier. After his initial stay at the Hotel Havana, he had been house-sitting in San Antonio for a friend of Brad's. When Brad's friend returned, Eddie had to move out. Besides, Eddie felt like he needed to get back to Houston to check on his own house. Not that there was much to check on. There were probably some spoiled cold cuts in the fridge and a stack of bills to pay. It would be a miracle if Jerome, his only house-plant, had survived his absence, even though it was accustomed to neglect.

On the three-hour drive to Houston, and Eddie let his mind wander at random from Carlos and Sofia to the Black Horse to the tunnels of Cu Chi. He wondered whether his car was due for an oil change and whether he should get a cat. He resolved to read more novels and play less computer solitaire. Eventually, as his eyelids began to droop, he began thinking how he'd like a cup of coffee—not a cup of highway convenience store coffee in a plastic cup, but a cup of dark roast coffee from Java, made from freshly ground beans.

But no matter where his mind wandered, it kept coming back to Raelynn. He had enjoyed her company. She was smart and nice-looking, and short like himself. But so young! He had felt more like her chaperon than her date. More than anything, he couldn't get over the fact that she worked at B.J.'s. It was a massive coincidence, and he had to find a way to talk to her about it.

When Eddie finally pulled into his driveway, he knew immediately that something was wrong because the garage door was slightly open. He rolled the door up and saw that the door from the garage to the kitchen had been kicked open. Inside it looked like a tornado had passed through. Dishes were in pieces on the kitchen floor. In the living room his couch and leather chair had been slashed open and the lamps broken and scattered on the floor. The place had been ransacked. His file cabinets had been dumped out, his mattress tossed, his phone line cut, his medicine cabinet emptied. His desktop computer was gone.

On the kitchen table there was a note that said, "Welcome home, Ed. Stay away from Brownsville. Otherwise...." Next to the note was Jerome's ceramic pot. The plant had been snapped off at its base.

"Subtle," Eddie muttered.

Except for his computer, nothing seemed to be missing. Any current documents were on his laptop that he had taken with him along with his camera and his gun. He didn't have anything else to steal anyway. The vandals weren't looking for anything, he concluded. They just wanted to leave him a message. So, message received, loud and clear. There was no doubt who had done it or why. The only question was: what should he do about it?

Eddie spent the next few hours cleaning up the mess and putting things back in order. At times like this, he was glad he didn't have a family to worry about. On the other hand, he wouldn't mind a little help with the clean-up, and someone to talk to would be nice. As he scooped up the broken dishes and righted the overturned furniture, he considered his next move. He was tempted to get in touch with Raelynn because she might provide some inside information on Lucero and B.J.'s. The problem was she might think he was just using her—and she might be right—which would be the end of a burgeoning friendship. No, Brad was the person he needed to call.

He reached Brad that evening and told him his house had been trashed.

"Shit. I'm really sorry, Eddie. I'll pay for the damage, of course."

"That's not the point."

"I know it. The point is you've touched a nerve and if you don't back off they'll come after you."

"Right. And I don't like looking over my shoulder all the time."

"I don't blame you. Is it time to come in from the cold?"

"That's not what I meant. When someone's bugging me, my instinct is not to back off. It's to turn around and go after them—or better yet, to go after whoever is pulling the strings on these yo-yos."

"You mean Henry Lucero?"

"Maybe, but I doubt he is the majordomo. And neither is Delmore Briggs. My gut tells me Mike Delaney is the head honcho."

"So you've said," said Brad. "But just seeing Briggs at the Black Horse is a pretty weak hand. We need some stronger evidence to make either of them for the big man."

"I think we should go to ICE. I have a contact there who will help us, I think."

"Yeah, I guess," said Brad weakly. "Can you leave out the black-mailing?"

"Can you have a full house with four cards?"

Chapter Twenty-Seven

A few days later, Eddie got an email from Raelynn.

Dear Gramps,

I had a great time with you the other night. Really. You are such a gentleman. Nobody ever gave me flowers before. I was touched. Thank you. I would like to see you again sometime, but don't get any ideas. You know what I mean. I'd like to have that beautiful friendship. I want to hear more stories! You must have a lot of them. Stay in touch. Please.

Raelynn

Eddie wrote back.

Thanks, Raelynn. I enjoyed it too. You are good company for an old geezer like me. Whether you know it or not, you are sitting on one of the biggest stories of the year. I'll explain when we meet again. Soon, I hope.

Eddie

Okay, Raelynn replied, *you've aroused my curiosity. When and where can we meet?*

They decided to meet in Corpus Christi, about halfway between Houston and Brownsville, although Raelynn was nervous about being so close to her mother. They rendezvoused at a coffee shop near the college campus, the last place her mother would go.

After some small talk about the long drive, the heavy traffic and the wildflowers alongside the highway, Raelynn got serious.

"So what gives?" she asked. "After that drive, this better be good."

"Could be good, could be bad. Knowing your views on illegal immigration, I'm not sure which way you're leaning on this."

"On what?"

"Drug trafficking."

"Well, I don't like the trafficking part. But I believe drugs should be as legal as alcohol or cigarettes."

"I'm not talking about marijuana."

"Neither am I. Heroin, cocaine, crystal meth…whatever."

"Even though forty-some thousand people have died in Mexico on account of the drug trade? Innocent people?"

"If the drugs were legal, the deaths would not have been necessary at all. Making something illegal only makes it more valuable and more dangerous. And by the way, no one is innocent."

"I don't know how to talk to you," said Eddie. "Should nothing be illegal?"

"Crimes against children," Raelynn answered promptly. "Child prostitution, child pornography, abuse. Bad things should not happen to kids. You want to tell me what this is all about?"

Eddie paused. "I will, but promise me you'll keep it to yourself, all right?"

"I guess so. On second thought, maybe I'll sell it to the paper—or to a television station."

"Too late for that, Raelynn." He produced a recent newspaper clipping and put it on the table for Raelynn to read.

Brownsville Bugle
September 5, 2010

Mexican Heroin Floods South Texas
DEA Blames Matamoros Cartel

By ANDREW SANCHEZ

BROWNSVILLE — A new supply of heroin is inundating south Texas, say agents at the Drug Enforcement Agency (DEA).

A drug trafficking organization based in Matamoros, Mexico is the probable source of the heroin, according to a DEA press release. The agency points to a sudden rise in street-level sales from Brownsville to Albuquerque.

"In the past few months we've seen a sudden spike in the availability of heroin," said spokesman Dennis Kloss. "It showed up in Brownsville first and has been making its way north and west."

The DEA estimates that over $1 million dollars' worth of heroin passes through Brownsville every week.

Kloss closed the press briefing with a warning to drug smugglers. "We are watching with constant vigilance. If you are pedaling drugs, we will find you and prosecute you."

So far there have been no significant arrests.

Raelynn read the clipping and said, "So? What's this got to do with me?"

Eddie lowered his voice and dipped his head toward Raelynn's ear. "I've discovered that B.J.'s is involved in this drug ring."

Raelynn let out a loud yodel of laughter that was hard to read. It betrayed neither shock nor surprise. It was just a piercing burst of giggles, and people turned to look at her. Raelynn's face returned to neutral. She looked at Eddie and shook her head.

"What's so funny?" he asked.

"A drug ring?" Her tone was incredulous.

"Quiet, Raelynn! Keep your voice down. Please."

"Sorry. It's just that a drug ring at B.J.'s is highly unlikely. Mr. Lucero hates drugs. His workers get random drug tests. He thinks junkies should have to do hard labor. He puts dealers in the same category as baby killers."

"So he's a law and order conservative, NRA type?"

"Not consistently. He respects some laws and ignores others."

"Ignores which ones?"

"Labor laws, mostly. He hires illegals, pays them less than minimum wage, overworks them…you know."

"Yeah, I do. Let me tell you a secret, Raelynn."

"Oh, good. I love secrets."

"There's a tunnel under the Rio Grande in Laredo that serves as a means to bring immigrant workers into the States. Sometimes they come through the tunnel carrying drugs, heroin, I think. Their handlers drop off the workers at factories and plantations along the Gulf, including B.J.'s. And B.J.'s is also a drop-off point for the drugs."

"How do you know all of this?"

"A few weeks ago I slipped in with a group of workers and came through the tunnel with them. Got dropped off at B.J.'s and worked there until they got wise and kicked my ass out. Rotten job anyway."

"Wait a minute. You worked at B.J.'s?"

"Yeah, under the name Tomás Aguilar."

Raelynn shook her head in disbelief. "Why?" she blurted out.

"That's a long story."

"Well, you better get started!"

Eddie sighed and recounted the entire stream of events. He told her about Brad and Briggs and Delaney. When he was finished, Raelynn was silent for awhile, sorting it out in her head. "Briggs," she said. "He's the creep who comes in to talk to Mr. Lucero, right? With the briefcase and bow-tie?"

"Yes."

"He's a blackmailer?"

"And a drug dealer. And he supplies B.J.'s with illegal workers."

Raelynn was silent for a moment, thinking. Then she said, "Are you using me, Eddie?"

"What?"

"We meet online, which is supposed to be anonymous. But who knows. We have this brief email exchange, then a date. I tell you where I work, and it just so happens that you're, what, investigating B.J.'s?" Her voice was getting louder with each sentence. "Did you know about me beforehand? You didn't seem too surprised at where I work. Did you research *me*?" Raelynn asked with a crescendo.

"No, no, not at all," whispered Eddie, trying to keep the volume down. "I had no idea. It was just a coincidence."

"A coincidence? I don't know. And if it was a coincidence, why didn't you say anything?"

"Raelynn, I swear. I didn't know where you worked. I was just shocked, you know. I didn't know what to say. I just wanted to have a nice dinner and forget about B.J.'s for awhile."

"But then you figured: *Wow! She works at B.J.'s. She could be useful.*"

"No, Raelynn. It's not like that at all."

Raelynn shook her head. "Why should I believe you?" she asked.

Eddie raised his eyebrows and tilted his head. "Sometimes you just have to trust people."

Silence lay between them like a frozen mountain lake. Their eyes locked for several seconds, until Raelynn sighed and looked away.

"So now what?" she asked. "You going to write about it?"

"No, Raelynn. I'm done with that. I may just go to ICE with the story and let them handle it. That's one reason I wanted to talk to you. You might want to be looking for another job."

Raelynn tilted her head. "Seriously?" After a thoughtful pause she asked, "What happens to the drugs?"

"Well," Eddie started. "This is going to sound crazy, but the drugs go out on the shrimp delivery trucks. I don't know where exactly, but they come in blocks about the size of a Bible, wrapped in plastic, and then they're hidden in with the rest of the items on an order."

"I don't know. I'm skeptical. Like I said, Mr. Lucero is very anti-drug."

"Maybe he doesn't know. Could the smuggling be going on behind his back?"

"I doubt it. He's pretty aware of everything that goes on at B.J.'s."

"Have you noticed a spike in revenues lately?"

"No, but if there was drug money, he'd hide it somehow. I'd never see it."

"True. Well, maybe greed overtook his ethics."

"Maybe, but I still can't believe he's involved in a drug ring. It's just doesn't make sense. Sometimes he'll go off on the evils of drugs, the moral depravity. 'Drugs will be the end to civilization as we know it,' he'll say. 'Goddamn drug dealers should be lined up and shot.' Stuff like that."

"Was there a time recently when he was broke? Sometime when he really needed money? A lot of it in a hurry?"

Raelyn thought awhile. "I don't know," she said. "But I'll tell you something. Mr. Lucero is a gambler. He likes to bet on sports. Every day Marcy—that's his secretary—will have his coffee ready for him at eight o'clock, sitting on his desk right next to the sports section. He'll spend quite a while looking it over, jotting things down, making calculations."

"How do you know he gambles though? Maybe he's just a sports fan."

"Right, but he's got this safe in his office where he keeps petty cash?" she said, as if it were a question. "I have a standing order to withdraw an extra $1,000 from the bank for petty cash every week when I make the payroll draw from the bank. I don't know what he does with it all, but lately he's been asking me for more than a thousand."

"How much?"

"Five thousand. Seven thousand. Ten thousand last week. What else could it be besides gambling?"

"No new cars?"

"Nope."

"Private plane trips to Martinique?"

"Nope."

"New girl friend?"

"Not that I know of."

"Has he been drinking more? Behaving erratically?"

"Hmm, maybe. A few weeks ago he got pretty freaked out after reading the paper. He's normally a very calm person. Calculating, canny, but relaxed. Anyway, he was pacing around his office, and I could hear him talking to himself, which was really weird. Couldn't really make out what he was saying, except a couple of times he said, 'Seven to one! Seven to one for Chrissakes!' I had no idea what was going on."

"Does he bet online?" Eddie asked.

"I don't know. I think he goes somewhere."

"Has he ever mentioned the Black Horse Saloon?"

"Not that I remember. Eddie, this is feeling more and more like an interrogation."

"Sorry, but I need to figure this out. It could get really dangerous for both of us."

"For you, maybe."

Eddie paused. "You want any more coffee?" he asked. Raelynn shook her head.

"So what happened that day Mr. Lucero was so distraught?"

"Nothing. He calmed down eventually. But. . . . The next day, or maybe it was two days later, this man dropped by the office. I'm guessing it was Delmore Briggs by your description. He comes by every week or so to see Mr. Lucero. Comes with a briefcase. They close the door and talk, so I don't know what goes on. But whatever it was, it made Mr. Lucero feel better. I wouldn't say it put him in a good mood, but he was different after Briggs left."

"Drugged up?"

"No, no. Relieved. Not happy, exactly, just more relaxed."

"Then what?"

"I remember he went home early, which is unusual for him. The next day Briggs came by again with a package for Mr. Lucero. When Briggs left, Mr. Lucero went out and took the package with him. I don't know what was in it."

"I do."

"What?"

"Money."

By the time Eddie and Raelynn had finished their talk, the sun was low in the sky. Neither of them was eager to make the three-hour drive back home, especially at night. Eddie suggested a motel. Raelynn said fine, as long as it wasn't close to her mother's trailer park. They settled on the Cottonwood Inn, a reasonably quiet motel off the main drag. The Cottonwood projected a vintage Western charm in an otherwise bleak neon landscape. They booked adjoining rooms for the night.

After sharing an unremarkable dinner at a nearby Chinese restaurant, they strolled back to the motel together.

"Want to watch a movie?" asked Raelynn. "It's still early."

"Sure," said Eddie. "Let's see what they've got."

Raelynn wanted to watch another black-and-white mystery like *Casablanca*. They settled on *The Thin Man*, in which detective Nick Charles and his socialite wife, Nora, live on martinis and witty remarks as they solve a murder mystery. Eddie and Raelynn stretched out on the bed together to watch the film. About halfway through Raelynn fell asleep with her head on Eddie's shoulder. Eddie had seen the film several times before and didn't need to see it again, but he watched it to the end just to smell Raelynn's hair and feel her body pressing on his.

When the film was over, Eddie got up carefully, trying not to wake Raelynn. He had his hand on the doorknob when Raelynn murmured, "Is it over?"

"Yep."

"I guess I fell asleep." She propped herself up on her elbows. "Who did it?"

"The attorney," said Eddie.

"Why?"

"For the money, of course."

"Oh. Eddie, stay with me tonight."

Eddie paused. "Are you nuts? I already paid for my room."

"I don't want to fool around," Raelynn said, ignoring Eddie's little joke. "I'm just tired of sleeping alone."

Eddie stripped down to his boxers and gave his T-shirt to Raelynn.

"Thanks," she said, turning out the light.

They got under the covers and snuggled up to each other. Eddie kissed her gently on the back of her head and again on her neck.

"Tell me a story," Raelynn said in a drowsy voice.

Eddie took a breath. "Once upon a time," he said, "there was a young girl who lived with her mother in the village. Her father had died in the war. One fine spring day, the girl took a walk into the countryside. Flowers were blooming everywhere. The girl began to pick some flowers to take back home with her. She picked some yellow and white flowers; then she noticed some red flowers down the road a bit and went to get those too. Around the hill she found violet-colored flowers that she added to the others. Gathering flowers as she went, she walked past the fields outlying the village and into the nearby woods. It began to get dark, and the girl decided she better go home. But when she looked for the path toward the village, she wasn't sure which path to take. She realized she was lost. As she wandered slowly through the dark woods, it began to snow. Then just ahead she saw a small cabin with lights on inside and smoke coming out the chimney. The girl went to the cabin and knocked on the door.

"In the cabin lived an old woodsman. He harvested firewood and sold it in the village. He had lived alone ever since his parents died, which was a long time ago.

"'Good evening sir,' said the little girl to the woodsman. 'I live in the village, but the snow has covered up the path, and I've gotten lost. Can you help me find my way home?'

"The woodsman invited her in and gave her some hot soup. 'Of course, I can help you,' he said to her, 'but we will have to wait until morning. Now it is too dark and stormy to ride to the village.' The man made up a bed for the girl by the fire, and they both went to sleep.

"When the man got up the next morning, the girl was gone. Although he looked everywhere, he could not find her. 'Maybe it was all a dream,' thought the woodsman. 'Maybe the girl was not real at all.' He went back in the house convinced that it had all been a fanciful dream. But when he went in the house, he saw the bouquet of flowers was lying on the table."

Eddie stopped talking. Raelynn had fallen asleep. He closed his eyes too.

"Good night, Raelynn," he said.

Chapter Twenty-Eight

The next morning Raelynn was in the shower when Eddie woke up. She emerged from the bathroom dressed, with her hair wrapped in towel. "I'm hungry," she said. "Let's get some breakfast."

"Right," said Eddie. "I look like a bum, though. I didn't bring my razor."

"You look great. A two-day growth is in, you know."

"Except that mine is gray."

"Gray is the new black."

They found a diner down the block and ordered pancakes and bacon.

"I need to tell you something else," Eddie said. "Maybe I should have told you last night, but I chickened out. Besides…."

"I know. It was nice."

"Yeah, it was. But now I need to tell you the rest of the story."

"Which one?"

"About the drug ring."

"There's more?"

Eddie said, "You sell something called 'Fishcake?'"

"Yes."

"What is it?"

"Well, extraneous fish get caught in the net with the shrimp. Instead of throwing them back, we clean them, throw them in a grinder and mix in potatoes and spices. Then they're formed into blocks and packaged in a plain yellow wrapper that says 'Fishcake' on the top and bottom. Asian restaurants shape it into patties, bread it and deep-fry it."

"Like crabcakes."

"Yeah, only fishier."

"Okay, then. What's 'Premium Fishcake?' Comes in an orange wrapper."

"I'm not exactly sure. It's a new item for us. It's not even listed on the invoice yet."

"Do you know how it's different from regular fishcake?"

"No. But I have a feeling you do."

"Yeah. It's actually heroin."

"Get out! This whole story seems a bit fishy, Eddie. S'cuse the pun."

"Let me finish. When a shipment of heroin comes into B.J.'s—after coming through the tunnel in Laredo—it is hidden in citrus boxes. The truck driver stashes them in B.J.'s back room, behind the Bossman's office, and someone repackages each brick in a red custom wrapper labeled 'Premium Fishcake.' The Bossman makes sure that they get put on the appropriate trucks. The heroin is delivered to fish markets that double as drop-off points for the middlemen in the ring."

Eddie paused, and Raelynn just stared at him. Then she said, "Do you know how nutso this sounds? Like wacko, crazy, totally ridiculous. B.J.'s is distributing heroin? Disguised as fishcake?"

"I couldn't make this stuff up, Raelynn."

"How do you know about this?"

"I've been there. I saw it happen. The thing is, I don't know which fish markets are legit and which are the fronts. So, Raelynn," Eddie said after a long bit of dead air. "I want to ask you a favor. A big one."

"What's that?"

"I'd like to identify which fish markets are receiving heroin. They would be the ones with Premium Fishcake on the packing slip. Then I could find out who owns those joints." Eddie waited for a response but Raelynn was silent. "Ideally, you could copy those packing slips for the past few months."

"You don't want much, do you," Raelynn exclaimed. "You have a lot of nerve, mister. I thought you said you weren't using me! This is my job we're talking about. If Mr. Lucero found out I did that, I'd be so dead!"

"You can say no."

Raelynn didn't say yes or no. She said she'd think about it.

The next few days, Raelynn wished she was invisible at work. She tried to look normal, not spooked, striding around in a business-like way, tapping away at her adding machine and computer. Just the same, her eyes were roving the room, looking beyond her ledgers and spread-sheets. For what she wasn't sure. She made up an excuse to go visit the Bossman. She found him on the work floor supervising the unloading of a catch. "I brought you a two-week inventory report—number of pounds processed on each shift so you can see who's being most pro-ductive."

"Sounds helpful, Raelynn, but I'm kinda busy right now. Will you just put it on my desk?"

"Sure thing, Bossman," said Raelynn, leaving him to his task.

Raelynn walked into the Bossman's office. The door was not only unlocked, but standing open. The Bossman was in and out of there twenty-five times a day. Raelynn put the report on his desk, clearing a space amidst the bills of lading, Department of Labor news releases, immigration documents and half a dozen phone messages from Marcy. Behind the desk, down a short hallway, was a door to the back room. Raelynn opened it and peeked inside. One table was devoted to citrus boxes. Next to them sat a box of wrappers labeled "Premium Fishcake" in red lettering. Any doubts she had about Eddie's story evaporated.

That afternoon Lucero left mid-afternoon, headed for the Black Horse, and Marcy left at five o'clock, as always. Raelynn was at her desk as Marcy was leaving.

"Working late tonight?" Marcy asked.

"Just a little while. I want to finish booking these invoices."

"Well, you have a good night, Raelynn."

"You too, Marcy. See you tomorrow."

There were still workers on the floor, but the Bossman was gone for the day. Charlie was supervising them. Raelynn had the office to herself. The packing slips were arranged by company, and within that by date. Starting with the A's, Raelynn leafed through the pink packing slips, signed by the person who had received the order. After an hour she hadn't found any packing slips listing Premium Fishcake. She was up to letter L when she hit the mother lode. A chain of markets called Little Saigon Fish Co. ordered Premium Fishcake every week. There were twenty Little Saigon outlets in the franchise located throughout south and east Texas with a few over in Louisiana. Raelynn checked the packing slips against the invoices. They matched. She made copies of those packing slips from the past two months and put all the copies into a mailing envelope addressed to Eddie Maez in Houston. No return address.

Chapter Twenty-Nine

Two days later Eddie received an anonymous parcel in the mail. He felt like a kid at Christmas. He ripped open the envelope and looked through the sheaf of packing slips with a grin on his face. All of the Premium Fishcake was sold to a company called Little Saigon Fish Co. When he looked up the company in the Texas Registry of Corporations, he found that the chain of stores was incorporated as Little Fish, L.L.C. with one shareholder: Michael T. Delaney of Brownsville.

He never got tired of the feeling he got when he had the goods on someone. In his gut, though, he felt a bit sick for Raelynn's sake. He hoped she would not have to testify against her boss—with all the publicity that would follow—but she might.

Eddie had one solid contact at ICE, Immigration and Customs Enforcement, a young and ardent officer named Gary Stone. When Eddie did an immigration story—and he had done several—he frequently got anonymous information from Stone, to whom he referred in print as "a high-ranking official at ICE." Over the past few years they had become friends, even collaborators at times. Gary took his job seriously, but he didn't have that tough-cop vibe that annoyed Eddie. And Eddie was not condescending to Gary about his age. They made a good team.

Eddie talked to Brad and explained that he would like to take their story to Gary Stone at ICE. Of all the agents and officers he knew, Gary was smart and easy to work with. He was also the youngest, which meant he ended up with more of the cases that no one else wanted—too complicated, too much paperwork, too little evidence to convict. Gary enjoyed the challenge and was willing to go to bat for immigrants who were sincere and deserving but didn't have a good case.

Eddie called Stone and said, "Hey, Gary, I've got a smoking gun for you if you wanna use it."

"In the form of what?"

"Packing slips. Innocuous, bureaucratic, pink packing slips—that pinpoint a few stops on a heroin trail. Would you like to see them?"

"Sure. I enjoy a proper packing slip."

"Wise guy. I'm on my way."

There were three handicap parking spaces in the ICE parking lot, all empty. Eddie resisted the strong inclination to steal a handicap slot and eventually found an empty spot in the back near the dumpster. He rushed up to the second floor office and wove his way through the cubicles to Gary's desk, dropping the envelope of documents on top of everything else. Gary took a few slips out and looked them over.

"You want to explain this to me, or am I supposed to guess?"

Eddie explained the entire enterprise, from the illegal workers coming through the tunnel to the drug drops at the Little Saigon Fish Co., with a stop along the way at B.J.'s Shrimp Co. to repackage the heroin as "Premium Fishcake." He mentioned Henry Lucero, Delmore Briggs and Mike Delaney by name, but not Brad or Raelynn.

"You said heroin is listed as "fishcake?" asked Gary Stone.

"*Premium* fishcake."

"And you say all these markets, the Little Saigons, belong to one guy...."

"Michael Todd Delaney."

"Who uses them to funnel fishcake—excuse me, *premium* fishcake—around the state?"

"And into Louisiana."

"And Delaney is buying the dope from...."

"I wish I knew. Someone in Mexico, because it's coming in through the tunnel I told you about. Delaney bought the seafood chain just to have drop spots for the street-level pushers, and now the Little Saigons are doing a booming business in premium fishcake."

"Sick," said Stone with admiration. "What happens to the heroin after it's dropped at the fish markets?"

"I don't know. I had to leave something for you to work on. Jeez, Gary, I'm handing you the operation on a platter. All you have to do is follow the fishcake."

Gary laughed. "Okay, dude, this is all very slick except for one thing."

"What's that?"

"Where is the money? Who is buying the drugs? Lucero?"

"No, not Lucero. He's got a gambling problem and is broke half the time. I think Mike Delaney is your man. Besides owning the Little Saigon chain, he runs a sports betting parlor in the back room of a place called the Black Horse Saloon. I'm guessing he got into the drug business with the profits from his gambling operation. Real bootstrap capitalist. But I don't know who the supplier is."

"What we should do, I guess," said Gary, "is to put a man on each Little Saigon, log their distribution schedule, and then go after all of them at the same time."

"Yeah, that would be spectacular."

"But it won't happen, 'cause where are we going to find twenty agents to take on a new assignment? What are we going to do—pull them off their current duty? Import them from Arizona?"

"You can't let this slide like it was nothing. You've got Delaney cold—and he's smuggling illegals in too!"

"Yeah, well, at least they're working somewhere. They're not pounding on our door for help. We got dozens of immigrants pouring in every day. We don't have to chase them down; they're chasing *us* down. And we're running out of room."

"This is unbelievable! I'm giving you a no-brainer bust, and you don't want it?"

"Oh, I want it all right. You want to help us bust Delaney? Then write it up and put it on the front page. Name names, identify the fish stores, get more specifics, expose the tunnel.... Put it all in the paper and create a public outcry. That will put pressure on the Federal Marshals and the DEA, and we'll *have* to make the bust. That's probably the only way it's gonna happen."

"There's a problem. I retired from the paper."

"You what? It sure as hell doesn't sound like you've retired. Who's paying your expenses?"

"The Brownsville Chamber of Commerce."

"Oh, I see. Protecting your sources? Well, if you're not working for the paper, you don't have that right any more."

"What difference does it make where I got the information? If you don't believe me, go stake out the tunnel, raid B.J.'s Shrimp, bust into the back room at the Black Horse. Christ, man, you're the law, not me."

"Yeah, and I could haul you in for obstruction of justice if you don't reveal your sources. We have to corroborate your story, dude."

"What's wrong with you? The way to corroborate my story is to walk in there flashing your badge and asking for a tour of the facilities."

"Like I said, we don't have the manpower to do that without some hard evidence in hand. The packing slips are good, but they aren't good enough to base the entire case on."

"What would be good enough?"

"Some workers who will tell their story and testify as to their documentation, their wages, their hours, their treatment...."

" Yeah, well, you know no one's gonna talk because it'll get them sent back home. There are other ways to document their exploitation. Seize their books, man!"

"And if we don't find anything, we look like fools."

"Well, you *would* be a fool for not running down a solid lead. And don't forget you've got two cases here: the illegal workers and the heroin ring. One leads to the other."

Gary Stone had to admit the situation presented a pretty enticing case. It would require the cooperation of several different agencies and some delicate diplomacy to get everyone working together on it. But that would get him the resources he needed to take it on in a comprehensive way.

"Even if I did write the story," Eddie said, "you would totally lose the element of surprise. If the story comes out in the morning paper, they'll have their act cleaned up by noon. You won't find anything but some empty fishcake packages."

"Cool your jets, dude. I'm with you. I like our chances to nail 'em all. Just give me some time to think about it."

In his days as a reporter Eddie would have jumped at the chance to write the story. But now he realized that if he wrote it he couldn't protect Brad. Eddie could spin the story so that Lucero, Delaney and Briggs got all the attention, along with B.J.'s, the Little Saigons and the Black Horse…. But sooner or later someone would ask Brad if he knew about the tunnel, and if so, why didn't he say anything? And if not, why not? *Someone is going to find out about the blackmailing,* Eddie thought. *I just hope it's not through me.*

When Eddie had gone, Gary Stone repeated the story and allegations to his superior, Wayne Tomlinson, the Assistant Director of the Houston field office.

"Who is your source for this information?" asked the Director.

"A reporter I know. I've worked with him before. He's a straight shooter."

"Name?"

"Eddie Maez."

"Maez. I know that name. He broke some big stories, right? Corporate corruption, illegal toxic dump sites, that kind of thing."

"That's the guy. Damn good reporter."

"I don't get it. Is he giving us fair warning before this story breaks?"

"Not exactly. Says he's retired now. Wants us to take the ball and run with it."

"Who's he working for?"

"Didn't say. Maybe he's flying solo on this one."

Tomlinson grunted. "I don't know, Gary. We're stretched pretty thin right now. I'm not sure we've got the time and resources for this. I mean, these days the cartels are bringing narcotics in by the planeful. I'm more concerned about them than about some small-time crooks running a few ki's of dope through a tunnel."

"Dope and illegals," reminded Stone.

"Right. Well, let me think about it. In the meantime, keep it to yourself."

"Sure thing, boss."

The Assistant Director, Wayne Tomlinson, was a stout middle-aged man with a bald head that glowed incandescently. ICE agents wondered if he used olive oil or hairspray or some secret polishing agent to keep it so shiny. Wayne essentially ran the office, since the Director himself—a political appointee who had very little concept of the day-to-day operation of the ICE office—was usually away in Washington for hearings or meetings.

Texas may be a big state, but some of its social circles are small. Wayne Tomlinson was acquainted with Mike Delaney because Wayne was married to one of Delaney's sisters. He knew about Delaney's sports book operation, but despite his position at ICE, he looked the other way, given the family connection. Besides, gambling was beyond his purview. However, he had made it clear that Mike better keep a low profile and not get any big ideas. The two men did not like each other. Their conversation, when it occurred that evening, was not cordial.

"You son of a bitch," Wayne began, "we had an agreement, and now I hear you've gotten involved in a shitload of other activities. Criminal activities like smuggling illegals, smuggling and distributing drugs. I don't even want to know what else. What the fuck are you thinking?"

Delaney kept his composure. "Take it easy, Wayne. This is just a short term deal. I'm helping out a friend in the shrimpin' business. The government cut their season short again."

"Like that's going to make any difference to a grand jury."

"I swear, I can opt out any time."

"How about yesterday?"

"Look, who knows about this, Wayne?"

"We got it from a newspaper reporter. If this comes out in the paper, you're going down, bro."

"Hold the phone a second, Wayne." Briggs was sitting nearby. "What's the name of that P.I. who's been snooping around, Briggs?"

"Eddie Maez."

Delaney returned to the phone. "Wayne, is this reporter a guy named Eddie Maez?"

Silence from Tomlinson, then "So what if it is?"

"I know who Maez is, Wayne. Let me deal with him. I can contain this."

"Famous last words."

"Who else knows anything?"

"Nobody. Just the agent who told me about it."

"Who's that?"

"Oh, no you don't. That's all you're going to get from me."

"All right then. Just sit on it for a few days, and I'll clear it up."

"Okay. Three days, then you better…. You bastard! Do you realize what an impossible situation you've put me in?"

"Difficult, but not impossible. Don't worry, Wayne. I'll handle it."

"Handle it discreetly, Delaney. I don't want blood on my hands."

Chapter Thirty

When Mike Delaney found out what Eddie knew, and that he had already gone to ICE with it, he decided he had better eliminate Eddie Maez. Delaney didn't care what Tomlinson had said about being discreet. The guy wouldn't take a bribe. Violence was the only alternative, and death the only logical outcome. Delaney told Briggs to "take care of" Eddie Maez.

Briggs knew that Delaney did not mean for Briggs to see that Eddie got box seats at an Astros game, yet he didn't know any contract killers.

"Who should I contact, sir?" Briggs asked.

Delaney cast a disparaging look at Briggs. "Never mind. I'll do it," he said.

Delaney got in touch with Billy and Axel, his go-to thugs, and told them to arrange a hit on Eddie Maez. They were happy to oblige. They thought Eddie was a smart-ass who had already been warned off three times and had run out of chances.

Their plan was simple. They would catch him at home late at night when the whole neighborhood would be asleep, including Maez. Say, four in the morning. Axel would drive and Billy would be the shooter. Billy didn't want to go in through the garage like they had when they had ransacked Eddie's house because it was noisy and took too long. They had been lucky none of the neighbors had heard them breaking in.

In back there was a half-stairwell with a door that opened onto a landing and steps that led down to the basement or up to the kitchen. Billy, who was good with locks, would go in there, sneak in through the kitchen, walk quickly down the hall to the bedroom, and nail him in his sleep. He would use a silencer. It would all be over in a few minutes.

Billy would walk out the front door; Axel would be waiting by the curb, motor running. They would drive away quietly and ditch the gun in the Buffalo Bayou on their way out of town.

With this plan in mind, they left Brownsville for Houston around dusk, arriving in Houston just after midnight. It was a moonless night, as dark as the inside of a gun barrel. They didn't want to be seen by anyone who might place them in Houston that night, so they stayed out of bars and restaurants. At three-thirty they drove to Eddie's neighborhood, killed the headlights and stopped in front of his house.

What the thugs didn't know is that, after the recent break-in, Eddie had a burglar alarm installed, so when Billy ever-so-carefully picked the back door lock and gently opened the door, the alarm went off. It was an ear-splitting siren that caused lights to go on in houses up and down the street. Eddie immediately rolled off his bed onto the floor, grabbing his gun that he kept on the nightstand. Billy and Axel realized that their nearly foolproof plan had one fatal flaw, and that they had best get the hell out of there.

Already inside, Billy panicked and ran to the front door where he wasted precious seconds fiddling with the double lockset. In desperation he blasted the locks apart and flung open the door. The silencer didn't muffle the sound of wood splintering and Eddie got to the door as Billy was sprinting toward the car.

"Freeze!" Eddie yelled above the screech of the alarm. "Freeze or I'll shoot!"

Whether Billy heard that command or not, Eddie did not know. In any case, Billy kept running and Eddie fired at him. He saw Billy drop his gun, clutch his leg and pitch forward like a running back diving for extra yardage. He hobbled toward the car as fast as he could.

"Freeze!" Eddie yelled again. He took another shot, missing Billy but putting a hole in the front fender. Axel had opened the passenger-side door, and was impatiently racing the engine. Billy reached the car and managed to pull himself in. Axel roared off, tires squealing, the front door hanging open until a sharp right turn slammed it shut.

The gunshot wound was serious. The bullet had pierced a major artery and blood was shooting out like water from a leaky hose. Police sirens whined in the distance, and Axel slowed to the speed limit.

"I need a doctor," Billy groaned. "I need a doctor bad."

"I don't know any doctors here," said Axel. "We could go to the ER at a hospital, but that'll mean talking to the cops."

"Shit. I'm starting to feel kinda woozy."

Axel turned into a dark street and stopped by the curb. He popped the trunk lid and rummaged around until he found a piece of rope.

"I'm going to put a tourniquet on your leg," he said. Billy was flopped over on his side, semi-conscious. The blood was thick and sticky, covering the seat and floor. Axel opened the passenger-side door and cut through the denim fabric of Billy's pantleg with his knife. His hands were soon covered in blood, and they were so slippery that it was hard for him to grasp the knife. The blood was no longer spurting but was oozing out in pulses. Axel wrapped the rope around Billy's thigh above the bullet hole and pulled it tight enough to slow the bleeding. He wiped his hands on the grass by the curb. Billy lay awkwardly on the front seat, barely breathing. Axel slid behind the wheel and pulled into the street. His eyesight was blurry from tears.

He drove northwest out of Houston, toward Waco and Abilene, away from Brownsville. He didn't know why, but he could not stand the thought of returning to Brownsville—maybe because they had failed in their assignment and Axel was afraid to face Briggs and Delaney. Or maybe because the cops would be more likely to look for them in Brownsville. Or maybe because he was scared and confused, and had no plan except to drive and keep driving.

The sun was rising behind them as they reached Waco. Axel stopped to gas up at a convenience store. He burned his tongue on some bitter coffee as he pulled back onto the highway.

Axel was pretty sure that Billy was dead. He hadn't moved in a long time, and he didn't seem to be breathing. Blood had stopped coming out of the wound. It had dried on his skin, turning a darker red, almost black. Billy's blue jeans were stiff as cardboard where the blood had soaked into them. About 100 miles from Abilene, Axel pulled off the highway at a deserted exit. He drove a mile or so down a dirt road and then stopped. He felt Billy's neck and wrist for a pulse but only felt cold rubbery skin. Axel opened the trunk and removed a blanket. He pulled Billy's body from the car and hoisted it into the trunk. He spread the blanket over the front seat to conceal the blood that was drying slowly in the humid air of central Texas.

Axel continued to go northwest on the highway, past Lubbock and into New Mexico at Clovis. The sun was high in the sky and bright as a mirror. Axel didn't know where he was going, but he remembered a childhood camping trip to New Mexico, and he chased his memories of that trip: fresh mountain air, a gurgling stream, the scent of pine needles. When he turned north toward Santa Fe he began to see snow-covered peaks on the blue horizon. He drove toward them.

In Santa Fe, Axel stopped at a thrift shop and bought some blue jeans, a flannel shirt, a snow parka and a clean blanket. He had a plan now. He wanted to bury Billy someplace in the mountains, someplace peaceful and secluded. He owed him that much. Billy was his oldest friend, his best friend. His only friend. Then he would continue going west. He wasn't going back to Texas.

North of Santa Fe, Axel turned onto a state road. The mountains loomed much larger. Piñon and juniper trees dotted the red hills. Late in the day, steely gray clouds massed behind the snowy peaks. As darkness descended, Axel turned onto a Forest Service road—a dirt road that led into the Sangre de Cristo mountains. The piñon and juniper gave way to tall firs and ponderosa pines. The ground was covered with snow that got deeper as he climbed higher into the mountains.

Axel had not slept in over 30 hours. He pulled off the service road at a wide place. The blanket in the front seat was caked with dried blood. He got into the back seat with the clean blanket he had bought and fell asleep.

The next morning was clear and bright. Mist was rising from the trees as the snow evaporated in the sun. The only sounds were of dripping snowmelt and occasional clumps of snow sliding off the trees to the ground, flecked with bird chatter. Axel put on the snow parka and opened the trunk. He took off Billy's shoes and undid the tourniquet. Then he cut the jeans down the side like he was skinning a deer and peeled them off of Billy's stiffening legs. He wrapped the jeans in the blood-soaked blanket and stuffed the whole wad in a corner of the trunk. He turned Billy so that his bare legs stuck out the back of the trunk, and then forced his legs into the jeans he had bought. They fit okay around the waist but were a little long in the leg, so Axel rolled them up a couple of turns, then put Billy's shoes back on. He grasped Billy under the arms and turned him 180 degrees so he could put the flannel shirt on him. Billy's arms were almost too stiff to straighten out, but Axel managed to get the shirt on and button it up to the neck. He took off his bandana and tied it around Billy's neck. Then he pulled him out of the trunk and carried him a ways into the silent, snowy woods. He was looking for a swale to lay Billy in before he covered him with dirt.

Then in the distance, Axel heard voices. He laid Billy down under a Douglas fir and moved deeper into the woods, away from his car, and hid behind a thick clump of snow-covered bushes. Two men on horseback appeared in the clearing.

"Holy shit!" said one of the men. "Is that what I think it is?"

"Looks like a dead body to me," said the other.

They dismounted and inspected the body. They felt for a pulse but found none. They looked for a weapon or signs of blood but found nothing. Axel could barely see them through the brush, but he could hear them discussing what they should do. One of the men tried his cell phone, but he didn't have a signal. Finally they decided to leave the body there and go call the police. They mounted their horses and left.

Axel waited five minutes to make sure the men were gone, then emerged from his hiding place in the bushes. He picked up Billy and carried him back to his car, which was parked in a different direction from the way the cowboys had come and gone. He put Billy back in the trunk, turned around and drove out to the main road. He drove several miles, finally turning off onto another Forest Service road. This time he went looking for a swale, leaving Billy in the trunk. He found a depression in the soil about three feet deep and six feet long. The ground was soft there, a nest of rotting tree branches and pine needles. Axel went back to get Billy, who seemed to be getting heavier, or at least harder to carry. But Axel hoisted him onto his shoulder and carried him to his grave. He lay Billy down in the swale and covered him with soil and branches with his bare hands. When Billy was blanketed with earth and no longer visible, Axel returned to the car and drove back to the main road to continue his journey. He didn't know exactly where he was going. He supposed he would drive until the road ran out. He had never seen the Pacific Ocean.

Chapter Thirty-One

The police arrived at Eddie's house about five minutes after the shooting. Although Eddie had not seen the face of the intruder, nor the getaway driver, he figured that they were the two thugs who beat him up outside of the Black Horse Saloon. He didn't tell the police this or anything else except for the bare facts of the incident. He told them he didn't see either man's face and had not gotten a good look at their car. He didn't tell them about his conversation with Gary Stone. He didn't want to say anything that would cause the cops to interfere with Gary's investigation.

Eddie said he fired two shots: one got the intruder in the leg, the other missed. The police found a gun on the lawn, smeared with blood. They also found the slugs that Billy had used to break the locks on the front door. They put out an APB for two men, one with a gunshot wound in the right leg. They didn't find the slug so they assumed it was still in the assailant's leg. That's all they had to go on. Officers canvassed the neighborhood to see if anyone could identify the men or the make of the car, or possibly the license plate, but no one could. The assailants wore dark clothing, the neighbors said, and they thought the car was a dark color, maybe a Honda, a Toyota or a Ford. Big help.

Of course the police checked Eddie's P.I. license and gun permit. They made sure he didn't have a criminal record or any outstanding warrants. The lieutenant in charge of the case asked Eddie to call him if he thought of anything that might be helpful. Eddie said he would. The lieutenant asked Eddie to keep his phone handy in case something came up on his end. Eddie said okay. The cop said their best bet was to check with hospital emergency rooms for men with a gunshot wound in the right leg. Eddie said good idea.

It was nearly seven o'clock when the police left and the neighbors went back to their morning routines. Eddie phoned a 24-hour locksmith to come fix his door. While he waited for the locksmith, Eddie paced the floor and drank coffee, trying to sort through recent events and make any connections he could. The locksmith installed a makeshift lock but said Eddie needed a new door. When the locksmith was gone, Eddie called Brad and told him about the break-in and the foiled attempt on his life.

"Shit, man," said Brad. "This is getting too weird. But those guys didn't act on their own, right?"

"No, I'm sure they were following orders. I'm just not sure whose orders."

"Who knows what you know?"

"Only a few people. You, for one. Gary Stone at ICE. And Raelynn Weeks."

"Who is Raelynn Weeks? You been holdin' out on me, Eddie?"

Eddie gave Brad a quick sketch of Raelynn and his relationship to her.

"She works there? Christ, Eddie, what were you thinking?"

"Give me a break, man, I didn't even know until halfway through our first date."

"You mean you've had a second date? Are you nuts?"

"Hey—without Raelynn we wouldn't have any evidence."

Brad said, "Could Raelynn have said something to Lucero that made him suspicious? Maybe he threatened to fire her if she didn't come clean."

"Maybe, but I doubt that Lucero suspects her of anything. She's a cool customer. I'll talk to her."

"Why rule out Lucero?" Brad asked. "He remembers you from B.J.'s. He had you fired. He was probably the one who had the thugs scramble your house. And he knows about the heroin smuggling—or at least about its distribution."

"True, all true. He's friendly with Delaney too, but I don't think he is aware of Delaney's involvement in the drug ring. To Lucero, Delaney's just a saloon-tender with a sports book in the back. I don't think he knows or suspects that Delaney knows Briggs or owns the Little Saigon chain or any of that shit."

"What about Gary Stone? You trust him, I assume. But did he talk to anyone about you?"

"I hope not. He knows that our conversation was confidential."

When Eddie finished talking to Brad, he called Gary Stone and started to explain the situation.

"That was you?" Gary interrupted. "It's all over the news. I heard it on my way to work. '*ARMED ASSAILANTS BREAK INTO SOUTH HOUSTON HOME. Two men considered armed and dangerous*.' Tell me what happened?" Eddie gave him the short version.

"Shit, that's heavy stuff, Eddie. Did you mention *me* to the police?"

"No, I didn't mention you or anything we talked about. You think I should?"

"Well, here's the thing, Eddie. If you keep it to yourself and the cops find out, you could be charged with withholding evidence. On the other hand, if you tell them what you told me, it's going to get very messy. The Houston cops will call in the State Police and possibly us or the FBI or DEA. Your investigation is going to get hijacked, possibly derailed by all these competing agencies."

"Yeah, that's what I figured. Either somebody will get killed, or the bad guys will skip town before the law figures out who's in charge."

"Something like that."

"That can't happen. That's the reason I came to you in the first place, Gary. I could have gone to one of those other agencies, but Homeland

Security scares the piss out of me and the others are all dysfunctional. I know I can work with you. Besides, ICE covers all the areas in my investigation."

"I appreciate your confidence, Eddie, I really do. How about we—you and me—come up with a plan, a comprehensive plan to nail 'em all."

"I'm game if you are."

"I'm down, man."

"One other thing, Gary. I need to know if you told anyone about our conversation."

Stone was quiet for a moment before he said, "One person. My boss, Wayne Tomlinson. I felt he needed to know, since he would make the decision on how we would handle the case. He said he'd take it under advisement and to keep it to myself for now."

"Maybe I should meet this guy, Tomlinson."

"Okay. I'll set it up."

That evening Eddie called Raelynn and told her what had happened.

"My God, Eddie. Someone's trying to kill you? Are they still, you know, at-large?"

"As far as I know, yes. All the hospitals in the area are on alert for someone with a gunshot wound to the leg. So far, all they've turned up is a couple of hunting accidents with the wrong blood type."

"It's because of the drug smuggling, right? You know too much."

"I don't know what else it could be. Look, Raelynn. Was there anything unusual at work that happened since you copied those packing slips for me? Any chance Lucero knows about that?"

"No, everything has been totally normal at work."

"Good. Good. I'm going to come down to Brownsville in a day or two. I'll find a motel and call you."

"You want to crash on my couch?"

Eddie felt a pang in his chest that went away as quickly as it came. "That's really sweet, but no thanks. I'm toxic right now, Raelynn. I don't want you to get hurt. We have to be careful, and staying at your place? Not a good idea. I want everything to look as normal as possible."

"Got it. Well, then, be careful. And call me."

"I will," Eddie said aloud. "*If I can*," he said to himself.

Chapter Thirty-Two

Over the next few weeks, Eddie and Gary worked out a detailed plan to, one, torpedo the tunnel; two, raid B.J.'s; three, bust into the back room at the Black Horse Saloon; and four, seize all the Premium Fishcake at the Little Saigons. Gary enlisted the help and cooperation of the FBI, the DEA, and the IRS, giving them specific tasks on a timeline, limiting their role so that they could take some credit without taking over the operation. When it was tentatively set up, Gary scheduled a briefing with Assistant Director Tomlinson, in hopes of getting his approval to move forward with the plan.

The Director listened intently, tracking the timing and the logic of the plan.

"How many agents will you need, and for how long?" he asked. They told him. "Where will you put detainees? How will you secure the evidence? Who will catalog the records and determine their usefulness? Who will handle interrogation? Who will handle the press?"

The Director hammered away with his questions until he was sure they had considered all corners of the plan, and until he was satisfied that it had a reasonable chance to succeed. He wanted convictions. He didn't want to make a big splash only to have to release everyone due to lack of evidence.

"Okay," he said after a thorough examination, "let's do it. There's just one more thing. Eddie can't participate. This is an official action, and Eddie, you don't work for ICE. You are a private citizen with a strong interest in the situation but no standing. So you are a spectator. Sorry. I'm sure Gary will be in touch to keep you apprised of the events as they unfold."

Eddie didn't object. He told Gary he would be nearby to observe. In an emergency he could help out.

They finalized the plan and set the timing, fully aware that something could go wrong. They had fall-back plans for different complications, but the X-factor was always in play. Ultimately, the Director gave his approval and they set a target date for the action at the end of September. Gary would coordinate the communication between agencies and obtain the necessary warrants.

The night before it was all set to go down, Eddie called Raelynn.

"Tomorrow night," Eddie said. "Don't go out after midnight."

"Are you joking? I never go out after midnight. Why? What's happening tomorrow night?"

"It's the night."

"You're being way too mysterioso, Mr. Maez."

"Sorry. It's just that...." Eddie didn't finish the sentence.

"Just that what?"

"I mean, I'm concerned for your safety." He struggled to express his feelings. "I care about you, Raelynn."

"Wow, that's the nicest thing anyone's said to me in...well, in a long time. But why would I be in danger?"

"There's going to be a bust at B.J.'s. You'd likely be arrested if you were there."

"That's the last place I would be after midnight, tomorrow or any other night of the week. What about you? Where will you be?"

"I'll be observing from a distance. I'm not supposed to participate."

"But you're going to anyway."

"Yes."

"Come to my place if you need a place to hang out...or hide...or whatever. I'll be here."

"Thanks, Raelynn. I might do that. We'll see how it shakes out."

About the same time, Mike Delaney was alone in his office when his cell phone played a few bars of the *Mission: Impossible* theme. He was sick of that ring-tone and kept meaning to change it. He silenced the jingle by answering the phone.

"Delaney," he heard someone say. "Don't ask any questions. Don't even speak. Just listen, because I'm only going to say this once. You fucked up, and now you are in big trouble. Conspiracy to murder, drug smuggling, human trafficking…. Life as you know it is about to change. This is the only warning you will get from me."

The caller hung up. Delaney slowly put down his phone. He was sure it had been Wayne; he knew his voice. He was also sure that Wayne was serious and only giving him a heads-up for the sake of his wife. Something was about to come down hard on him and his operation. He knew he should flee. And now.

Where should he go? Should he tell Briggs? Lucero?

Delaney took two suitcases out of a closet in his office. Opening the larger safe, he filled a suitcase with bundles of hundred dollar bills. He started to do the same with the smaller safe, shuffling bundles of bills from the safe to the other suitcase. Then he heard footsteps on the stairs. He felt a bump of adrenaline. Someone knocked on the door.

"Who is it?" asked Delaney.

"It's me, boss." It was Briggs.

"Come in."

Briggs entered and saw one bulging suitcase, the door to the larger safe standing open, the safe empty. "Going somewhere, Mr. D?"

"Yeah, I am. Spur of the moment decision." He continued to move money from the smaller safe to a suitcase, balancing on one knee. "You should take off too, Briggs, as soon as you can."

"What the heck?" said Briggs.

Delaney looked up. "The feds are going to bust us. Maybe as soon as tonight. Everything is in jeopardy. I suggest you get out. Take the rest of the money." He nodded toward the small safe, which still held several thousand dollars.

"Where are you going?" Delaney shook his head. "Do you want some company?"

Delaney shook his head again. "Are you coming back?"

"I doubt it, Briggs."

Chapter Thirty-Three

When Delaney walked out of the Black Horse Saloon with $300,000 stuffed into two suitcases, no one seemed to notice. And, if they did, they knew enough to know it was none of their business. Delaney tossed the two suitcases into the trunk of his car and drove away. He stopped briefly at his house where he picked up clothes, toiletries and his passport, folding all of it into the suitcases. His wife was out shopping. Delaney thought about leaving her a note, but he didn't know what to say: *Goodbye? Don't wait up? Something came up—I'll call you?*

It was late afternoon. Delaney drove to Port Isabel, looking for a boat that would take him up-river to Matamoros. He saw a number of outfits that ran charter boats for deep sea fishing, diving and dolphin-watching in glistening white yachts with the latest boating technology, deluxe cabins and full bars. They were not what Delaney was looking for. He was not going out into the wide-open Gulf. He was going through the delta and up the shallow, twisting, clotted river. He stopped at a pier where a beat-up skiff was docked. The red paint on the unnamed boat was peeling off, showing a layer of blue underneath; the chrome fittings were pocked with rust. The only thing new about the boat was a coil of rope lying on the bottom. Sitting on-board smoking a cigar was a man with a deep tan and deeper wrinkles. Delaney approached him.

"Ahoy there. Are you the captain of this vessel?"

"Captain, first mate, deckhand and pilot."

"Are you taking on passengers?"

"Might. Where you headed?"

"Just to Matamoros."

The sea-weathered sailor puffed on his cigar and squinted at Delaney. "Why don't you drive across the bridge? It's only a three-dollar toll."

"I've got my reasons. Would five hundred dollars cover it?"

The captain spat over the side without getting out of his seat. "Got any luggage?"

"Two suitcases."

"Five hundred for one. A thousand for two."

Delaney smiled. "All right," he said.

"In advance."

Delaney opened the trunk of the car and extracted a thousand dollars from one of the suitcases. He reached around behind the spare tire, found a pistol he kept there, and tucked it into the back of his pants, pulling his shirt down over it. Then he set the suitcases on the ground and closed the trunk.

"What about your car?" asked the skipper. "If it's here more'n three days, they'll tow it."

"I'll send someone to pick it up."

The captain nodded. "You ready to go then?"

"Yeah, let's go." Delaney picked up his suitcases.

"Need a hand with those?" asked the skipper.

"I got it," Delaney replied. He stepped aboard with his suitcases, then handed the skipper ten one-hundred dollar bills. The old salt stashed the bills in a pocket and started up the engine. He steered the boat around the docks into the ship channel and eventually up the Rio Grande, which at that point was as squiggly as a child's handwriting. As the sun set they passed under a bridge.

"Whereabouts do you want to dock?" asked the skipper.

"Someplace safe, if you know what I mean."

"I know what you mean, but I'm not sure anywhere in Matamoros is safe as long as you've got those two suitcases in tow."

"I just don't want to run into any customs officers."

"Who does? But you better have a couple of bills ready in case you do."

Half an hour later, in the waning light, the skiff slipped up to a small inconspicuous dock surrounded by thick brush that grew out over the water. A narrow dirt path led away from the river into the brush.

"End of the line, boss," said the skipper.

"Okay. Just let me make a quick phone call before you go." Delaney punched in the number he had for El Flaco.

"*Sí?*" said a voice.

"Mike Delaney calling for El Flaco."

"*Momentito.*" Thirty seconds later an English-speaker took the phone. "Mr. Delaney, El Flaco asks what it is you want."

"I need to see Mr. Flaco. I'm in Matamoros, on the riverfront. Can someone pick me up?"

"Where are you exactly?"

"Hang on a minute." Delaney called over to the skipper. "Where are we?"

"St. Jude's Landing," he answered.

Delaney spoke into the phone. "I'm at St. Jude's Landing."

"Okay, I'll be there in twenty minutes. Wait for me at the dock."

"I'll be here."

Delaney disembarked with his suitcases, and the small boat vanished into the near dark.

Delaney stood on the deserted dock. There were no lights, and the dirt path disappeared into pitch blackness. Somewhere in the distance, Delaney could hear the muffled sound of traffic. The water slapped against the side of the dock. A bloated dog carcass floated by on the slow current, leaving behind the stench of rotting flesh.

The darkness was complete when Delaney finally heard a rustling sound. Someone was coming down the path. A moment later he was blinded by the beam of a flashlight.

"Delaney?" a voice said.

"Yes."

"Don't move."

A man approached and patted Delaney down, while another man held the flashlight on him. The man confiscated Delaney's gun, then said, "Follow him." Delaney picked up his suitcases and followed the man with the flashlight. The other man trailed Delaney, holding a gun at his back. They soon came to a car parked on a rocky road. The man with the gun motioned for Delaney to get into the back seat. He got in back as well, holding the gun to Delaney's ribs. The other man turned the flashlight off and took the driver's seat. "We go now," he said.

El Flaco lived in a walled compound on the city's east side. In the daytime, one could see that the grounds were a manicured mix of palm trees, colorful flowering plants, succulents and vines. The house was a two-storey block of ice-blue stucco with iron bars on all the windows. But it was dark when the car pulled into the drive and Delaney saw only vague forms as the metal gates silently closed behind them.

He was escorted into the house through a side door, up a flight of stairs and into a large office, outfitted with dark wood paneling, leather-covered chairs, a Turkish carpet, rich with reds, and a large screen television. Smoke hung in the air. El Flaco was seated in an armchair smoking a cigarillo and watching a soccer match. He clapped his hands once, then yelled something in Spanish at the television screen. He clicked the TV off with his remote and turned toward Delaney.

"Monterrey is very good this year," he said in English. "I think no one is better." He rose from his seat and walked over to Delaney with his hand extended. "I am surprised to see you, Mr. Mike. How are you?" The two men shook hands.

"Stayin' alive, Mr. Flaco. And you?"

"Very well, thank you." They greeted each other with proper Mexican etiquette but in English. "But why only 'staying alive,' Mr. Mike? Do you not prosper also?"

"Yes. Our operation has been doing very well. Until now."

"I do not understand."

"The feds are going to shut us down, amigo. I have it on good authority that *some*how they know about our smuggling business and about my sports betting game, and they're going to shut them down. I don't know when, but soon. Maybe even tonight."

"If that is true, it is very unfortunate." El Flaco's voice had become as cold and mean as barbed wire. "There is a, *como se dice*?—a leak? A snitch?"

"Yes. Probably one of the workers. I don't know."

"How am I to believe you, Mr. Mike?"

"Trust me, man. Something's goin' down. I advise you not to use the tunnel until we see what they're going to do."

"Fuck that!" yelled El Flaco, spitting venom. "We will come prepared for a fight. Nobody shuts El Flaco down."

"You'll lose this one, bro."

"Like hell I will."

El Flaco frowned in anger and jammed his little cigar into an ivory ashtray. He sat down and motioned Delaney to sit as well.

"You have *dos maletas*," he said pointing to the suitcases.

"Yeah. All the dough I had on-hand. Figured we'd split it, fifty-fifty."

"*Que magnánimo.*"

"It's only fair. *Es justo, no?*"

"I think no. I think you come to El Flaco for protection. You have nowhere to hide and you want to buy protection. *Verdad?*"

"We are partners, Mr. Flaco, right?"

El Flaco looked at Delaney with a wary stare. "*Abrien los!*" he said to one of his underlings. The man opened the suitcases. He piled Delaney's personal possessions in one place—clothes, passport, gun—and then spread the money out in stacks.

"*Cuenta lo,*" El Flaco ordered. For several minutes, the room was silent except for the sound of money being counted by three men. They used a calculator to add it all up, and one of them announced there was $307,000.

"That is not very much," El Flaco said. "That much money comes through the tunnel every month, no? But now you say the tunnel is shutting down, and I am losing that income. Is that correct, Mr. Mike?"

"Yes, I'm afraid so."

"You are afraid?"

"It's an expression. It means it is unfortunate but true."

"Yes, very unfortunate." He spoke to his men. "*Pon lo en la caja de seguro. Todo.*" The men repacked the money into the suitcases and took them out of the room.

"Hey, wait a minute," said Delaney. "Half of that is mine. You can't take it all."

"Yes, Mr. Mike. I can. I am afraid so." He laughed. His laugh was malicious, bitter, piercing, and utterly without joy. "It belong to me now. In return I will protect you."

"I'm beginning to think this was a bad idea," Delaney said. "I don't want your protection, Flaco. I only wanted to tell you that our operation is going to be shut down by the feds. I didn't want you to think that I was double-crossing you. I didn't want you to come after me. I know you would have."

"Yes."

"So in a gesture of good will and cooperation, I came to you."

"Thank you, and I assure you, you will be very comfortable here, Mr. Mike."

"I appreciate the offer, but I must say *No, gracias, mi amigo.* If I could just have my things and one of those suitcases, I'll be going now."

"I think not, Mr. Mike. I insist that you stay with us. You know too much about me now. You know where I live."

"Flaco, I am not your enemy."

"Good. Then you accept my hospitality."

"With all due respect, Flaco, I must decline."

"Your room has a full bar and a hot meal waiting. I have another appointment now, but we will dine together tomorrow." To his bodyguards he said, "Take him," waving them away with the back of his hand.

Delaney stood, seeming to acquiesce at last. Then, in a blink, acting on instinct more than reason, he grabbed the jacket of one bodyguard and pulled it halfway down his arms, pinning them against his sides. Then he seized the gun from the guard's shoulder holster and trained it on El Flaco. The guns of the other gang members came out, all aimed at Delaney.

Flaco scowled and his face turned dark. "Kill him," he uttered.

Several guns erupted with firepower, hitting Delaney multiple times. Any one of the shots would have killed him, and one did. But Delaney had fired first, a sliver of a second before the others, hitting El Flaco exactly in the middle of his forehead. Flaco toppled over backwards, spilling blood on his carmine Turkish carpet.

Chapter Thirty-Four

Delmore Briggs was alone in Delaney's office. He stuffed the remaining bundles of bills into his briefcase. He knew that Delaney kept an extra gun in his bottom desk drawer, if he hadn't taken it with him. He hadn't. Briggs put that in his briefcase too, after checking to make sure it was loaded.

Briggs had several customers who paid him to deliver the illegals he imported through the tunnel, but because of the heroin his most important client was Henry Lucero. Briggs knew his other clients could finger him as their supplier of cheap labor, but only Lucero could name him as part of the drug ring. Lucero and Charles McPherson, the Bossman. He wanted both of them out of the picture. Briggs could think of only one sure way to guarantee their silence.

Delaney had left in a hurry, and Briggs wondered who had tipped him off. The bust could happen at any time, so Briggs was anxious to go, too. But first he had to wait for Lucero. He had observed that Lucero usually came in to the Black Horse about 7:00 and left around 9:00. It was 7:30, approaching that time of the evening when things are seen in silhouette or not at all. Briggs went downstairs with his briefcase and approached the back room.

"Is Mr. Lucero in there?" he asked the security guards.

"Yes, sir."

Briggs nodded. Then he went outside, located Lucero's car and found a dark place to wait. He grabbed the gun from his briefcase and held it loosely in his hand. The parking lot was half-full, but when Lucero came out, just before 9:00, there was no one around except for a couple of drunk bikers having a pissing contest in the back of the parking lot. Lucero was humming to himself when he got into his car. Briggs approached him quickly as Lucero fastened his seat belt. He knocked on the driver's side window. Lucero lowered the window.

"Hello, Briggs. How've you been?"

Briggs didn't answer. He just raised his gun, placed the barrel on Lucero's forehead and pulled the trigger. The drunk bikers turned to look, but Briggs was already walking away in the darkness. No one else was around to investigate the sound of the gunshot, which wasn't an uncommon sound in that neighborhood anyway. Lucero slumped sideways, dead as a gutted gopher.

The operation began at 10:00 that evening, while the body of Henry Lucero was still warm. FBI agents took the lead in the initial sub-op. Five agents walked into the Black Horse Saloon waving a search warrant. That sports gambling transpired in a back room of the Black Horse was an ill-kept secret, so three agents went immediately to the betting parlor and flashed their badges at the beefy bouncers. The other two agents stayed out in the bar.

"Put your hands on the table where we can see 'em," said an agent to the patrons of the bar. "Leave your drinks alone, don't light any cigarettes. Just sit there quietly." He motioned to the bartender to come out from behind the bar. "You too, buddy. Go sit at one of the tables." Both agents had their guns out for all to see, pointed down.

"This is not a robbery," said the head agent. "This is a raid. FBI," he said holding up his badge, although it might as well have been a Sheriff Scotty badge for all anyone could tell. "If you've done nothing wrong, you have nothing to fear from us. Line up single file, ladies and gents. Keep your hands out of your pockets—or anyone else's pockets too. When it's time to dance, you're going to walk outside and get on a bus that will take you downtown. You will be frisked before you get on the bus. Anything you don't want us to know about, drop it into the bag Agent Scully is holding. No, you will not be able to pick it up later."

Meanwhile, the other three agents confronted the bouncers, who offered no resistance. The bouncers didn't care if the men holding guns were FBI or Dixie Mafia. This was a job to them, not a cause, and they damn sure weren't going to get shot over a job. They willingly surrendered their weapons.

"After you," said one agent to the bouncers. The muscle pushed through the door to the back room with the FBI guys right behind them. The door led to a small landing with a half-flight of stairs descending to the main floor. "You boys go stand over there," the FBI mouthpiece said to the bouncers, motioning to a spot along the wall.

The two agents stood on the landing, looking like actors in a balcony scene. "Everyone stay where you are and shut the fuck up!" shouted one agent over the din, which gradually died down until it was as quiet as a wake. "FBI! We are investigating a report that sports gambling is taking place here. That is an illegal activity in violation of federal and state laws. You are all invited downtown to be interviewed. If you come voluntarily, we will not cuff you." There was no other exit from the room, so the twenty or so people in the room—some bookies, but mostly gamblers—had little choice but to cooperate. One man who tried to break away was quickly taken down by an agent and cuffed. Seeing this, the others went quietly.

An additional FBI agent met the drinkers and gamblers and patted down each one before they boarded the bus. Those on the bus were muttering to each other. The agents picked up words and phrases like, "Got nothin' on me...just having a beer for Chrissake...can't hold me for anything...I'm clean."

When everyone was seated on the bus, an agent searched Delaney's office, but he didn't find much there. There were two safes, both open and empty except for some pornographic photos and an external hard drive, which they confiscated. Then they sealed off the gambling den where a covey of computers, phones and other devices would be examined for evidence.

One of the FBI agents, checking the outside of the building, found a car in the parking lot, with a very dead Henry Lucero strapped into the driver's seat, and the passenger side covered with blood and brains.

***

The next phase of the operation began at two in the morning at the tunnel in Laredo. Gary Stone was leading a squad of ICE agents, who were stationed in strategic places around the yard of Neighbors for Health. At 2:00 the truck arrived. The ICE agents waited until the suspects had unlocked and opened the gate and backed the truck up to the loading dock. An ICE agent closed in on the truck's doors before the men in the cab could get out.

"Federal agents," said one. "Don't move."

The driver swung open his door as hard as he could, directly into the shoulder of an ICE agent. He reached for a gun hidden in a pocket on the door, but the ICE agent slammed the door on his hand, crushing several fingers. The driver screamed in pain and the ICE agent smashed his gun into the man's head. That silenced him, and he fell to the ground. After witnessing this, the driver's helper offered no resistance.

Moments later, people started to climb out of the tunnel. The first man out—El Flaco's courier—stood at the rear of the truck. Normally at this point he received a backpack full of money from a confederate in the truck. This time was different. Instead of the backpack of money, he got the muzzle of a gun in his face. Seeing this, another of Flaco's drug runners bolted for the tunnel. An ICE agent stepped out of the shadows and leveled a gun at the runner, who disappeared down the tunnel like a white rabbit. The agent never had a clean shot, so the runner got away, even though he was swimming upstream against the flow of illegal workers who were coming through the tunnel. One by one the illegals who emerged from the tunnel were taken into custody. ICE agents seized and impounded the drugs taped to their bodies. Everyone was put on a bus and taken to a holding room at the local ICE office.

Meanwhile in Brownsville, several ICE agents and an empty van rolled up to B.J.'s security gate.

"Federal agents," said the commander of the raid, flashing his badge. "Open your gate." The guard, drowsy and flustered, pushed a button and the gate slid open. The van and three cars of agents drove through the gate. They rounded up the workers on the graveyard shift, along with those who were asleep in the bunk houses, and told them to sit on the floor in a group. A Spanish-speaking agent explained that they were looking for undocumented workers. He told them to get any identification they had and get into the van. He said they would be taken to ICE headquarters. If they had legitimate papers they would be released, if not they would be detained and deported.

The ICE agents sealed off the offices with yellow crime scene tape until FBI and IRS agents could examine B.J.'s records. They also sealed off the Bossman's office, cluttered with boxes of paper records stacked around the room two deep and three high, some of them slumping into an adjacent box or collapsing onto the floor. The agents looked at each other wearily. God knows what was hidden away in those cartons—a mix of boxes labeled Old Grandad, Early Times, Red Delicious apples and Ruby Red Grapefruit. The ICE agents thumbed through some of the paperwork—years of invoices, order sheets, bills, government forms and time cards. They were not systematic and almost overlooked the

Ruby Red Grapefruit boxes amidst the jumble. But one agent eyed them and pulled one aside. He slipped the top off, and—bingo!—25 kilos of black tar heroin. There were four Ruby Red boxes, all layered with blocks of smack repackaged and ready for delivery.

"Jackpot," said one of the ICE men laconically.

His partner looked into the box. "Nice haul. Let's check the others."

"Good intelligence," said the first in a bored monotone.

The other agent examined a block. "So this is what fishcake looks like," he said.

"Funny guy. Coupla of those would put Jeannie through college."

"Or me through Leavenworth."

The ICE agents tagged the boxes of heroin as evidence and hauled them away for the FBI to deal with.

***

Unable to sleep, Eddie had watched the bust from a hiding place across the street. It had been a swift and efficient operation, forty-five minutes from start to finish. Although he had not seen Carlos or Sofia, he assumed they had been arrested along with the other workers.

About four a.m. Eddie had gotten word from Gary Stone that everything had gone according to plan. The only unforeseen event had been the murder of Henry Lucero outside the Black Horse.

"What about Briggs and Delaney?" Eddie asked.

"Good question. Delaney's safes were open and empty, except for some porn. He wasn't at home, but his car was gone. Briggs is MIA. It's like they knew this was coming and they split town."

"What happened to the porn?"

"I don't know. The FBI probably seized it. Why? Is it important?"

"To my client it is."

Gary Stone grunted. "Maybe I can track it down," he said.

Stone wasn't all that concerned with the porn, though. He wanted to know what had happened to Briggs and Delaney. The two biggest fish in the pond—aside from Lucero, who was dead—were nowhere to be found. FBI agents had searched their houses, finding no one but a very distraught Mrs. Delaney. Had someone tipped them off? Gary Stone and Eddie Maez had been scrupulous in their planning. They had divided up the operation into discrete parts, assigning specific tasks to each partic- ipating agency, so no one knew its full scope, except for them and As- sistant Director Tomlinson—Delaney's brother-in-law. If Stone knew about this connection, he declined to mention it to Eddie or to confront his boss.

When the Little Saigon Fish Marts opened, the workers were greeted by DEA agents there who cataloged the inventory and seized all blocks labeled as Premium Fishcake. Some regular fishcake was also taken by mistake. In a few days the evidence locker was filled with blocks of heroin that smelled overwhelmingly of rotting fish.

**

Early that morning, at about 5:00 a.m., Eddie stood in front of Raelynn's door and called her on his cell. A few birds were heralding the new dawn.

"I'm standing out front," he said. "Can you let me in?"

Raelynn opened the door and threw her arms around Eddie.

"I was so worried about you," she said.

"It's okay," Eddie said. "Everything went smoothly. Textbook." He suggested that Raelynn take a sick day.

"Why?" asked Raelynn, who was still in her nightgown and bath- robe.

"The place will be crawling with federal agents who will be hauling away all of B.J.'s records, including, probably, your computer. If you show up to work, you can expect to be grilled by the FBI. Do yourself a favor and call in sick."

Raelynn left a message for Marcy that she wasn't feeling well and wouldn't be in.

Eddie wanted to tell Raelynn that Henry had been murdered, but he knew that would be a mistake. If the cops arrived to question Raelynn before the news became public, she would either have to lie or implicate Eddie as the source of her inside information. No, to be safe she should hear it on the news like everyone else, unless the cops showed up before then.

Eddie had been up all night. At Raelynn's suggestion, he lay down on her bed to rest. Raelynn went into the kitchen to make some coffee. Eddie was just dozing off when his cell phone rang. The caller was his former editor in Houston who asked him what he knew about the story.

"Did you know what was going to go down?"

"I really can't comment on that, chief."

"I'll take that as a yes. Give me a name or two, Eddie. Who are they after?"

"I really can't say, chief."

"Look, Eddie. You want an exclusive on this story? We'll pay you five grand a week to cover it."

"Nice try, chief. I'll call you when the dust settles."

The rich aroma of coffee drew Eddie into the kitchen. He knew he shouldn't fall asleep at Raelynn's. What if the cops showed up?

Over steaming mugs of strong coffee, Eddie and Raelynn talked about what happened and what might happen. Raelynn insisted she had no direct knowledge of wage violations at B.J.'s. Wages were paid in cash. The workers clocked in and out, but it was not Raelynn's job to check to see whether the hours worked matched the wages paid. That was the Bossman's job because he prepared the weekly pay envelopes based on the workers' time cards, which were signed by the workers. When pressed, Raelynn admitted to Eddie that she suspected the Bossman doctored the time cards, paying less than minimum wage, but she hadn't questioned it.

A few days earlier, Eddie had called Brad Collins to give him a heads-up about the bust. He told Brad that the feds would want to talk to him. Eddie said he would ask Gary Stone to assign himself to interview Brad. Now, early in the morning after the bust, Eddie called Brad to bring him up to date.

"Briggs and Delaney have disappeared," he said. "I think the blackmail photos were confiscated by the FBI. They will probably be stashed in an evidence locker, labeled as porn and forgotten about. Nobody's looking for porn. I'll try to keep you out of it, but I probably won't be able to. You should expect a visit from Gary Stone. He's going to ask you what you know about the tunnel and about the smuggling. Figure out how you're going to play that."

"Can they give me some kind of confidentiality agreement? Because if they can, I'll just tell the truth."

"What a concept. But just remember: the truth won't necessarily set you free. You could still be indicted for abetting a felony, namely, human trafficking and smuggling illegal goods."

After talking to Brad, Eddie checked his watch and decided he'd better leave. The cops could arrive at any time.

"Where are you going?" asked Raelynn.

"Back the motel, get some sleep."

"Okay, call me later. We could have dinner together," she said, thinking, *If you don't get yourself killed first.*

235

Before he left, Eddie washed one of the coffee cups, dried and put it in the cupboard.

"I was never here," he said to Raelynn.

Chapter Thirty-Five

It was still dark at 5:30 when the Bossman, Chester McPherson, drove from his house to B.J.'s, as he did most mornings, expecting on this day to meet a truckload of workers and another shipment of heroin. But as he approached the plant, he could see something was wrong. Only a few lights were on, and the plant appeared deserted. There was no guard at the gate, which was sealed with a new lock and a heavy chain. Inside, he could make out yellow crime scene tape disallowing entry to the offices, including his. He drove by slowly but didn't stop. He drove home, a short distance from B.J.'s, grabbed some bolt cutters from his workshop and drove back to the plant, parking two blocks away.

The street was empty when McPherson cut through the heavy chain and entered the plant. He swung the gate closed. The plant was eerily quiet. The conveyors were silent and all the Bossman could hear was the buzz of fluorescent lights and the sound of water dripping onto metal. Clearly there had been a bust that night. Some federal agency had rounded up the entire crew. He was not surprised. *You can fly under the radar for quite a while, but not forever,* he mused. He was unsure whether the truck would show up or not. McPherson's most urgent concern was whether the feds had found the heroin in his office, which was packaged and ready to ship. He slipped under the crime tape that sealed off the steps to his office and ascended the stairs.

He flipped the lights on, but one quick look told him the heroin was gone. A more thorough inventory of the cardboard boxes piled in his office turned up whiskey boxes and banana crates but no grapefruit boxes.

All this time—for the past few hours, in fact—Briggs had been watching, hiding in a dirty doorway across the street from B.J.'s, under the cover of darkness. He too had seen the yellow crime scene tape and noted that the gate was heavily padlocked. By the time he had arrived, the raid was over and all the badges were long gone, but he was guessing that McPherson didn't know about the raid in Laredo, and that he would be there to meet the truck at its normal time, around 6:00. Briggs knew there would have been a load of heroin on the truck, but he didn't care about that. He was there for one reason only: to silence the Bossman. Actually, Briggs was delighted that there had been a bust that night. Now there were fewer potential witnesses to concern him.

Briggs saw the Bossman arrive, slow down to survey the scene, and drive off. *Unfortunate*, he thought. *I will have to devise another plan.* He continued to sit there, mulling it over. He was still sitting there ten minutes later when McPherson returned, on foot, with his bolt cutters. Briggs smiled. He watched McPherson cut the chains and go to his office—looking for the heroin, Briggs figured—and was about to make his move when another car drove up slowly and stopped by the gate. After a moment the car parked and a man got out. From his description, Briggs realized it was Eddie Maez. Eddie closed the car door gently. He had been on his way to his motel when he decided to take a detour by B.J.'s, just for the satisfaction of it. But now Eddie realized that the chain on the gate had been cut. Puzzled and curious, thinking he might find Briggs or Delaney lurking about, he pulled his gun from his shoulder holster and slipped through the gate. He unintentionally scuffed his shoe on a concrete incline. He lifted his feet more carefully as he walked around the edge of the processing area, looking around every corner, then going outside onto the loading dock where three empty trucks were parked. Across the side panel of each truck, in large letters, was the company slogan, "B.J.'s Shrimp…Fresh from the net." It was twenty feet from the edge of the loading dock to the warehouse where the walk-in cooler and freezer were installed, side by side.

In his office upstairs, McPherson thought he heard a car door close. A moment later he heard another noise, a scraping sound, and realized he was not alone. He peeked out the window and in the pre-dawn light recognized Eddie Maez walking stealthily around the perimeter of the plant. Eddie had his gun out and was checking every door, looking in every nook, stopping to listen, then proceeding. It reminded McPherson of the Army, being on patrol in Afghanistan, clearing houses, hugging the walls.

Eddie was not the only one with a gun. The Bossman pulled out his Army-issue M9 pistol and gripped it by the barrel. The Bossman waited patiently for Eddie to reach his office.

Eddie went back through the processing area and looked up at Lucero's office, where Raelynn worked. The lights were off and doors were closed and striped with yellow crime scene tape. Then he skirted the room to the wooden stairs leading to the Bossman's office, where the lights were on and the door was open. This felt wrong to Eddie. He edged up the stairs, putting his feet down carefully in the middle of a step, alert to squeaky nails.

He crouched down to slip under the yellow tape. Also, he knew from experience that a lower position makes a smaller target. Memories of Vietnam came flooding back: patrols searching for Viet Cong, moving through the forest slowly, spread out in a line, M16s pointed down. Even though he was there as a reporter and walked behind the patrol, he always felt lucky to survive those lonely marches. Eddie thought about the one guy who offered to sell his patrol duty for a thousand bucks. Everyone scoffed at him, derided him and ostracized him. Now the poor guy had no choice. He had to go on the "death patrol," as the grunts called it, or go into the brig for disobeying orders. And sure enough, as if there might be justice or retribution in the universe, the kid was blown up by a land mine that afternoon.

All these memories, and the feelings they evoked, floated through Eddie's mind as he inched up the stairs. He reached the top and peeked around the corner. Eddie didn't see anyone or hear anyone. He crept under the yellow tape, went into the office and straightened up slowly.

Then the lights went out.

Before Eddie's eyes could adjust to the suddenly dim light, something hammered him on the back of his head. He fell to his knees, stunned and in pain, blood running down the sides of his head from the blow.

"I guess I'm not the only one who wanted those grapefruit boxes, eh, Maez?" said a voice behind him. Eddie was down on all fours, still seeing stars. "Well, looks like the feds got here first. I get nothing. This is what you get." His assailant kicked him viciously in the ribs, then in the stomach. He collapsed onto the floor. As Eddie fought for air, he felt his gun being taken from his hand. "You won't be needing this," said the man. "Or this," he said, finding Eddie's cell phone in his jacket pocket. "Now get up and go down the stairs."

Eddie lay on the ground, breathing now but not moving. He opened one eye to see his attacker and verify what he already knew: it was the Bossman.

"I said get up," the Bossman ordered. He grabbed Eddie by the collar and pulled him to his feet. "You shouldn't have gone sticking your nose into our business. That was a big mistake, Maez. Now, move!"

Eddie tried to resist, but his small beat-up frame could barely stand, much less do any damage to a man as large and strong as the Bossman. They went down the steps, ducking under the crime scene tape. "Put your hands behind your head," said the Bossman. He gripped Eddie by the collar and marched him across the production floor. They went onto the loading dock, Eddie hoping for a chance to run away. No such luck. The Bossman jerked open the big freezer door and pushed Eddie into it. The push was strong enough to send Eddie stumbling forward until he lost his balance and went down. The lights went out and the freezer door closed. On the outside, the Bossman put a lock through the door handle and snapped it shut. He dropped the keys into his pocket. The temperature in the freezer was twenty below zero.

Chapter Thirty-Six

Eddie lay on the floor of the freezer. He held a handkerchief to his head where blood was still oozing. The cold felt good at first, like putting ice packs all over his hurting body. His head had settled into a steady throbbing rhythm; he felt dizzy and nauseous. It was as dark as a tomb. He got up slowly and felt his way to the door. It wouldn't budge. Eddie realized with a shock that it was locked from the outside. He pounded on the door a few times, but he knew the door was six inches thick. No one would hear him. The luminous dial on his watch said it was 6:30.

Out of habit, Eddie reached in his pocket for his cell phone but then remembered that the Bossman had taken it. He felt around the door for a light switch and realized that the switch was on the outside, too. He patted his pockets for a lighter but found only a pack of gum. Even after his eyes adjusted to the darkness, he could barely make out the sparse contents of the freezer: totes filled with bags of shrimp, a pile of nets and buoys, rolls of shrink wrap, a pile of pallets, not much else. He kicked something on the floor—not a flashlight, just a renegade wrench that he put it in his jacket pocket.

Eddie wore a cotton shirt and a light sports coat. Soon the cold began to seep through his clothes. He crossed his arms and squeezed his hands in his armpits. His eyes teared up from the cold. He jumped up and down to keep warm; it did little good. Within an hour his hands and feet ached; his neck and shoulder muscles tightened up and ached too. He began to shiver uncontrollably. He knew his muscles were trying to generate heat by rapid movement; he also knew it wasn't going to work for very long.

In the darkness, Eddie could make out the giant cooling units hanging from the ceiling. *Where were the controls?* he wondered. He patted down the walls near the door and found nothing. He made a stack of pallets and climbed on top of them so he could reach the condensers. He felt around for a switch or a dial but didn't find any. So he climbed down, moved the stack of pallets over a few feet, climbed back up and felt around in a different area. Still no luck. After moving the stack of pallets several times, he found two round units, encased in glass, sitting at the bottom edge of the condensing unit. Eddie took out the wrench he had found, wrapped its cold metal handle in his handkerchief and climbed back up on the stack of pallets. He smashed the glass that protected the instruments. He couldn't tell what kind of controls they were, but there were no moving parts, no switches or dials. He began pounding them with the wrench, hoping to shut down the system. The condensers kept on working, blowing out frigid air.

All that activity, stacking and re-stacking the heavy wooden pallets, had warmed Eddie somewhat. In fact, he was sweating and his breathing was faster. A few minutes later, however, his clothes absorbed the sweat; ice crystals began to form on his shirt. He felt a surge of panic ripple through his body.

Eddie's hands and feet hurt, his head ached, pain pierced his ears, and he felt tired. He curled up in a fetal position on a pallet, feeling pain and fatigue. He looked at the luminous dial on his watch. It was 8:30. Eddie couldn't remember what time it was when the Bossman had thrown him into the freezer. He lay on the pallet, the thoughts in his mind wandering aimlessly. He thought of the warm days he had spent on Padre Island walking barefoot through the surf. He envisioned Raelynn walking with him, holding his hand. He thought he heard someone call his name once, twice, then no more. He closed his eyes and drifted off.

Briggs had slipped into the plant while the Bossman was busy with Eddie. He hid underneath the wooden stairs where it was dark. The gun Briggs had used to shoot Lucero was in his hand again as he watched McPherson hurry toward the entrance to the plant. After the Bossman passed through the processing room—where the shrimp were beheaded and shelled—Briggs stepped out from the shadow of the stairs. "McPherson!" he said in a harsh whisper. The Bossman stopped and peered into the gray morning light.

"Briggs?" he asked, surprised.

"Who else?" Holding the gun with both hands, Briggs brought the gun up swiftly, arms straight out, as he had seen in countless films and television shows. He fired point blank into McPherson's forehead. The big man's knees crumpled under him, and he went down. With great effort, Briggs managed to drag the heavy body into a closet and closed the door, leaving a smear of blood on the floor. He went out the front gate, closing it behind him.

***

From the Brownsville/South Padre Island International Airport, a traveler has the choice of two destinations: Houston or Dallas. Delmore Briggs did not plan on going to either city. He parked his car in the longterm parking lot and rented a different car. He fled east, towards Louisiana, towards New Orleans, towards the Tremé and a hide-out on Toulouse Street, where he would retreat to look for another scheme, another scam, another opportunity. On the way he stopped near Breaux Bridge and tossed the gun into the bayou.

Chapter Thirty-Seven

All morning Gary Stone had been busy overseeing the investigation. ICE didn't issue a press release regarding the multi-pronged, multi-agency action, but word had begun to seep out, and the media were calling. Stone delegated himself as the press contact, so he was fielding inquiries from radio, TV and print reporters, as well as bloggers and other on-line media hounds. Stone was vague on the details. He declined to say exactly where the tunnel was or who was suspected of operating it or what was being smuggled. Stone had seen investigations undermined by a frenzied media looking for a sensational story. He was determined to maintain control this time. He gave the reporters a few crumbs of information and left them to undertake their own investigations.

Shortly after nine that morning a Brownsville resident reported to the local news media that he had seen the FBI removing computers and file boxes from B.J.'s Shrimp Co. As a result, a few reporters descended on B.J.'s, trying to find someone who knew something about somebody. They knew that the owner was named Henry Lucero, but he didn't appear to be on the premises. In fact, the only employee there was Lucero's secretary, Marcy, who was being questioned by the local police, with the DEA, IRS and ICE waiting their turn.

Later that day the police-beat reporter for the *Brownsville Bugle* learned that a man had been murdered outside the Black Horse Saloon—shot in the head at close range, according to the coroner. The police identified the man as Henry Lucero, the owner of B.J.'s Shrimp Co. The police spokesman admitted there was probably a connection between the murder of Lucero and the investigation of his business, but he declined to draw any conclusions. He said the police had not identified any suspects in the murder, nor did they have a motive. He referred reporters to the FBI for comments on the investigation at B.J.'s Shrimp Co. The FBI referred them to the IRS who referred them to DEA who referred them to ICE who stonewalled them.

Not long after that, an FBI agent noticed blood on the floor of the plant and followed it to a closet where he discovered the body of Chester McPherson. A ballistics report would later confirm that the gun that killed McPherson also killed Henry Lucero. It was registered to Michael Delaney, owner of the Black Horse Saloon.

About 3:00 that afternoon, two detectives came to Raelynn's apartment, a man and a woman with the Brownsville Police. The news of Henry Lucero's death had not hit the media yet. It would be the lead story at 6:00, so at 3:00 Raelynn was still unaware of his murder. The detectives identified themselves and said they wanted to ask Raelynn some questions, informally.

"About what?" asked Raelynn.

"May we come in?" Raelynn stood aside and let them enter. The woman cop identified herself as Detective Lorraine Dunlap. She asked the questions while her partner took notes.

"Ms. Weeks, do you work at B.J.'s Shrimp Co.?"

"Yes."

"But you didn't go to work today?"

"I called in sick this morning."

"Okay. Who is your boss at B.J.'s?"

"Henry Lucero, the owner."

"When is the last time you saw him?"

"Yesterday when he left work."

"Have you spoken to him since then?"

"No, I left a message that I wouldn't be in today. What's going on?"

"Ms. Weeks, Mr. Lucero was killed last night."

Raelynn was genuinely shocked. "What? Killed? Oh my god! Seriously? How?"

"He was shot in the head while sitting in his car outside the Black Horse Saloon."

"Shot? I can't believe it! You mean murdered?"

"Yes, it appears so."

"Why would anyone murder Mr. Lucero?"

"We are hoping you can help us answer that question. Can you think of anyone who had a grudge against Mr. Lucero or any reason to kill him?"

"No. He doesn't have any enemies that I know of."

"No business competitors? Disgruntled employees?"

"I don't think so."

"What about Mr. McPherson?"

"What about him?"

"Did he and Mr. Lucero get along? Was there any friction between them?"

"Not that I ever noticed."

"Did Mr. Lucero have money problems? Was he in debt?"

"The business is solvent, I know that. But as for his personal finances...I have no idea."

"Ms. Weeks, I have to ask: Where were you last night?"

"Me? I was here all evening, all night. You don't think I...killed him, do you?"

"Did you?"

"God, no!"

"Did you see anyone last night? Can anyone verify that you were home?"

"No. I didn't see anyone."

"Do you own a gun?"

"*No!* I had nothing to do with this."

"Did you get along with Mr. Lucero?"

"Yes. We have a cordial professional relationship," she said, still speaking in the present tense.

"Were you unhappy with your salary or the hours you worked?"

"No. He pays me very well, and I work a standard 40-hour week."

Detective Dunlap was just fishing now. When she ran out of bait, Dunlap handed a business card to Raelynn. "If you think of anything that might help us find out who killed Mr. Lucero, please give me a call," she said. "Anything at all." Raelynn took the card and stuffed it in the pocket of her jeans.

When the police were gone, Raelynn fixed herself a cup of herbal tea. She needed to calm down. Her pulse was still racing from the police visit and the news about Lucero. The tea was still too hot to sip when the doorbell rang again. Two men identified themselves as agents from the Drug Enforcement Agency.

"Drug enforcement?" questioned Raelynn. "What do you want with me?"

"May we come in?"

They moved to Raelynn's spartan living room. The two agents sat on the couch, Raelynn in a wooden rocking chair. There was no coffee table, so the two agents had to balance their papers and notebooks in their laps and on the arms of the couch. Raelynn slipped off her shoes and sat cross-legged in the rocker. She sipped her tea.

"Did you go in to work today?" asked one agent.

"No, but I have a feeling you already know that. I called in sick."

"Why?"

"Because I wasn't feeling well? Flu-ish. Some kind of bug. Don't get too close."

The agents exchanged looks. One asked, "Do you know about Mr. Lucero, your boss?"

"Yes, the police were just here. They said he was apparently murdered yesterday but didn't give me any details."

"Did you know that there was a raid at B.J.'s last night?"

"A raid? What for?"

"So you didn't know about it?"

"No! What is going on?" Raelynn asked, tired of being grilled.

"We'll get to that in a minute, Ms. Weeks. What is your job at B.J.'s Shrimp?" asked the agent.

"I'm the bookkeeper. I pay the bills, track invoices, balance the books, work up cash flow spreadsheets.... That kind of thing."

"So you are familiar with B.J.'s products and its customers?"

"Yes."

"Does B.J.'s have a distributor?"

"No, we have our own delivery trucks. Three of them."

"How many accounts would you say these trucks service?"

"We have 135 active accounts."

"How often do you deliver?"

"Twice a week. But we only offer a few products."

"Can you list them for me?"

"Well, shrimp, of course. Fresh or frozen, depending on the season. That's our main product. We also sell cocktail sauce and fishcake."

"Fishcake? What is that?"

"It's a mixture of ground up fish, potatoes and spices. It's usually deep fried before it is served. See, fish will get caught in the net with the shrimp, and rather than throw them back, we make fishcake with them. In fact, sometimes a fisherman will get more bycatch than shrimp."

"Bycatch?"

"Yeah. Fish we're not fishing for: pogies, mullet, croakers, flounder."

"In Mr. McPherson's office we found some packaging labeled Premium Fishcake. What is that?"

"I'm not really sure. It's a new item for us. A better grade of fishcake, I guess."

"I thought you said you are familiar with B.J.'s products." Raelynn glared at her interrogator.

The other agent jumped in. "Do you recall an account called the Little Saigon Fish Shop?"

"Yes, that's one of our newer accounts. It's a chain of about twenty stores."

"I noticed that they buy a lot of Premium Fishcake. Hardly anyone else does."

"Huh," said Raelynn. "I wonder why. You could ask them, I guess."

"Ms. Weeks," said the first agent, "it appears that the packages labeled as Premium Fishcake are actually not fishcake at all."

"I don't understand."

"Those packages contain heroin, not fishcake."

"What?" exclaimed Raelynn in apparent surprise. "Heroin?" She uncrossed her legs, put her feet on the floor and leaned forward.

"It seems that Mr. Lucero was involved in a heroin ring. The drugs are smuggled into the U.S. from Mexico and then B.J.'s distributes them around south Texas through the Little Saigon Fish Shops."

"No way. I don't believe it."

"You had no inkling that this was going on?"

"No, not at all. I'm...I don't know what to say." There was silence in the room until Raelynn said, "It doesn't make sense. Mr. Lucero is...was very much opposed to drugs. I can't believe he would be involved in anything like that." No one spoke for a moment. The first agent tried to straighten his papers which had slipped off his lap onto the floor. When he picked them up, he knocked the papers on the arm of the couch onto the floor too.

"How often do the workers get paid?" asked the other agent.

"Once a week, on Friday."

"By check?"

"No, in cash."

"Don't you think that's a bit strange, Ms. Weeks? You must have had thousands of dollars on hand to meet payroll every week. Aren't you worried about a robbery?"

"Oh, I see where you're going with this. Drugs are a cash business, right? But, you see, most of our workers are guest workers. They are only here temporarily. Most of them don't even have a bank account. Besides, the closest bank is at least a mile away."

"Then where do they keep their money?"

"Every employee has a locker for their personal possessions. Or we will keep it for them, in a safe. Many of them go over to Walmart and wire the money home to their family in Mexico or wherever."

"Where do you keep the payroll?"

"In the Bossman's safe."

"And who tracks the cash that goes in and comes out?"

"I do. Look. Here's the way it works. The Bossman gives me the time cards. I total it up and call the bank. Charlie picks up the money. Charlie and I divide it up and put it in pay envelopes. Then the Bossman distributes it to the workers."

"Ever come up short?"

"No, never."

"Ms. Weeks, do you know a man named Delmore Briggs?"

"I wouldn't say I know him. Mr. Briggs comes in the office every week or so to see Mr. Lucero."

"Would you say Briggs is a business associate of Mr. Lucero's or a friend?"

"Maybe both. They go into Mr. Lucero's office and close the door. I don't know what they talk about."

The second agent tapped her watch and the first agent nodded.

"That will be all for now, Ms. Weeks," he said. "Thank you for your time and cooperation."

When the DEA agents had gone, Raelynn sat down and gradually absorbed the fact that Henry Lucero was dead. This meant she didn't have a job, which in turn meant she was free to chart her future. She had saved up enough money to live on for a while, even enough to move somewhere else. She pulled up a map of the U.S. on her laptop. Locating Brownsville, she was struck by how tiny and insignificant it seemed. It was just a dot among thousands in America, just one leaf on a towering tree.

Chapter Thirty-Eight

By the time the last of Raelynn's interrogators left it was dark. Raelynn was surprised she hadn't heard from Eddie yet. It was past 6:00. She punched his cell phone number into her phone. It rang several times and then went to voicemail. This bothered Raelynn. Eddie always picked up right away. Maybe he was still asleep.

Raelynn got in her car and drove to Eddie's motel. His car was gone. She knocked on his door anyway, but there was no answer. Then, without quite knowing why, she drove to B.J.'s. Eddie's car was parked in the front lot. FBI and IRS agents had been there in the morning, hauling away computers and other evidence. They had turned off the lights and locked the front gate. Raelynn wondered if Eddie had been arrested. Or maybe he was in the plant somewhere.

"Eddie!" she called. No answer. "Ed-dee!" she called again, louder.

Raelynn felt in her pocket for the card the police detective had given her. Her name was Lorraine Dunlap. Raelynn called Dunlap's number.

"Homicide. Dunlap. Can I help you?"

"Yes, Detective Dunlap, this is Raelynn Weeks from B.J.'s Shrimp?"

"Yes, Ms. Weeks."

"I'm calling because, well, I don't know who else to call."

"What's the problem?"

"I was supposed to meet a friend for dinner. Eddie Maez is his name. But he didn't call, and I went looking for him. I found his car outside of B.J.'s. I'm here now. The plant is all locked up. I'm worried about Eddie."

"Do you have reason to believe he is in danger, Ms. Weeks?"

"Not exactly. It's just that I don't know why Eddie's car would be here. Something's not right."

"Did Mr. Maez have anything to do with Mr. Lucero? Would he know something about his murder?"

"I don't know. But …." Raelynn hesitated. She didn't want to say anything that would get Eddie in trouble. He had so many secrets. Raelynn decided to tell one of them.

"But what?" asked Detective Dunlap.

"Eddie was investigating B.J.'s for possible tax fraud and labor law violations. He may have made some enemies here."

Dunlap considered the situation. "I think we should search the plant," she said.

"Okay," Raelynn replied.

"Sit tight. Lock your car doors. I'll be there in ten."

Dunlap arrived with a police locksmith who opened B.J.'s locked gate with ease.

They searched the plant, asking Raelynn where this or that stairway went, what was in this room, where did that hallway lead. The locksmith opened all the doors that were locked and locked them again when they left.

"That is my office," said Raelynn, pointing to another locked door. She opened it with her own key. There was no one there, but Raelynn was shocked to see that her computer was gone and her file cabinets were empty. Her desk drawers had been searched too.

After a half an hour they had found no one, dead or alive.

"What's back there?" asked Dunlap pointing to the open-air area out the back.

"That's the loading dock. The walk-in cooler is back there. And the freezer too."

Dunlap exchanged a look with the locksmith. "Let's go," she said, running towards the freezer.

The locksmith and Dunlap opened the lock with a master key. Detective Dunlap opened the freezer door and they discovered Eddie huddled on a pallet, unconscious. Blood was frozen on his head. Dunlap called in an urgent request for an ambulance. They pulled the pallet out of the freezer onto the loading dock. Eddie had been in the freezer for over 12 hours.

Raelynn put her cheek next to Eddie's mouth and felt a very light, shallow breathing.

"He's still alive!" she told the detective. Raelynn rubbed Eddie's cold hands in her warm ones.

When the ambulance arrived a few minutes later, it backed up to the loading dock. The EMTs transferred Eddie to a gurney, wrapped him in a thermal blanket and raced off to the hospital with the siren wailing. An EMT alerted the hospital that they were bringing in a case of profound hypothermia. At the ER Eddie was placed on a heated mattress and administered a warm saline solution intravenously. The doctor knew that if the body warmed up too fast, it could cause the heart to spasm.

Eddie's limbs were stiff. The hospital staff cut off his clothes with scissors and covered him with blankets. They monitored his heartbeat and his temperature. His heartbeat had slowed to 25 beats per minute and his body temperature had dropped to 79 degrees. Warm saline solution flowed through Eddie's abdominal cavity, into one catheter and out another. Very slowly, over the course of two hours, his body began to warm up. His limbs relaxed; his pulse inched up. The doctor warned Raelynn that Eddie might lose fingers or toes to frostbite. Worse, there might be brain damage.

Detective Dunlap had been called to cover another crime. She said she would be back later to talk to Raelynn. "Obviously, someone tried to kill Mr. Maez," she said. Dunlap left thinking it was a curious coincidence that there was one murder and one attempted murder in the past 36 hours, and Raelynn Weeks knew both victims.

Raelynn slumped in a waiting room chair, exhausted. She heard the beeping of the heart monitor, and watched a parade of emergencies come into the ER. She tried to ignore the television mounted on the wall, spewing obnoxious commercials. She tried to get comfortable in the chair, rested her head against the wall and dozed off. She dreamed that her car was stalled at a traffic light and when the light turned green her car wouldn't start. All around her drivers were honking at her angrily. Someone was shaking her....

"Ms. Weeks. Ms. Weeks, wake up!" It was a nurse. "Mr. Maez is starting to stir."

Raelynn followed the nurse to Eddie's bed. His eyelids were fluttering.

Raelynn put her mouth near his ear and whispered his name. "Eddie. Eddie. Can you hear me?" Eddie opened his eyes, squinting against the light.

"Raelynn?" he asked.

"I'm right here," she said.

"What?... Where am I?"

"At the hospital. You were trapped in the freezer at B.J.'s." Eddie looked at her blankly.

"He probably has amnesia," the doctor said. "Don't push him."

Raelynn put her hand on Eddie's hand. "It's okay," she said. "How do you feel?"

"Tired." Eddie closed his eyes again.

"Let him sleep," the doctor said. "He can talk, which is a very good sign."

By now it was almost midnight. Raelynn went home to get some sleep too.

Eddie lived. Not only did he live but he retained all his fingers and toes. Another hour in the freezer and he would have lost most of his digits to frostbite, the doctor said. Another two hours and he would have died. In addition to the frostbite, he had a concussion from the Boss-man's blow to his head and a gash that required six stiches, along with a broken rib and a variety of bruises. *Nothing like a near-death experience to focus the mind*, he told himself.

When Eddie was out of danger, Raelynn took him to her apartment and set him up in her bed. She slept on the living room couch. Raelynn babied him for a few days until Eddie convinced Raelynn that he was fine and needed to go see Brad Collins in San Antonio.

Raelynn said, "When will I see you again?"

"Soon, I hope. But who knows? You're out of a job now. This is your chance to get the hell out of Dodge."

"I know. I've been looking at different cities online. I'm ready for a major change. What about you?"

"Not sure. I'll decide when I get back."

"Back from where?"

"Vietnam. I've decided to try to find Kim and An."

Raelynn jumped up and gave Eddie a big kiss on the cheek. She gushed about what a good idea that was, completing the circle, finding his past, taking responsibility for....

"Stop, please stop," Eddie said. "I'm already nervous about it."

When he was ready to go, they hugged and promised to stay in touch.

"I don't want this to be the end of a beautiful friendship," Eddie said.

Chapter Thirty-Nine

Carlos and Sofia had been sleeping when the ICE men came. Bleary-eyed and fuzzy-brained, they were escorted to a van by men in uniform and taken to the ICE offices with the other workers. Intake agents were assigned to interview the workers. It was mid-morning by the time Carlos and Sofia's turn came.

"*De donde eras*?" asked the agent.

"*Hondurás*," Carlos said.

"IDs? Visas? *Pasaportes*?"

"No," Carlos said.

"*Familia* in USA?"

"No."

"Why are you here?"

Carlos understood the question and tried to answer it. "*Hondurás es muy peligroso. Las gangas controlen todo y no tienen respeto a la vida humana. Pedimos asilo político. Nosotros estamos preocupado por nuestras vidas en Hondurás.*"

The agent interviewing Carlos got the gist of this—that Honduras was a dangerous place and they were seeking asylum—but didn't speak more than ten words of Spanish, and he had already used half of them.

"Do you have any other documentation? Anything at all?"

Carlos understood the word "documentation." He dug into his pack and came up with a newspaper clipping, dated seven months prior, that listed all the marriage licenses issued that week, including one for the marriage of Sofia Maria Guzman to Carlos Cruz, which also named a village in Honduras as their home. He also had a photo of his family taken by a traveling photographer. Carlos kept the photo and the clipping in a grimy envelope to protect them.

The agent looked at the photo and the newspaper clipping. *This was all they had?* He knew they would be sent back to Honduras. Normally, most undocumenteds wouldn't get any farther than "No documents" before they were shuttled to a holding tank for illegal migrants. The holding rooms consisted of large windowless rooms with cots but no chairs—one room for men, one for women—where glaring fluorescent lights buzzed day and night. A single exposed toilet serviced all the detainees, some of whom slept on the cold cement floors because of a shortage of cots. But these undocs picked up at the shrimp processor were a bit more complicated because they had already been working in the country for several weeks or months. The IRS would want to know if they had paid taxes and whether the employer paid his FICA and Social Security.

He handed the envelope back to Carlos who put it back in his pack.

"You are allowed one phone call," said the agent, pointing to the phone and holding up one finger.

Carlos dug out Eddie's card buried in the bottom. He handed the card to the agent who was interrogating him. "This is who you want to call?" he asked.

"*Sí.*"

"Okay." The agent picked up the desk phone and punched in Eddie's number. In a closet at B.J.'s Seafood Co., in the pocket of Chester McPherson, Eddie's phone rang. No one heard it.

The agent shrugged. "No answer," he said.

Carlos and Sofia were returned to the holding cell. Theoretically they were allowed a public defender and a court hearing, but sometimes the government agents skipped a few steps, especially in a case like this where the migrants had no leg to stand on. The next day, an officer came for Carlos, Sofia and several others. He returned their personal belongings, including their money belts. They were then driven to the airport, along with several other Hondurans being deported, and put on a plane for Tigucigalpa.

Before boarding the plane, Carlos and Sofia had been given deportation papers. When they presented the papers to the Honduran customs officials, they were ushered into a drab office where they were fingerprinted, photographed and questioned. Carlos asked if they could get Honduran I.D. cards. The official rubbed his fingers together. How much, asked Carlos. For one hundred U.S. dollars they each were issued official I.D. cards. Then they were released into the dangerous darkness of Tigucigalpa.

Carlos and Sofia were still a long way from home. Eventually they found a bus station where they could buy tickets for a ten-hour trip that would get them close to their village. The station was crowded with people and luggage. Some children raced around screaming and laughing and others were crying. Chickens crowed in their cages. Vendors were urging people to buy their goods—everything from ice cream bars to stuffed monkeys. Waiting in the ticket line, Carlos was bumped from behind and then felt a tug at his waist and heard a knife ripping through fabric. He turned around in time to see a teenaged boy running off with his money belt.

"*Oi!*" he yelled, running after the thief. In the crowded terminal, Carlos pushed past people, leapt over luggage, skipped around trunks and boxes, keeping the young thief in view. "*Para ese niño!*" Carlos yelled. People looked around to see what was happening, but no one joined the chase. The boy had the advantage of knowing the territory— places to hide, shortcuts, exits. Still, Carlos was gaining on him. He swerved around a man selling lottery tickets and slipped by another selling something in a newspaper cone. Carlos saw the boy run into a fruit vendor, spilling oranges on the floor, but the boy barely slowed down. Then a porter pushing a trolley loaded with suitcases emerged from the crowd, directly in Carlos's path. He dodged the trolley but slammed into an ATM standing in his path. His head hit the pavement, and when he looked up, he could not see the boy. Carlos got up and continued running in the same direction, looking for the nearest exit. When he got outside, lines of buses obscured his view. He climbed up on the back of a bench to see over the buses, but the boy was gone.

He raced back inside, looking everywhere in vain. Heartbroken, Carlos walked back to the ticket window. Sofia had their tickets and was waiting anxiously. "He got away," Carlos said with tears in his eyes. "He stole my money belt."

Carlos felt a staggering mix of emotions: fear, anger, resentment, failure. It was a feeling without a name, something beyond his comprehension. It was about a lack of hope and money, about blood and death, about something as complex as the struggle to live and as simple as twisting the head off a shrimp.

Chapter Forty

There was one thing that bothered Gary Stone: how did the perps have access to the yard at Neighbors for Health? He was able to stage the bust because Eddie gave him the combination to the locked gate. But how did Eddie get it?

Stone went to see Eddie in the hospital. When asked how he got the combination to the lock, Eddie hesitated. Then he said, "My client gave it to me, who got it from Briggs."

"Well, how did Briggs get it? Did your client give it to him too?"

"I can't tell you that, bud," said Eddie. "It's privileged information. Just trust me on this."

"Well, I trust you, Ed, but I still need to know. If your client was complicit in the smuggling, he or she should be part of the investigation."

Eddie didn't reply.

"Okay," said Gary, "I'm going to assume that your client is someone at Neighbors for Health. To find out for sure I could interview the folks there, starting with the Chairman of the Board and the Executive Director."

Eddie sighed. "I wish you wouldn't do that."

"Look, Eddie, somebody there knew about the tunnel. How else would you get the combo to the lock? Why are you trying to protect them?"

Eddie was feeling cornered. "Because they're innocent?" he explained, raising his eyebrows.

"Oh, so now you are the judge and jury in this case?"

"No, but my client was being blackmailed. He had no choice."

"Blackmail is against the law. If he was being blackmailed, well, all the more reason to talk to me."

"My client doesn't want to press charges on the blackmailing."

"Because why?"

"Because it can only lead to heartache."

"Don't get sentimental on me, Eddie. I'm going to find out one way or another. It would be a lot easier if you just tell me the story."

Eddie had known this moment would come sooner or later. As a newspaper reporter he never gave up his sources, but he had the whole newspaper and its lawyers behind him. But now he had no one.

"All right," he said at last. "My client is the CEO, Brad Collins. As far as I know, no one else at Neighbors for Health knows about the tunnel. I warned Brad that you would probably want to talk to him. I could give you the story, but I think you should get it directly from Brad."

***

Gary Stone was ten years younger than Brad Collins. They had grown up within a mile of each other and gone to the same high school. At a meeting at the ICE field office in San Antonio, they spent half an hour trading stories.

"Remember Mr. Sturdevant, the chemistry teacher?" Gary asked.

"Sure," said Brad. "He was a madman. He liked explosions, as I recall."

After the stories and memories tapered off, Gary got suddenly business-like and said, "I need to ask you about the tunnel, Mr. Collins. You know what I'm talking about?" Brad nodded. "Eddie did his best to keep you out of it, but he can't. As you know, last week we busted up an illegal operation that was using a tunnel that goes under the Rio Grande and comes out at Neighbors for Health. Did you know about the tunnel or the illegal activities?"

"We did not know about the tunnel when we bought the property last year."

"When did you find out about it?"

"In February. I was approached by a man named Delmore Briggs. He told me about the tunnel. I didn't believe him at first. The entrance to the tunnel is very well hidden."

Gary Stone waited for Brad to continue. After a minute of silence, Gary said, "Look, Mr. Collins, I can drag this out of you one question at a time, or you can just tell me the story. It's in your best interests to be cooperative."

"Can this just be between you and me?"

"No, I'm afraid not. I can try to keep it out of the press, but I can't promise anything. If it ends up in court...." Gary shrugged.

"Right." Brad plunged ahead. "Basically, Briggs blackmailed me into giving him access to the tunnel. He had some, um, compromising photographs and video of me with a woman who was not my wife. He threatened to release this material to the press or to my Board of Directors if I didn't cooperate with him."

"So you gave him the code to the locked gate?"

"Yes."

"Did Briggs tell you what he was going to use the tunnel for?"

"No. He said it would be better if I didn't know. So then I hired Eddie to find out what was going on. He investigated and discovered it was being used for, you know, smuggling drugs and undocumented workers. I was hoping that I could find a way to shut down their operation and keep the incriminating photographs from going public, but the operation was too big and there was too much money at stake. So Eddie went to see you."

"Good thing he did, too."

"Do you know where the photos are?"

"I believe the FBI has them, but as far as I know, no one has connected them to the case. If you're lucky, no one ever will."

Chapter Forty-One

From the first October snowfall, the Sangre de Cristo Mountains remained under a white blanket until the spring thaw. The snow melted gradually, and just as gradually the hikers and campers returned to explore the trails of the high country. In early June a pair of weekend hikers looking for mushrooms and wildflowers noticed the tips of two boots sticking up through some wet leaves. Carefully scraping away a layer of dirt and pine needles, they discovered a dead body in a shallow grave. They immediately turned around, retraced their steps and reported their find at a nearby ranger station. A ranger called the county Sheriff and they asked the hikers to lead them to the body. Later that day the county coroner examined the badly decomposed body.

The victim's fingers were too far gone to obtain useable prints, so the coroner had to use dental records to identify the corpse. Two weeks later the coroner announced that the dead man was William Bonner of Brownsville, Texas. He'd been missing since the previous October when he was identified as a suspect in an attempted murder in Houston. A man named Axel Rodd was wanted for questioning regarding the same incident, but he too had been missing since then. The New Mexico State Police conducted a search of the area within a mile of where Bonner had been found, but the search yielded nothing.

The coroner's report indicated that Bonner had died of massive hemorrhage due to a gunshot wound to his right leg. Axel Rodd remained a suspect wanted for questioning.

Brad Collins continued his efforts to bring medicine and medical aid to people in Central America. The damning photos of his tryst with the woman in San Francisco were impounded by ICE and later destroyed as evidence unrelated to the case. The case itself—the U.S. vs. B.J.'s Shrimp Company, Inc.—was a brief one since Henry Lucero and his right-hand man, Chester McPherson, were dead. A warrant was issued but never served for Delmore Briggs, who had disappeared into the shadows of New Orleans, where he acquired a new name and a false passport and began to plan his next move. Michael Delaney was also wanted by the FBI, but he had vanished without a trace.

Raelynn Weeks didn't know she had a drawl until she moved to Seattle. Then it quickly became apparent, since people were constantly saying (politely), "You're not from around here, are you?" Or "I just love a Southern drawl. Where are you from?" And when she said she was from Texas, the response was usually, "Wow, that's a big change. I hope you like rain."

But Raelynn didn't move to Seattle for the weather. She moved there because it was totally different from Brownsville and 2,500 miles away from the grim realities of her childhood. Of course Raelynn had seen pictures on the Internet, but she was still surprised at the size of Seattle—the skyscrapers, the crowds, the traffic. Green replaced brown, hilly replaced flat, urban replaced small-town, trendy replaced traditional. About the only similarity between the two cities was the availability of fresh fish.

Finding a job was not a problem. There were several companies looking for a bookkeeper, and Raelynn accepted an offer from a large sporting goods store. She found a pleasing second-floor apartment in the Greenlake area, half the space and twice the cost of her apartment in Brownsville. There were many people her age, and in just a few months she had acquired lots of friends. She had left Brownsville and all that had happened there in the rear-view mirror. She had begun her life anew.

Chapter Forty-Two

From the air, Vietnam is a vast green expanse that looks solid enough to walk on, level enough to land on. Eddie had ridden in many helicopters during his stint in Vietnam—with foot soldiers, with medics, with brass, and of course with the dead and injured. He was always struck by the illusion that he could rest on the canopy of treetops like a frog on a lily pad. Now, as the jetliner came in for a landing in Saigon, he smiled at the thought. A tsunami of memories washed over Eddie— he heard women screaming and children crying. He heard explosions, smelled diesel fumes and felt the choke of the smoke of battle. He was transported back to a tent, where he wrote dispatches by lantern light, deep into the night, when the screech of insects displaced the sounds of war.

Eddie felt a chill as he stepped off the plane, despite the breathless wet heat of Saigon. Even forty years later it still felt dangerous.

Eddie collected his luggage and passed through customs. Most of his fellow travelers were American and European tourists, along with Vietnamese businessmen in Western suits. Eddie took a tuk-tuk to his hotel. The driver followed his own route to get there, squeezing between cars, driving on sidewalks, swerving around lorries, and pushing aside bicyclists. Eddie tipped the driver well.

He checked in and followed a boy with his luggage to his room, which overlooked the sprawl of the city. Across the boulevard, two-storey stucco buildings, painted white or pastel with red-tiled roofs—remnants from the colonial days—stood side by side with taller modern structures.

His hotel room was hot and close.

"Air-conditioning?" he asked the boy. "I was supposed to have air-conditioning."

The boy pointed at a ceiling fan revolving slowly over the bed.

Eddie had come to Saigon to find Kim and An. Now that he was here, he hadn't a clue how to begin. He took a shower and changed into a white linen shirt, lightweight khaki pants and sandals. He found a bar near the hotel and ordered a beer. It arrived cool, not cold. Eddie sat at a table outside the bar, shaded by a large awning. He watched as throngs of people passed by. He had booked a hotel in old Saigon—now known as Ho Chi Minh City—in hopes that the territory would look familiar…but it did not. He was pleased to see a few Buddhist monks in their bright saffron robes, and the vermillion poinciana trees still shimmered in the breeze of his memory. But where were the heavily made up and mini-skirted hookers? Where were the wooden ox carts piled high with goods? So many things had changed in 40 years.

That night Eddie went bar-hopping, but the bars he remembered were gone. A few bars had live music, mostly young men and women performing popular Vietnamese songs or singing karaoke. He had wondered if Kim still sang in bars and clubs. It was a thin thread to follow, but it was nearly all he had.

Eddie had brought along a photo of Kim, a faded Polaroid of a young woman sitting on a railing with one leg bent to her chest, smiling. He showed the photo to dozens of people—mostly men his age—none of whom recognized Kim. At the end of the evening, the only evidence of his efforts was a headache.

The next day Eddie went to the American Embassy and asked how he might find the person in the photo. A clerk gave him the address of a government building where they kept records of births, deaths and marriages.

The records building was a pre-war structure with a high atrium that encompassed the first two floors and a sweeping stairway rising to the second floor. It was cool inside and sounds echoed in the large open space.

"Do you speak English?" he asked the receptionist.

"A little."

He handed her the photo. "I am looking for this person. Her name is Nguyen Kim. The picture was taken in 1970."

"Oh, is very long time ago. Where she was born?"

"I don't know. In a village outside of Saigon. Can you look her up by name?"

"Yes, but is very common name. I look."

The woman disappeared down a staircase. Fifteen minutes later she returned carrying a long file drawer filled with index cards.

"Many women name Nguyen Kim. When she was born?"

"About 1950 or 51."

The clerk examined the cards and extracted a pile of them as thick as her thumb.

"Nguyen Kim, all born 1950." She handed them to Eddie, but of course they were all written in Vietnamese.

"What do they say?" he asked.

The woman began reading the cards, one at a time, and distilling the vital information to a few words each. "She die, she missing, she live in Saigon, she live in village, she die, she live in Hanoi…. Many different story. Also, many card not here. Lost in war."

"What about her children?" Eddie asked. "Is there any information about her children?"

"No. Childrens have own card."

"Yes, of course. Could you check on one other person, a daughter of Nguyen Kim?"

"Name?"

"Nguyen An, born in 1970 or 71."

"Also very common name. But I check."

This stack of cards was much thicker than the first. Eddie realized it was almost an impossible task to find his daughter in the stack of cards. He would need a translator and a driver. Eddie thanked the clerk for her help and turned to go.

"Wait," the clerk said. "You look on Facebook?"

"Yes," said Eddie. "No luck there."

Facebook was a new tool for Eddie. As a journalist he had occasionally found it useful in finding people and tracking them. But he was not comfortable with it. He was more at ease with old-school journalism—using the telephone and the face-to-face encounter to get a read on someone. He liked to see how a person reacted to queries and questions in the moment.

Before he booked his ticket to Vietnam, Eddie had tried to find Kim and An using Facebook. He had found 35 Facebook users with the name Nguyen Kim and over 300 with the name Nguyen An. He filtered out as many as he could, based on photos, birthdates and other information posted in their profiles. To the most hopeful candidates, he sent a friend request adding a note that explained he was looking for a 60-year old woman (Kim) or a 40-year old woman (An) born in Vietnam. Many of his friend requests were granted, and to those he sent a detailed message about who he was and who he was looking for and why. This approach netted some interesting replies but no solid leads. Eddie figured they didn't use Facebook, or maybe they had gotten married and changed their surname. Or they were dead.

Their death was a depressing but real possibility. When the war ended in 1975, and the last Americans fled the country in grim desperation, the victors were not kind to those who had aided the American enemy. South of the DMZ over 150,000 were killed and more than a million were arrested and sent to "re-education camps," which meant hard and even deadly labor, clearing the jungle for food production, digging wells and latrines, and sweeping fields for land mines. Malnourishment and disease were rampant. The distinction between well and sick was blurry, between the sick and dying even more indistinct. The dead were carted off into the jungle and buried in unmarked graves. Families were split up, children frequently landing in an orphanage where neglect or abuse was common. Yes, Kim and An might well be dead.

Failing to find Kim or An through friend requests on Facebook, Eddie tried a different approach. He posted a message on his Facebook page, telling his story, and asked his network of friends to share his post with others, hoping that the ripples would reach out far beyond his own small band of friends, and that someone somewhere would see his post and make a connection. But after weeks of waiting with no responses, Eddie had decided to go to Vietnam.

When Eddie left the Bureau of Records, he returned to his hotel. He hadn't checked his Facebook page in several days. His room did not have Wi-Fi, but there was a small room off the lobby where he could hook up his computer to the Internet. He logged on and found a new message waiting for him.

"My name is Ann Parker," the message read. "My maiden name was Nguyen An. I was born in 1970 in Vietnam. My mother's name was Nguyen Kim. After the war, my mother was sent to the country and I was put in an orphanage. I never saw her again, and I barely remember her. When I was eight an American charity brought me to Los Angeles where I was placed in a foster home. I still live in Los Angeles."

Eddie was thunderstruck. Could it be that his daughter had been living in Los Angeles all these years? He quickly replied, asking Ann to post a picture of herself. He explained that he was in Vietnam searching for her.

In post-war Vietnam, orphans were treated harshly, especially those with blue eyes and fair skin, the stranded offspring of American soldiers. Kim was lucky. Eddie had Mexican and Mayan blood, so his skin was dark, his eyes were brown, and he was shorter than most Americans. Except for her big bones and stocky figure, Kim looked thoroughly Vietnamese. When a photo of Ann Parker appeared on his Facebook page the next day, Eddie immediately recognized himself in her face. He told Ann that he would fly to Los Angeles tomorrow if she would see him. "Yes!" she replied, and sent her address and phone number.

When Eddie landed at LAX a few days later, he called Ann Parker. She answered the phone on the second ring.

"Hello?"

"Hello, this is Eddie Maez. Is this Ann Parker?"

"Yes."

"I am at the airport. Would this be a good time to come see you?"

"Yes, yes. Come right away. Do you need directions?"

"No, I have your address. I know where it is."

Eddie was surprised that Ann had no accent. He had expected a Vietnamese inflection, but there was none. He rented a car and drove to Ann's house in Glendale. He drove slowly through a neighborhood of modest stucco houses, looking for the street and then the number. Finding it, he stepped out of the car and could hear children inside yelling, "He's here! He's here!"

He was halfway to the front door when Ann emerged. Three children, between five and ten years old, peered through the living room window. Eddie and Ann stopped about three feet from one another and locked eyes. Neither of them was embarrassed by their long gaze, neither wanted to look away from the other's deep brown eyes. A single tear rolled down Ann's cheek. Eddie reached out his hands and Ann took them. He pulled her to him and they embraced. Eddie smelled the scent of jasmine coming from Ann's long black hair, which was pulled back in a ponytail, revealing her smooth skin the color of acorns.

They pulled back from their embrace and resumed their looking, now blurred by tears, still holding hands. Something intimate passed between them, some acknowledgement, an unspoken understanding. They each felt an undeniable connection to the other, stretching over a void, bridging culture and time. Ann sniffled and wiped her eyes.

"Come in and meet your grandchildren," she said.

On Sale Now!

For more information
visit: www.SpeakingVolumes.us

www.ingramcontent.com/pod-product-compliance
Lightning Source LLC
Chambersburg PA
CBHW020608260626
47157CB00003B/916